WITHOUT MALICE

A Novel

KURT MACH

CROSSWATER BOOKS

Two Worlds Media
Brush Prairie, Washington

© 2019 By Kurt Mach

Published by Crosswater Books
A division of Two Worlds Media
Brush Prairie, WA

All rights reserved. No part of this publication may be reproduced, stored in a retrieval system or transmitted in any form without the prior written permission of the publisher. Brief quotations for written reviews or fair use with attribution is permitted.

ISBN: 9781073361434

FIRST EDITION

Printed in the United States of America

DEDICATION

This book is dedicated to my mother, Lillian McFarlane. She was and is the most influential person in my life. To know her was to know you are loved.

ACKNOWLEDGMENTS

Giving honor where honor is due, I must give thanks to my cousin Judy La Salle for her consistent, faithful encouragement throughout this project. I may not have continued otherwise; also my dear friend Stella Sigmund, whose willingness to read and re-read, offering defining insights and constructive criticism that made it a much better read; My dear wife Revell, who has patiently put up with me through this, and so much more for the last 45 years; and The Boys, whose antics made the story so much more interesting and entertaining. Last, but not least my buddy Dan Mayhew of Two Worlds Media who actually turned this into a real book. I am more thankful to you all than I can adequately express. If I knew anyone famous whose name I could drop, I would… but I don't.

Contents

Business as Usual 1

The Shot 8

Dead or Alive 26

Green Lake 30

Armed 38

Boldly Forward 43

Talk and Walk 52

More In 64 64

A Change of Venue 72

A New Set of Wheels 95

A New Way of Life 100

Redefined 109

The District 144

Old & New 174

The Grass Is Greener 184

A New Direction 193

Into the Great Unknown 212

Disclaimer

This story contains language that some may consider offensive. It is included solely for the purpose of authenticity – never gratuitous.

WITHOUT MALICE

Crime, Violence & Forgiveness

(1970)
Business as Usual

The place was crowded, but Friday nights always were. Will was sitting at one of the small round tables set close together throughout the main room. Pool tables, pinball machines, and restrooms were toward the back of the building. Legal occupancy might have been 150 to 175, and the owner was careful to never allow more than 250 or 300 in at one time. Live music was not offered, it cost too much and took up too much space, but the 18'X 18' dance floor in the center of the main area was well used. Top 40 songs blared continuously from the juke box near the front door.

Four other people shared the table with Will, although it was almost impossible to distinguish one group from another; the press of humanity, sitting, standing, and moving about was such a blur amidst the mingled fragrance of spilled beer, cigarette smoke, perfume, popcorn, and sweat. No small part of Will's blur came from the volume of beer he had already swallowed, and his almost constant inhalation of cannabis. The highly desired hashish known as Charis, imported from India, was his favorite. All manner of drugs were available in abundance in 1970 Seattle.

The predominant beverage of choice was Rainier Beer, flowing without interruption from two banks of taps behind the long "L" shaped bar near the front of the building. A relatively small number of people bought drinks one serving at a time in 10 oz. glasses, known by the locals as schooners. But the vast majority had the golden brew delivered in 60 oz. pitchers made of very heavy glass, almost ½ inch thick at the bottom. The

1

glasses had to be considered a consumable operating expense, so many walked out the door never to return. Even more ended up smashed to bits when they hit the floor for one reason or another. The pitchers, however, were virtually indestructible.

Regular patrons constituted about two-thirds of those present on any given night, in addition to a significant number of sailors who found their way over from the Naval Air Station just across the street. Regulars said the place had live entertainment… a fight every ten minutes.

Will was enjoying what for him was a peaceful and relaxing evening in a comfortable environment he considered home turf. He probably had no less than two dozen people who could be called friends, at some level, on the premises that very moment. One of those people, Butch, had been his close friend since junior high school.

The truth was, Will was not old enough to even be there. He was 19 and the legal drinking age in Washington State was 21. But he looked older. The first time he'd been served in a bar he was 15, and he had been a regular at OUR PLACE since he was 17. He had even worked checking I.D. at the front door.

Out of nowhere, something exploded on Will's head and drove him into his seat. It was a good thing he was sitting down or he would have been knocked to the floor. He had no idea what had happened, or that he was now soaking wet. Instinct and conditioned response kicked in as he spun on his chair to his left. Standing over him was a huge enraged man he did not recognize, but the fire in the other man's eyes, and the shattered remains of a beer pitcher in his hand convinced him immediately the man was his enemy.

He sprang from his seat like a coiled snake, planting his right foot to drive from as he thrust his right fist at his assailant's head. With the punch on its way, nothing could be done to avoid the jagged, broken pitcher the other man lifted to block the blow. Will's clenched fist slammed into the broken glass, slicing two fingers open to the bone. He couldn't feel it. Things were happening very fast as the two young men kicked, swung and clawed at each other, both determined to bring the other's aggression to a halt.

When he jumped to his feet, he sent his own table sprawling just as his friends' heads were turning to see where all the flying beer had come from. They watched the two combatants crash through the place, patrons fleeing as they cleared a path where tables and chairs stood seconds before. Butch, a genuine brawler, watched in delight as they settled into a more focused contest in the confines of a corner.

He had once boasted strategy to Will, saying, "I don't care how good you are… you're going to get hit a couple of times in a fight. I'll take mine on the way in." Butch had lifted weights since they were 13 years old, now weighed 255 pounds and could bench press in excess of 500 pounds. His method usually worked well for him. Once he had his hands on someone the outcome was a foregone conclusion.

Will was not nearly so strong. Neither did he enjoy fighting like his friend did. In fact, he preferred to do whatever he could to avoid it. He hated to get hit. Butch seemed to be energized by it. Will was not small, and at 6'2" and 230 pounds he could put up significant resistance, even convince most antagonists to look elsewhere for sport. But this guy was huge at 6'6", 260 pounds, and Will was no match for him.

With a jarring thud he landed with his back down on a table that did not go over. As the attacker dove in Will kicked him hard in the chest and guts several times. It seemed to have little effect on the guy. The worst of it was that he still held the broken pitcher in his hand, and whenever he got in close enough he stabbed Will in the head with it. Blood was flying everywhere.

Will was sobering up quickly, and just as he began to think this could turn into serious trouble, the guy was gone… no more blows to block, no more giant target to drive futile kicks and punches into. He blinked, caught a breath, and rose to his feet. The man lay motionless on his back, blood spurting three feet in the air from a severed artery in his right forearm and Butch standing over him like a gladiator.

"What the hell took you so long!?" Will shouted.

Butch didn't take his eyes off the fallen victim as he said to his friend, "I just thought you guys were having a good fight. I figured I'd give it a few minutes to see how you did. When I saw him stabbing you with that broken pitcher I stopped him." He arched his eyebrows and shrugged his shoulders as if to say, "Sorry."

"I need to get out of here," Will said, as he started moving toward the door. "The cops are going to be here in a hurry." Not being old enough and getting caught would spell trouble for everyone, including the owner who enjoyed their lucrative thirst and knowingly ran the risk of serving minors who looked older, or had phony I.D.

He burst through the door, but half way across the parking lot he realized he couldn't see well. He reached up and rubbed the back of his arm across his face to clear his eyes. Dropping his arm, he saw it was covered with blood and realized it was flowing heavily from his head and filling his eyes again. And his glasses were gone.

He turned and began marching back toward the tavern for a towel, having no good ideas beyond that and getting away from the place quickly. About 15 yards from the door the young woman he had come with crashed through it with his glasses in one hand and a couple of bar towels in the other. She was a nursing student at the University of Washington and had a plan of action.

"Give me your keys," she said. He did.

She wrapped one towel around his head, and then clapped his left hand on top of it to hold it in place. "Keep that there," she said next. He did.

She then cleared his eyes with the other towel, tossed it on the ground, and put his glasses on his face. Amazingly, they were not broken. She grabbed him by his right arm, spun him around and marched him to the passenger side of his car. She unlocked the door, swung it open and placed him in the seat with the skill of a seasoned police officer. With the door closed, she walked around to the driver's side, got behind the wheel and slid the seat up to accommodate her 5'4" frame. She started the engine, depressed the clutch, and slipped the shifter into first gear, then tore out of the parking lot headed for a hospital.

He didn't know it yet but the unprovoked attack would change his approach to the threat of violence for the rest of his life.

Three hours later the Emergency Room doctor tied and clipped the last of several dozen stitches needed to close up Will's wounds, most of them on his head.

"You might want to consider a less exciting form of entertainment," the doctor said. They had talked some while he worked. Will didn't withhold relevant details.

"A little late for this weekend, Doc."

"I'd like to see you live to see 25," the good doctor said with resignation, his eyes revealing his lack of confidence.

"You've lost a lot of blood. I don't want you drinking any alcohol for the next 30 days. And please don't rip the stitches out of that hand. You could lose feeling in those fingers... maybe even some movement or control. You'll just have to wait and see. No guarantees."

"Your hairline is receding, and may well go beyond the cuts in your head. I did the best job I could under the circumstances, and I don't think the scars will be too bad a few years down the road. Try to take a little better care of yourself, okay?"

"I'll try, Doc."

As he drove his friend home he thought, "Great way to show a girl a good time you idiot." She was genuinely beautiful and he had hoped they would develop a liking for each other.

Pulling his car to a stop at the foot of her parent's driveway, he put the transmission in neutral and set the parking brake, but left the engine running. Turning to her he said, "Thanks," with a sheepish smile.

She leaned over, gave him a kiss on the cheek and squeezed his arm. "I'll see ya," she said, then slid over, got out, and walked up toward the house.

"Yeah," he said to himself as he pointed his car toward home in the early morning hours. Her parents would probably be pissed about him bringing her home so late.

Monday Morning

Walt looked up at Will as he walked into work. "What happened to you?" he asked.

When Will gave him the three minute version, Walt said, "Well...that probably wouldn't happen to you in church, would it?" Walt was in his late 50's, a man of few words, and he liked Will, who looked back at him with a sigh that said, "Brilliant, Walt."

"What?" Walt asked. "God didn't do this to you."

Will headed for his own office in the basement. Church was the last thing he wanted to hear about. He knew what went on there, and why, and had been deliberately avoiding them for several years now. He couldn't even bring himself to look at one while driving past.

He had a surprisingly good job for being almost 20. He worked at the largest car dealership of its kind on the west coast, and oversaw the delivery and processing of the new car inventory, often in excess of 500 vehicles. Three brands and a line of trucks made it a busy place, with more than 100 employees. Used cars were another department. He landed there after buying a new muscle car just before he turned 19, and quickly moved from a pre-delivery preparation job into the two man office.

He was not in charge, but he did have quite a bit of authority. When a transport truck full of new cars was delivered from the rail yard, many of them were damaged. Will's job was to inspect every car and record all damage. The transport truck driver would then sign to verify everything listed. The cars rode trains across country, often with bums as passengers, and had no external protection. He could always tell when a school vacation began because the cars showed up with boulders in the front seat, dropped from overpasses. Kids with too much time on their hands were job security for Will. Some cars served as moving targets for all manner of fire arms. If they had mag wheels the spare was gone, and nice factory stereos had little chance of reaching their destination.

Among other things, his job was to get those defects fixed, ASAP. To do that the company had accounts set up with vendors all over Seattle: upholstery shops, glass shops, stereo shops, even a body and paint shop nearby, since the dealer didn't maintain one of its own. One of the benefits was the jugs of high quality booze he received at Christmas for funneling work to local businesses.

He also had the opportunity to generate fictitious work for his personal needs. When the truck drivers had a need, he would balance things out for those who signed whatever he wrote down on the delivery inspection sheets. The shops made money, the manufacturer and transport companies paid the bill, and no one else needed to know. This enabled him to have nice tires, new paint, and a fine stereo in his own car. He also had a custom made leather bar in his home. The company used the same method to cover in-house damages, which were bound to happen with that many people moving that many cars around. Don't overdo it, and no undue attention was paid by anyone.

(1960)
The Shot

It was a beautiful, sunny summer day as Will and Skip sat on the waist-high wooden wall separating Will's front yard from the back, one world from another. His dog Pug was sunning herself on the ground between them. His parents got her as a puppy when he was two years old and she was always nearby when he was at home. At nine years old, he had never known life without her.

The back yard was a kid's world, for the most part. A paved driveway strip snaked in from the gravel alley all the way to the back door of the house, with a manhole cover about 15 feet from the house. In fall and winter the coal truck backed in, the driver removed the heavy iron lid, attached a steel chute from the truck, and dumped a load of coal into the underground cavern near the furnace in their basement. The truck usually came while he was at school, but if Will was home he got to help the driver. His father usually shoveled the coal into the furnace. If he wasn't home his mother did it. He had done it a few times, but the coal shovel was big and very heavy when heaped with coal.

Between the alley and the house, a picket fence extended half way into the side of the back yard, opposite the garage and up to the edge of the paved drive. Between the fence and the alley was a large wood framed playhouse that belonged to his older sister. There was a strip of grass along the wooden wall on the other side of the driveway, between the garage and the house, up to the gate near the kitchen door. At the other end of the back yard from the alley was a giant old cherry tree.

A year earlier Will had won a gasoline powered Go Kart in a shopping center drawing and embarked on one of the great loves of his life. On weekends they would load it into the trunk of the family car, the front wheels sticking out with the trunk lid tied to the bumper, and take it to various school grounds. Other families with karts would gather and have real races around the large paved playgrounds or parking lots. Everyone but Will and his dad had wrecked the kart at one time or another, but no one had ever been seriously injured. They would load it up and haul it home where his dad and his friend Art would pound it back into shape. He loved the kart and didn't like letting other people abuse it, but sharing was not optional in their family. Though he and his dad often clashed, the kart was something they were able to enjoy together.

Their huge backyard also served as a private track for the kart. Starting on the paved drive at the alley Will would floor it, swerve to the right just past the picket fence and out onto the grass. The cherry tree could be circled from the right or the left and allowed him to develop some skill hanging the tail out in either direction. Coming out of the turn, it was wide open back onto the pavement, then a big left-hand circle around the playhouse, out past the picket fence again and back onto the pavement for a whole lap, almost like a big figure eight. Once his sister didn't make the full turn around her playhouse and smashed right through the fence. His kart came through that one unscathed.

The grass did not survive the two big turns at both ends of the yard. Will's kart had knobby tires that gained good traction coming out of corners in the yard. These thrills and skills would serve him well a few years later when they moved to Seattle near Woodland Park and Green Lake.

It was summertime, warm, and not going to school was a pleasure every day. Will and Skip's parents were at work and the days were pretty much theirs to do with as they pleased. Once they had spent the day capturing about five gallons of pollywogs in an old, abandoned brick mill pond, south of Longfellow School, about a mile south of their house. They hauled them home in buckets in a wagon and put them in an old galvanized wash tub in Will's back yard with high hopes of watching them turn into tadpoles, then into frogs. Unfortunately, Will and his sister had pet ducks at the time, and none of the future amphibians survived the night.

Summer vacation was a simpler time in 1960. Neither of them had ever heard or known of anyone being kidnapped in their life. No one, adult or child, had ever shown up at school with a gun. Skip's and Will's houses faced each other across 38th Street, a typical quiet residential street in Everett. If either of them did anything deserving of punishment, any parent on the block was authorized to take charge and reign them in. Their own parents would deal with them later.

It was late morning and neither of them had come up with a good plan for the day. They both had bikes, balls, bats, and mitts. Outside one end of Will's back yard was a steep grass slope they could slide down on cardboard to the sidewalk below. Several blocks down Oak Street the home of United States Senator, Henry M. Jackson had an even bigger, better hill to slide down. He was usually not there and his housekeeper would come out and run them off, yelling about ruining the grass. One day the senator himself came out and told her to let them play. He knew they would grow up to become voters.

But nothing seemed to excite them on this particular day. Eventually their conversation found its way to Skip's grandpa, who lived upstairs with the family. The way Skip told it, he had led a very exciting and colorful life. One thing led to another, including war, and Skip said, "You know, my grandpa has a bunch of real bullets in his dresser drawer in his bedroom".

It didn't take long for Will to say, "It would be fun to take a look at those bullets. What do you think?"

Skip's sister was the only one home at his house, and she didn't want to be bothered.

They slipped in through the back door as quietly as they could, through the kitchen and down the hall near his sister's bedroom. She was playing 45 records and wouldn't hear a thing. They breathed a sigh of relief creeping up the stairs. His grandpa's room was at the other end of the hall, extending out over the garage. Even though they knew no one else was home,

Without Malice

Skip slowly turned the knob and gently pushed the door open just enough to peek in. All clear. He turned to Will and nodded.

Skip knew the contents of his grandpa's dresser drawers well. Most were meticulously organized with socks, shorts, tee shirts, and trousers all neatly folded. But the drawer with all the ammo was just a huge, indiscriminate jumble of bullets: large ones, small ones, long ones, short ones; some shiny and some dull, some complicated looking and others simple, but lots and lots of bullets. The boys' eyes grew wider and a hush fell over the room.

Will looked at Skip, then slowly reached out and picked up a big one. He brought it up close and turned it over and over as he looked at it. "Wow!" was all he said. His Uncle Bud was a real cowboy and rancher down in California, where Will was born. He had guns, but Will had never handled one. He'd had his own pocket knives since he was about seven, and he was a Cub Scout, but guns and bullets were a whole different matter.

There were so many of them, it seemed no one would ever notice if a few were missing. How could you tell? It was just a big mess. Later, they wouldn't be able to remember who started it, but they both began stuffing handfuls of bullets into the front pockets of their jeans. Satisfied they had enough for whatever they decided to do with them, they closed the dresser drawer, slipped quietly out of the room, down the stairs, and back across the street to Will's house.

One thing was obvious…nothing fun was going to happen with those bullets still in their pockets. Digging down with both hands at the same time, they heaped them into one big pile on the sidewalk. Standing there looking down at them was mesmerizing. Where had these bullets been? Will's dad and Skip's grandpa had both been to war and they had heard many stories about World War II. Scenes from the war movies they had seen drifted through their minds, marines storming beaches, soldiers pinned down in fox holes, sailors shooting enemy planes out of the sky, and new recruits in boot camp going through training exercises. Each boy imagined himself present in those dramatic events.

Later, neither one of them would be able to remember whose idea it was, but one of them said, "Wouldn't it be cool if we could get some of them to go off?" And pretty soon they had hauled the biggest rocks they could lift over to their cache of ammo. First one, then the other, and then both of them together at the same time, they began lifting the rocks above their heads and smashing them down on the pile of bullets with all their might. Over and over they pounded them down, urging at least one bullet to explode. "Come On!" Though the vigorous exercise may have tired them, adrenaline was building, and they became even more frenzied as they hoped to overcome their frustration with greater effort.

Then, just as they were about to give up, BANG!!!... A big explosion as one of the bullets finally went off. "YES," they yelled with jubilation, the smell of sulfur filling their noses as they jumped up and down with excitement at their success. Oh, this was so much fun! Then, Will looked down and saw blood pouring from Skip's foot... dark, red blood, running out onto the sidewalk.

"Hey, man... you've been shot!" he yelled.

Skip looked down, saw the blood gushing from his foot, burst into tears, and fell on the ground.

"Stay put," Will barked with authority, and he took off to tell Skip's sister to call an ambulance. Even though it took her a moment to believe him, he was so animated she ran to the phone on the little table in the hall, picked up the receiver, spun the dial number "O" around, and let it go as it ratcheted back – click, click, click, click, click. She then heard the ringing and waited for the operator to answer. As soon as he heard her shout, "My brother's been shot!" Will took off, back out the kitchen door, across the street, and into the garage at his house. He grabbed a bucket and ran to his fallen friend.

The fire department was not far away and it seemed they got there not long after Skip's sister arrived on the scene. She also called her mother at work as soon as she hung up from talking to the operator. When the firemen pulled to the curb with lights flashing and siren blaring, Skip's foot was in the bucket, and what looked like a lot of blood had filled the bottom of it. Skip's mom arrived before the firemen loaded him into the ambulance that showed up not long after they did.

Will's sister had come out in the midst of all the ruckus and he told her what happened while Skip was being tended to. Skip's mom jumped in her car with his sister and headed for the hospital right away. Will knew he would be telling her his version of it all before the day was over.

As Will and his sister stood there after everyone else had left, next to the big blood spot on the sidewalk and the bucket lying on its side, she gave him a look that said, "You are in BIG trouble this time." She turned and walked back into their house, leaving him to contemplate his fate alone. He wondered what God was thinking but didn't feel like he was in trouble with Him. He did know he'd catch hell from his dad.

He would often remember that day over the years.

The Throw

One month later Will was standing alone on a bluff, high above the dark blue/green waters of Puget Sound on the south end of Vashon Island, feeling more alone than he ever had in his life. He had never heard of Alfred Dreyfus, this was not Devil's Island, and he was not banished for his crimes. He was at Camp Burton, the summer Bible Camp run by his family's church, the First Baptist Church of Everett, Washington.

He had arrived with a flood of other church kids on Sunday afternoon and would return home the next Saturday. His weeklong stay could not be considered the consequences of shooting his friend in the foot, if that's what he'd done. It was scheduled long before the unfortunate incident. Skip was not with him. It wasn't just that their parents had agreed the boys should not be together for a while, but Skip's family was Roman Catholic. Neither family held their different faiths against each other, but Baptists and Catholics just didn't participate in each other's corporate practices of faith.

Walking through the woods from his cabin, he stopped and sat before the weathered cross of a little open-air amphitheater with log benches. "God," he said... "Things really stink right now and I don't know what to do about it."

He hadn't had a lot of conversation with God. He was always in Sunday school and his family rarely missed a Sunday morning worship service. They always prayed and thanked God before they ate meals together. They always said, "In Jesus' name." He knew the Bible stories and believed God and Jesus were real. No reason not to, really.

Then, swelling up all around him was an overwhelming sense that God Himself was right there! He jerked his head up and looked all around. Not another soul anywhere to be seen. Everything still and silent. But that presence was thick and real.

And then, he knew. He didn't hear a real voice, but he knew Jesus was real and He was somehow telling him He was right here with him, right now. He knew Jesus was telling him, "I'll forgive you, Will. Believe Me and ask Me. Trust Me."

"Please forgive me, Jesus," he said. At least he thought he said it. Just like a moment before, he knew it was true; he was forgiven, and then the presence was not there anymore. Now here he was, standing on the cliff looking down at the water.

He bent down, picked up a rock and threw it out toward the water. It felt good. It always felt good. He liked throwing things, and rocks were usually readily available. He liked throwing baseballs, too and had started playing on his first Little League baseball team two years earlier when he was seven. The throwing just came natural for him.

He reached down and picked up another rock, about the size of a lemon, a little larger than the first one. From way up on top of this cliff the water didn't look that far away, but his first throw had bounced off the rocky beach about half way between the base of the cliff and the edge of the water. He hadn't thrown it all that hard, anyway. This one had a little more heft to it, and he would put more muscle into it. He wasn't really trying for the water the first time.

Without Malice

Over his first three seasons the baseball coaches had made him a pitcher and an outfielder, positions that took advantage of his arm. He didn't get to play in games that often yet. The 11 and 12 year olds were so much better than the younger kids.

He liked pitching best. He didn't have to suffer the embarrassment of dropping a fly ball, and he could set up each throw on his own terms. From the outfield, he had to throw it in NOW! When pitching, he had control over exactly when he would throw it, and the batter had to wait for him. He was also always throwing at a well-defined target, the catcher's mitt. He fully intended for things to go his way.

The water below was much farther away than a batter's box, more like an outfield throw. But he imagined himself on the mound, none the less. He liked the whole pitch delivery motion. A target would help. He spotted an old rotted stump sticking up out of the water, about four feet from the shoreline.

He backed away from the cliff's edge a few feet. He intended to take a full stride. They had taught him to drive off of his back foot – for him that was his right – push off as hard as he could, lift his left foot and stride forward as his throwing hand came over the top with the ball. He would release it shortly after his left foot was planted, with all of his weight coming forward onto it. He liked a full windup.

Will closed his eyes. He could see the anxious batter awaiting the onrushing ball. Years later a guy he had grown up with told him they were often terrified in the batter's box. Will had some serious heat. Sometimes he did not have the most serious control. His last year of Little League he hit more home runs than anyone and was given the MVP trophy at the end of the season. On the way home his father explained to him why he did not deserve it, and that another kid should have gotten it. He just played all the harder.

He reared back, opened his eyes, started his motion, and picked up the stump as his left foot began its descent. Pushing hard with his right leg he felt the wave moving up his body, up through his butt and his back into his shoulder. He began to whip his right arm forward faster than his body rotation, and stuck his head out as he made the last pull to bring the ball to full release speed. What a satisfying feeling! Just before he let the rock go he thought, "I may launch this thing 10 feet past that stump."

He was actually looking beyond the stump when his fingers let go of the rock, still under full power and continuing into his follow through motion, when out of nowhere a small bird streaked into his field of vision from the right. In less than an instant, not more than 15 feet in front of him, the rock and the bird collided and the bird almost disintegrated.

He was stunned. For a moment he felt mildly ill. He liked animals, and to have so suddenly, unintentionally killed the bird was unsettling. First his friend's foot, now this innocent bird. He stood with his hands on his knees, his eyes closed, and breathing hard. His thoughts were swirling, and his commitment to throw more rocks until he hit that stump was gone.

Walking back to his cabin he felt like giving up. Was he stuck with this lousy feeling? He just wanted this week to be over. Maybe things would be normal at home.

Revenge

Returning home from Bible camp on the ferry from Vashon Island, the events of the previous month filled Will's mind. Other than the occasional neighbor's broken window, things had never gone so far off course in his life. What else could go wrong? As far as the windows went, his love of throwing rocks and the hilarity that consumed him at the sound of breaking glass did not always match up well.

Will was jarred from his daydream by the ear-splitting blast of its horn as the huge ferry began to churn violently in reverse to slow its approach to the dock, the tangy smell of saltwater boiling up around the hull. As the big boat bumped into the massive guide-wall posts on each side, his thoughts returned to the summertime fun of catching crabs off of the ferry docks. With some putrid meat in the bottom of his mother's old nylon stockings, he reeled them up on his fishing line. Once the crabs grabbed the nylon they couldn't let go.

The church bus picked them up at the ferry dock for the rest of the trip home. While most of the other kids were bubbling over with excitement, Will sat in silence, contemplating the remaining three weeks of summer vacation. How would he be received by his parents? Would he and Skip be allowed to play together again? Were things ever going to return to normal? How did he stand with God? He never intended to hurt anyone. His stomach was churning like the water around the ferry.

At the church he grabbed his suitcase from the pile and his mom got out of the car to greet him before opening the trunk.

"Hi, Honey." She gave him a hug and kissed him on the forehead, but something was different. Whether he was coming home from baseball practice or an overnight stay at a friend's house, she was almost always upbeat, asking him how his time was and spouting about something good they were looking forward to, even if it was only dinner. Will looked up at her, but made no reply. He was waiting for her to say something as they pulled away from the curb. She was looking straight ahead in silence, not even playing any radio music.

A couple of blocks from the church she finally said, "We have a problem at home."

OH, NO! he thought. His mind began racing through every horrible thing he could think of: Skip's foot had to be cut off, someone had broken into the garage and stolen his kart, a neighbor had exposed him for some prank he couldn't even remember doing …What? Without shifting his head or his eyes, he wondered; was he going to be punished for the trouble he had caused.

He looked over at her. She returned the look and said, "Let's wait until we get home." They rode in silence the rest of the way.

Pulling into the driveway his mother stopped in front of the garage, set the parking brake and put the transmission in park. She turned off the ignition key and softly exhaled. Will's eyes were on the open gate from the back yard. Where was Pug? Whenever they came home she came out to greet them. When he had been gone she was extra excited and came running toward the car. Where was she?

He looked toward his mom as her eyes came around to meet his. "Where is she?" he asked.

"We don't know," his mother replied. "We haven't seen her since Tuesday."

"WHAT!?" he blurted out. "Where can she be?" His face was a picture of torment, and his mother wanted desperately to comfort him.

"We've looked everywhere and asked everyone. She's not over at Aunt Lois's. We have some posters up. We don't know what else to do, Will. We need to keep praying."

Will bolted from the car, running all around the yard, then into and through the whole house, looking for what? He didn't know. Their yard was not exactly secure, but his dog was not a wanderer. She lived to be with her people and she never separated herself from where they were.

Pug was supposed to be a Boston Bulldog when his parents bought her for him. As she grew it became apparent her mother had had more than one suitor. When she crested 40 pounds, and her nose grew out, the breeders refunded his parent's money. By then she was a member of the family and they were all in it for the duration. She did have the appropriate dark brown and white markings.

Where was she? Will wandered out of the door from the kitchen into the back yard, looking completely lost. Walking through the open gate, his mother enfolded him in her arms. "We'll find her," she said. "We'll get her back."

"Dear God,", she prayed silently, "please bring my son's dog home."

Will began to cry and couldn't stop. He just couldn't hold it in any longer.

The next Friday, Pug had not been found. The whole family was avoiding the subject. A few years earlier their other dog, Becky, had been hit and killed by the milk truck, but this was worse.

Friday night Will's mom came home with some news. The dentist she worked for told her about a family who was moving and needed a home for their dog, a Wire-Haired Terrier named Pal. Would they be interested? In spite of his mother's cheerful enthusiasm, Will turned and left the kitchen, went upstairs to his room and closed the door.

After dinner his sister followed him out to the back yard. "Hey."

He turned his head toward her. "Yeah?" he replied.

"Let's go see the dog tomorrow. We might still get Pug back, but let's go see it anyway… okay?"

He closed his eyes and hung his head. She didn't say anything more. After a minute he looked up and said, "okay", without expression.

Pal turned out to be a fabulous dog. He loved to play. He lived to play. Balls, sticks, rocks, anything - he would play until he had worn out everyone around him. They brought him home.

It felt strange. Pug was his life-long friend: a family appendage, gentle, quiet, faithful but not real exciting. Pal was bursting with energy looking for a place to exert itself, not unlike Will. At home later that day, he threw a tennis ball that bounced up and stuck in the crotch of the big old cherry tree at the end of the yard. He started running to get the ball down, but Pal got there first, and to his utter amazement, climbed the tree and got it himself. Will stood in awe as this dog jumped down, ran over and dropped the ball at his feet, his head shifting in sudden movements from Will, to the ball, and back again.

A little before dinner time, Will and his sister started to play tether ball. As she hit the ball back to him, Pal came flying out of nowhere and slammed his nose into the ball, sending it right back at her. He dropped to the ground, and when she had it in her hands he began scooting and shifting back and forth, up and down, with his eyes darting from hers to the ball and back again. Will backed up several feet and said, "Do it."

She moved about halfway around the circle from Pal, raised the ball above her shoulder, and launched it in an arc around the pole. With perfect timing, Pal shot straight up and bopped the ball hard with his nose, like a soccer player making a header. Both kids squealed with delight, and took turns playing tether ball with a dog. When their mother called them in for dinner, Pal had to be tied to a fence post or he would keep playing tether ball with himself.

After dinner they brought Pal in and fed him. He seemed to understand that evening was a time to relax, and was lying in perfect calm just on the other side of the doorway between the kitchen and the dining room. Will's mom and sister were cleaning up the last of everything from dinner, and Will was sitting at the kitchen table, lost in thought… drifting. Three scratches at the kitchen door startled them all. Will's mom and sister looked to each other, and over at Pal. Will's head snapped around toward the back door. Scratch, scratch, scratch again, and he shot from his chair.

He jerked open the door. Pug almost got by him, her eyes bulging with anxiety, before he tackled her on the floor, crying as he spoke her name over and over. His sister joined the pile and his Mother ran from the room shouting for his Dad.

When he finally sat back and held her at arms-length, it was obvious to them all she had not eaten since she'd left; she must have lost 15 pounds. Looking closer, she had rope burns around her neck.

"She's been tied up," his Father said.

"Who would do that?" Will shouted in anger.

Looking up at the three of them, his Mother said, "I don't know, son. But let's be thankful she's home," and she thanked God for answering her prayer.

He hugged his dog around the neck until she began to wiggle free. Pal almost went unnoticed, dancing around them, and when Will released Pug, she sped past them all and emptied the water bowl.

His mom, dad, and sister all crowded around their faithful old friend, as Will sat on the floor seething and searching his mind for who did this to his dog.

The next week was a sigh of relief. Pug was home, eating and putting a little weight back on, though she was sticking close to the house, and never leaving the yard. Skip's foot was healing and he and Will were free to play with each other again, but even with the gate open she would not join them in the front yard.

Pug and Pal were getting along fine. Pal only wanted to play, all the time, and Pug didn't care about such things. There was no competition between them. After a week it looked as if their expanded family would do just fine.

The next Saturday Will's cousin Tom and his family showed up for a visit from California. One last hurrah before school started up again after Labor Day. Sunday after church, Will, Tom, and Pal headed for the old mill pond to catch some frogs. Tom's family was more free-wheeling than Will's, but he knew he was expected to be home in time for dinner. They didn't even have to call Pal. He was glued to them, excited about whatever action they might throw his way. He had his head stuck right in the middle of everything. If he drifted behind a bit on the way home, he then ran by them next, but never let them out of his sight. He was made for this kind of life.

They hadn't taken any containers with them and came home with only one frog each. They were hunkered down on the concrete drive in the back yard, prodding the frogs with sticks and hoping for a jumping contest, when Will's mom leaned out the back door and called them to wash up for dinner. "Where's Pug?" she asked. Will's head did a 360, and terror rose up in his heart. He jumped to his feet and raced around the yard calling her name. No Pug.

During a sleepless night Will had asked God to bring her back. In the morning he and Tom set out to find his dog. Their parents were off on an outing of some sort and Will's sister was trusted to keep an eye on things. Most of his night had been spent plotting what he would do to whoever had his dog. He would find her, and when he did… well, he'd deal with that when the time came. He had said little to anyone since going to bed last night. Now he began to confide in Tom, and he was on board for whatever they found. It didn't take long.

The biggest house in the neighborhood, on the biggest piece of property, except for Senator Jackson's place down Oak Street, was a huge old Victorian right across the alley from Will's. It had three stories and a basement, with a tall gabled attic above the third floor. The whole place was covered with fancy woodwork, but most of it could not be seen behind the massive trees and hedges that had grown up around it for decades. Two old spinster sisters lived there, and they didn't like kids.

Whenever Will and Skip had been spotted snooping around, the mean old ladies had yelled threats and insults at them as they ran away. It probably didn't help that Will's dog chased their cat whenever she spotted it crossing the alley. His sister had gotten in trouble once for smarting off to them on the party line of their telephone. Four houses in the neighborhood shared the same phone line and you had to take turns. The phone in each house had its own ring, so everyone knew which house was being called when it rang: one ring, two rings, a ring with a pause then another ring, and two rings with a pause then another two rings.

Of course, anyone could pick up and listen, but you weren't supposed to. If someone was taking too long, someone else on that party line may ask them to shorten it up a bit. Will wasn't sure if the sisters had told his sister to get off the phone, or if she had suggested they get off, but it hadn't gone well. Nobody liked them and they didn't like anyone.

At the very back of the sister's property, right on the alley and pretty far from their house, was a big old two-story storage building, probably a carriage house back in the day. The upstairs had a big wide door on one end that swung open, with a lift and pulley arm that stuck out. On the ground floor, on the side away from the alley, was a regular size door. Just inside that door, some old wooden stairs went up to the second floor. Will had never been up there. He was always afraid of getting trapped by the sisters and figured he didn't want to jump from the big upstairs door. But not today. He had a feeling, and was willing to risk anything to get his dog back.

They crept through the hedge at the back of the barn, and watched the house for several minutes. The sisters weren't out working in their yard. The boys tip toed up to the side of the house, and crouched down as they worked their way along the side toward the front, pausing at each window to listen. Nothing. After staying by the front porch for a bit, they decided the sisters were not home and turned to head back to the barn.

They stopped at the ground level door and listened for anyone coming down the alley. If the sisters were in the barn the door would be open. Very carefully, Will reached out and took hold of the old metal doorknob. Ever so slowly he began to turn it, sure it would screech. It turned quite nicely, and he pushed the door open slowly. The hinges didn't make a sound either. They paused and listened. Confident no one else was there, they stepped inside and closed the door behind them. It smelled old inside.

Will turned to Tom, nodded his head once and said, "Come on."

In the big room to the left was a space large enough for a car, with tall double doors on the end below the big upstairs door, and work benches along one side and on the other end near the stairs. To the right was a smaller room filled with more gardening stuff than Will had ever imagined. Bags and bags of fertilizer, and potting soil, and who knows what all lined one wall the length of the floor. A whole wall of shelves had cans, and jars, and bottles of powders and liquids, paints, and solvents and stuff - lots and lots of stuff. The place was crammed with things that had probably been there since before Will's parents were kids. Both rooms had all kinds of tools in them. Everything was quiet and still.

Will stepped out of the small room and started up the stairs with Tom at his elbow. Unlike the door, the stairs creaked and groaned all the way up. As they neared the top of the stairs, they could see there were no walls dividing the upstairs. It was all one big open space with windows on only one end. It was kind of dark, but if the big loading door was open on the other end lots of light would come in.

Will stepped up onto the floor of the loft and turned toward the darkened end of the building. There she was! His dog was tied up with a rope around her neck, and quivering in the corner. He sprang toward her and called her name, "Pug!" Running over he hugged her in his arms and buried his face next to hers. His emotions were bringing tears to his eyes, when suddenly they were completely pushed aside by rage… burning rage. They would pay for this!

Tom was standing over him as he untied her. "What are we going to do?" he asked.

"We get her out of here," he said, and they ran for the stairs, Will, then Tom, with Pug hot on their heels. They ran down the stairs and out the door, caring nothing for silence. They raced around the end of the barn, across the alley, into Will's back yard, and through the kitchen door. Pug headed for the water bowl as Pal jumped up to greet everyone.

Tom was staring at Will as he turned around. "What now?" he asked.

Will marched past him and closed the door hard behind them, leaving the dogs inside. He didn't break stride, and Tom caught up with him as they made their way back to the barn. The side door was still open and Will walked straight through it, making a sharp right turn into the room with all of the gardening stuff. He paused only a moment, surveying the contents, then reached over a bench and grabbed a hand sickle hanging from wall hooks, and started slashing the bags that were against the wall along the floor.

As soon as he saw Will's plan of action, Tom joined in. After Will slashed a bag open, Tom would kick it over and turn it upside down, spilling the contents on the floor. When they ran out of bags, they began smashing pots, and jars, and bottles on the floor and walls. It didn't matter what was in them. If they were breakable they would be shattered as soon as possible. The boys worked themselves into frenzy, and before they left, the paint cans had been pried open and dumped out too. The place reeked of solvents and fertilizer.

Walking away, Will was still steamed but he felt better, though he suspected God was probably not pleased.

Later that day, as Will and Tom rounded the corner of 38th street coming home from the mill pond, they saw the glow of the flashing red lights before they saw the two police cars idling in the alley. Coming through the gate into the back yard, they found two policemen talking with Will's mom.

The officers looked in their direction, and his mother turned to face the boys. "Will, these police officers are here because the sisters' barn was vandalized today. Did you boys hear or see anything?"

Will and Tom hadn't seen or heard a thing and told the police officers as much. They had been at the mill pond all afternoon.

"Oh," his mom said as the boys turned to go into the house, "Pug is home."

Their yard had two apple trees, and from that day on Will would fire apples at the old ladies' rotten cat whenever he had a shot at it.

(1970)
Dead or Alive

"Oh, God," he groaned. Will did his best to avoid God, but still looked in His direction when things felt hopeless. Sometimes he felt God's sympathy, and sometimes he thought His response was surely, "You got yourself into this. Live with it." He didn't plead. If the summer of 1960 was uncomplicated for him, the summer of 1970 was not.

He had never felt so horrible in his life. His head was pounding like it might split; it felt like someone was driving railroad spikes into his skull with a sledgehammer. His first conscious effort was fighting to keep from vomiting, a fight he lost. The putrid smell engulfed his head and prompted involuntary retching that could only lead to one thing.

One month to the day from the Emergency Room Surgeon's admonition, Will had some catching up to do. Maybe 30 days' worth of drinking was too lofty a goal for his first night. The half-gallon of cheap Sangria, on top of countless beers, was not his best idea.

His room was in the basement. The ground level window above his bed was completely covered. Darkness was his only friend... and silence. "Oh, God... this feels like hell," he moaned. If he could just stay still enough, long enough, maybe he would live through it.

BRRRIIINGGG!!! BRRRIIINGGG!!! The telephone on his headboard went off like a fire alarm in his head! His hand shot up and grabbed the hand set off the cradle just in time to stop it from assaulting him a second time. He flopped it down on the pillow beside him.

"Will? Will, Honey… are you there?" He could hear his mother through the tinny speaker in the ear piece of the handle he gripped too close to his head. This was years before the first cordless phones. It was tethered to the base by a strong curled cord and the thought of throwing one across the room had not occurred to anyone yet. "Will, Honey?" The urge to hurl welled up like a wave again.

"Not now, Mom," he croaked, and put it back on the base as softly as he could. Crawling out of bed he hoped to make it to the bathroom before he lost it this time. He lifted the vile thing off the hook, slipped it under the other pillow, and staggered off. The toilet was his only goal. He'd deal with the dial tone and the first mess when he got back. Having thrown the soiled bedspread out near the pile in the laundry room, he crawled back in bed to crash again.

He had no idea how long he'd been in the bliss of oblivion when he awakened to someone knocking on his front door. He would like to have screamed, "GO AWAY!!" But he knew they would never hear him from down there, and the scream would hurt. He didn't want anything escaping his body except the slightest of breaths through his nostrils. Total stillness, total silence, and total darkness were his deepest desire. Probably one of his buddies anyway. He didn't care who it was. There wasn't a soul on earth he wanted to see, much less hear from. Had his room been on the main floor, he may have heard the key in the front door.

Laying on his left side, curled up in a fetal position, his right eyelid popped open when he heard the first footfall on the basement steps. "Will, Honey… are you okay?" Clop, clop, clop came her shoes down the wooden stairs, right outside his open bedroom door. He didn't want a closed door to slow him down on his next dash to the toilet. He hated throwing up but hated cleaning it up even more.

She slipped her head around the door jam, peeking into his room. As softly as a lamb she whispered, "Will?"

He closed his eye, and rolled over onto his other side, ever so slowly. She tiptoed into the room and stood beside his bed. "Will?"

After a long, motionless silence, he asked, "What are you doing here, Mom?"

"Come to think of it," he thought… "how did I get here?" The last thing he remembered was being dragged into his friend Lamont's house by his armpits with his heels plowing through the gravel, and that was miles away. When she realized he had tuned her out and he wasn't in any real danger, she left as quietly as she'd come.

It was afternoon before he dared to wash up a bit, pull on some jeans and a T-shirt, and slowly stagger up the stairs into the kitchen. Though his stomach felt empty, it also felt volatile. He cracked the door of the fridge open slightly, fearing the light. Someone had had the good sense to close all the curtains and blinds on the main floor windows. Nothing in the fridge looked safe, and he eased the door closed.

He turned to his left, putting his right hand on the counter to steady himself, and his left hand on his head hoping to calm it before the jarring of any sight, sound or movement assaulted him. His eye lids were slender slits, allowing only the minimum sight needed to avoid bumping into something. Over by the toaster… a loaf of bread.

Twenty minutes later he was still sitting on the couch, beginning to believe the dry toast would stay down. He eased around, parted the curtains of his front room window just a crack, and peered outside. His car was at the curb. That was good news. After another ten minutes of planning, he eased himself up and shuffled over to the front door. Glancing back, the clock on the mantel told him it was a little after 3:00 PM. Thank God it was overcast when he looked out. His sunglasses were probably in his car.

His car… he could see it from the door, parked right in front. He couldn't see any dents from where he was. He could see a huge swath of dried puke flaring out from the passenger side window, all the way back to the rear wheel.

The passenger side? He could remember driving down I-5 toward downtown Seattle with his head hanging out the driver's door window, unloading far more than he thought he had swallowed. He closed his eyes and stood there. Faint images of doing the same thing out the passenger side began to drift through his mind. He shut the door, went back to the couch and lay down. Thank God it was Saturday and the week end. What a way to end it.

Years later, he would often look at the gift his mother brought him the next day, a sad, miserable, comical little figurine, slumped over with an ice-bag on his head, and the slogan printed on its base, "If you're gonna fly by night, you've gotta pay by day." His mother did have a sense of humor.

(1962)
Green Lake

In the summer of 1962 Will's family moved to a house his parents bought near Green Lake in the north end of Seattle. It was only a half block from the lake and paradise for a kid. Green Lake is bordered by Lower Woodland Park to the south, with a par 3, nine-hole golf course tucked in between them. The Aqua Theater rounded out the south end of the lake. Will's house was at the south end near the golf course. In the 1960's, Green Lake was not yet Mecca for every fitness devotee in Seattle, and felt like the private domain of those who lived near it.

Across Aurora Avenue from Lower Woodland Park was The Woodland Park Zoo, connected by three pedestrian overpasses spanning the busy arterial. Before I-5 opened up in 1965, Aurora/Hwy 99 was the main north/south traffic route through Seattle. There was no admission charge to the zoo, and the animals did not yet live in "Natural Habitat" displays where they could hide from the people who wanted to see them. Lower Woodland was a mass of baseball diamonds, large and small, a football field with a track around it, tennis courts, and a soap box derby racing hill.

Will soon added a soap box racer to his transportation stable, along with his Go Kart and bicycle. Leg power, gravity, and an internal combustion engine could all feed his growing lust for speed. His parents also bought a 1961 Thunderbird that summer. Because Will's family moved in June, he didn't know any of the kids his age in the neighborhood as summer got under way.

The second week there, Will sat on the rockery in front of their house with four guys who lived nearby standing around, the smell of freshly cut grass floating on the warm breeze. It was Will's first year of a life-long commitment to wearing loafers. About 20 minutes into their junior high bull session, a kid named George, who lived around the corner at the end of the block, reached out and slipped one of Will's shoes off. The conversation halted as Will and George eyed each other.

A sly twinkle sparkled in George's eyes, and the corners of his mouth turned up into a grin as he began flipping Will's shoe end over end in the air and catching it in the same hand. No one said anything as Will and George maintained eye contact and everyone waited to see how this would play out. Will sat on the rockery as still as one of the stones.

Then, as the drama reached what felt like a peak, George moved over to the grass parking strip between the sidewalk and the curb, smiling broadly. With everyone looking on, he deftly bent down and scooped up a pile of dog poop in Will's shoe as the hoots and howls exploded from the other neighborhood guys.

Will didn't know these guys yet, and they did not know him. He didn't like being taken by surprise, and tried to anticipate every foreseeable scenario he might face, especially confrontations with his dad. But he hadn't seen this one coming, and couldn't avoid it now.

The mischievous twinkle in George's eye slowly morphed through a slightly sinister gleam into a dead-serious stare. Will slowly blinked once, but never shifted eye contact with George. Everyone was still and silent. Will expected he may live with these guys for a long time, and living in the midst of enemies was not appealing.

The corners of his mouth began to turn up. He winked at George with his left eye – something he had seen his father do with his friends – then let out a chuckle and said, "I never liked those shoes anyway." He had also been working to perfect the blood-chilling stare of his Uncle Bud, but this was not the time or place for that. Will admired his Uncle Bud greatly, and by the time he was in High School he could make some girls cry without a word, strictly for sport. Will was not mean. Others who found themselves in its sharp focus were often uncertain, but suspected things could get very serious. It became known as "The Stare."

Laughter and relief erupted from them all, though George would have been happy for it to go either way. When the laughter died down everyone knew Will was accepted as one of the guys. George even cleaned out his shoe.

Taking it to The Streets

The first time Will rolled out his go kart that summer his status in the neighborhood went way up. His mom was at work all day. His dad worked graveyard and was asleep in their bedroom upstairs at the back of the house. Just in case, he coasted it down the street a block before starting it. Other than his buddy Ted, who lived two doors up, no one else knew he had it, and word spread quickly.

By the time the 1980's came around, the entire Green Lake/Lower Woodland area was constantly clogged with traffic. But in 1962 traffic was no heavier than any other neighborhood in Seattle. Being so close, Lower Woodland seemed like a natural destination. There were no cars to contend with at all, and there was an almost limitless expanse of grass, with a few paved drives and parking lots. The biggest grassy spaces were just east of Aurora, between Lower Woodland and the zoo, where Will could explore the limits of his kart's speed and handling. And the overpasses had no gates.

His favorite sport was to drive the kart across the overpasses into the zoo side of the park. A large forested area buffered Aurora from any animal displays where people congregated. Eventually he attracted the attention of park staff, who would attempt to give chase in their little park department Cushman pickup trucks. They couldn't stay close to him, much less match the kart's handling. He would speed back across the overpasses, down through Lower Woodland into the neighborhoods, a discreet distance from his house, and along the side streets to the safety of his garage. Only once did he come close to being caught.

Tooling home at an entertaining pace, he came around a corner right past a Seattle Police patrol car parked at the curb. The officer was looking down while writing something. Will looked back over his shoulder as he made a left at the end of the block, and saw the cop pulling out from the curb and accelerating. Halfway down that end of the block he turned left sharply into a driveway, and left again onto the sidewalk. As the squad car came around the corner, Will was rounding it on the sidewalk going the other direction. He knew the neighborhood like the back of his hand, and the cop never saw him again. He didn't bring the kart out for two weeks. That story placed him on unassailable status in the neighborhood. It wouldn't be the last time he got away from a cop chasing him for his driving.

The blocks in Will's neighborhood were mostly rectangles, very long down the sides, and only a quarter that distance on the ends. When the next summer rolled around he had given in to pressure from his buddies to let them drive the kart, too. Teenaged adventure and risk didn't take long to develop into competition. How to measure themselves against each other and gain bragging rights? A full block was not unlike a real racetrack, Indy being foremost in every kid's mind. The corners were just a little sharper.

Two brothers lived midway down one such block. Conveniently, both of their parents were at work during the day. The street in front of their house made the perfect start/finish line. They spread out around the block, with one kid at each corner to check for cars on the street as the racing kart approached, one kid mid-block on the back side to keep an eye out for adults and cars coming from garages and driveways, and two kids at the start/finish line with watches to keep track of each other's time. It was perfect. What could go wrong?

Each driver had one lap to get up to speed, then one timed lap, followed by a lap to slow down. Will was the most experienced and had the hot hand, though a few guys were gaining on him and he had his reputation to uphold. Half way through that summer race day had become a regular event, though they changed up the time and day of the week in case anyone was plotting to catch them.

On this particular day three guys had made their runs when Will climbed into the kart. Ted was at the first turn, one block up from Green Lake Way, where Ashworth intersected 54th. Will was completing his first lap and running full speed down Ashworth toward the start/finish line. Looking ahead he saw his buddy, Ted, vigorously waving him through with the big windmill cranking motion of his left arm. Will tightened his focus and swung the kart over near the curb to his right to give him the best possible angle, cutting the corner on his left. He would sweep out to the right side of 54th, then left onto Woodlawn, and run full tilt down the backstretch.

Just after he initiated the turn and fixed his eyes on the curb at the left-hand corner, he saw the car coming into his peripheral vision out the corner of his right eye. The driver of the car had no idea a kid in a go kart would come shooting out from the side street, and he had no time to even tap the brakes. Will was fully committed and already moving into the car's path fast, with no realistic options other than keeping his foot down and plunging forward.

He passed so close to the left front bumper of the car he was sure he could have reached out and touched it. The driver blasted the horn, as if that would do any good at this point. Will was glad he had no rear-view mirror. He could feel the bumper and grill right behind him. He hunched over the wheel, skipped the turn onto Woodlawn and shot straight up 54th as the sound of the car faded behind him.

By the time he wound his way around several blocks of the neighborhood and back down to Ashworth, all the guys were gathered at the start/finish line. Ted's eyes were wide open as he excitedly retold the scene to the others. When Will screeched the kart to a stop and sprang to his feet, Ted was laughing so hard he couldn't contain himself.

"Are You CRAZY!?" Will screamed at him. "You could have gotten me killed!"

Without Malice

"I knew you could make it," Ted laughed. Will's heart was pumping a mile a minute.

That summer Will decided it was time to expand his driving experience. In anticipation he discretely had a copy of his parents' car keys made. A two year old Thunderbird was a pretty nice set of wheels for a kid, and he intended to give it a try. He knew he wasn't likely to get his parents' permission, and it was August before the ideal opportunity presented itself. From then on he would never be without a set of keys for the family cars.

His mother's lifelong friend and her husband lived in Montana. In August of 1963 they came to Seattle for a visit, and the two couples went off for a short trip together. The Thunderbird stayed home. Will hadn't been caught for anything significant so far in his young life. His older cousin was left in charge of oversight and supervision, and she was not up to the task, or she didn't care.

A week later, when his parents returned, he was worried they would notice the 500 extra miles on the car. Not a word was ever spoken, and his enlarged operations were off to a good start. What better way to celebrate than adding some beer.

Will's family only had alcohol around for holidays, and then in very limited supply. His mother liked an occasional hot buttered rum at Christmas, and made a mean scratch egg nog with some very lively ingredients for parties. Ted's family drank all the time, and beer was stacked like cord wood in the kitchen and hallway. The refrigerator was always full. The thought of drinking and driving didn't seem outrageous to Will at all. Don't get caught. No harm no foul.

Will and Ted were in sleeping bags in Will's back yard, looking up at the stars. Will's parent's bedroom window was just above them on the second floor, over the kitchen, but Will's Dad was at work. His mom was fast asleep, and knew the boys were out there. Ted's parents didn't know where he was, but it wasn't an issue.

"Did you get it?" Will asked.
"Of course," Ted smirked. "You doubted me?"

"I don't know. We've snuck a bottle before, but never a whole six pack. I wasn't sure. How'd you get it? From your brother?"

"Naw. He might have given it to me. He lets me have a bottle or two in the back yard now and then. But if I asked and he said no, he'd be on the lookout. When nobody was around I just stocked the fridge from one of the cases in the hall and took a six pack with me. They will all figure someone else stocked it up and won't count. It's in the back seat of my brother's car".

Will looked over, and Ted was grinning. He looked up at his mom's bedroom window. Dark.

"Okay," Will said, and they slipped out and over to the open garage in front of Ted's house. Ted had been careful to make sure the car was unlocked earlier. The six-pack was on ice, in a small cooler on the backseat floorboard, under a blanket.

Will had managed several decent sips of the holiday hot buttered rum, and the equally lively egg nog and he liked them both. They not only tasted great, but the heat that grew in his chest felt good. The strange sensation in his head was unlike anything else he had ever experienced. Usually he just sat in a corner with a smile on his face, unnoticed by everyone enjoying themselves in the life-flow of the party. His mom and some others, young and old, played music and sang songs they all knew. Will had been taking piano lessons since he was five years old, but strenuously resisted playing for adults.

Sliding back into their bags in the back yard with the beer, Ted pulled a metal bottle opener from his pocket. They had one in Will's kitchen too, for opening bottles of pop, but if it were missing, it would be noticed. One among several at Ted's house would never be missed.

"Why do you call it a church key?" Will asked.

"I don't know," Ted said. "That's just what they call it." Ted had been required to attend the local Catholic elementary school, but transferred to public school in Junior High when his father was injured and out of work. Other than that, Ted didn't go to church.

Will was disappointed at how bitter the beer tasted, but there was no way he was backing out now. He didn't manage to finish the 3rd one, and was glad they were lying down. He would get used to it as the summer went on.

Will's family had become established in the Freemont Baptist Church when they moved to Seattle. One earlier summer, after a week at Camp Burton when Will had embraced Christ as his Savior, he was baptized in their church in Everett. He knew the difference between right and wrong. He knew he would be in trouble if he got caught. But he didn't feel badly about the things he did, except when he thought God was looking and didn't approve. He just had a strong, natural pull to cross the boundaries people set for him. He didn't like being told what he couldn't do. He didn't hurt people. If they never found out… so what?

Three years later, when he was 15, he and two other guys from the neighborhood were taking driver training together, sponsored by Seattle Public Schools. A third kid came along just to watch. One day as Will adroitly navigated the car through traffic, the instructor said, "My, Will… you have a natural sense for where the car belongs in the lanes of traffic." Laughter erupted from his buddies in the back seat.

(1970)
Armed

Will's bandages were off and the stitches were all out. The right front crown of his head looked like a road map, but the hair was growing back over most of it. Not yet 20, he could only hope that as his hairline continued to recede the scars would become less prominent. Years later they would not even be recognizable unless he was sunburned. It turns out the doctor on duty that night had training as a plastic surgeon.

The good doctor did not take such detailed care when sewing up his right hand. The largest of those scars, running across both middle sections of the second and third fingers stood out. Mixed in with the other scars his hands would acquire, they would just be part of the puzzle.

Unless he was drunk, Will didn't usually like fighting, though with Butch as a friend it was unavoidable sometimes. They could be outnumbered at a party where they hardly knew anyone, but when he saw that look in Butch's eyes he knew it was going to happen. He had tried to drag Butch away.

"Come on Butch. Let's get out of here."

But Butch would just shake him off with great force and forge ahead. He didn't want to fight Butch. They had tried it in the eighth grade, and Will knew it was best to be on Butch's side, no matter the odds. Most people knew when to stop. Not Butch. He had an "ON/OFF" switch, and once he started, he would not stop until his opponent was out, or he was disabled. Butch being disabled didn't happen often.

Now, one month after Butch may have saved his life in the bar brawl, his physical wounds had mostly healed, but not his mind or emotions. Thoughts of revenge contended for his attention almost daily. His body always healed amazingly fast. High metabolic rate, he figured. But he was determined to never be put in that position again. It didn't matter how well you could defend yourself. There was always somebody tougher. He had had enough, and believed an ounce of prevention was worth a pound of cure. When retribution was needed, it would help prevent a repeat offense.

One week after the bandages came off and the stitches were out, he was talking about the whole episode with his boss and office mate at work. Gus was only five years older than Will, but married with kids and of another generation. Things were free and open between Will and Gus. As Will told him how he was feeling in the wake of the brawl, his boss said, "Will... nobody defeats a gun."

Will looked at him and found a dead-serious stare looking back. Will had learned how to shoot in the Boy Scouts. They went to the range and got real training from licensed instructors. His parents had given him his own .22 rifle and a 410 shotgun when he turned 12. He and a pal had gone through a firearms course offered by the Forest Service at the Green Lake Fieldhouse when they were 15. He liked guns, like all things mechanical, and was a pretty good shot. He used to shoot crows out of trees, a block from his house at Green Lake. He would rest the barrel of his .22 on his parents' upstairs window sill, and never took more than one shot every few weeks. However, he had never owned a handgun.

The last time he had seen his Uncle Bud he was 11 or 12 years old and they were out in some fields in an old WWII Jeep. He had heard that his uncle's friends called him "One Shot Probert," and there was a pistol in a holster on the floor between the seats. He had forgotten what they were talking about when his uncle reached down, grabbed the pistol, raised it, and fired. He had no idea what he was even shooting at. They drove over a little way and found a rabbit with a bullet right through the head. Will was impressed, to say the least. Later his uncle took him to town and bought him a set of real cowboy boots, a shirt, and a hat. He wore the shirt out, eventually lost track of the hat, but kept the boots the rest of his life.

Now his boss was suggesting that he would never have to take a beating like that again, if he simply shot whoever tried to give it to him. Will was not sure about shooting someone, but was sure about never being the victim of an unprovoked attack like the one he had recently survived. God had saved his life on more than one occasion already, and he believed death was supposed to be His business. Several months before the dust up at Our Place, divine intervention had spared him from death twice in some serious car wrecks.

A few weeks after his conversation with Gus at work, they went to a secondhand shop run by his boss's friend. Some things were sold off the books. Will would be armed, and usually carrying, for most of the next 25 years.

A few months later Will was encouraged to talk with an attorney who was a friend of the family. He had been thinking about taking his attacker from Our Place out without notice, a total blind side. But he knew he would be the obvious suspect. He sued the guy instead, and when the money came through 18 months later, he bought his first house. It was small, repossessed, and condemned, but he got it cheap, fixed it up, and called it home for several years. He also bought the motorcycle of his dreams, a P11 750 Norton and it screamed! It almost got him killed, but also put him together with some guys who rode old Harley Choppers. Will was hooked.

Get a Hawg – Then we'll talk about it

Springtime 1972 was time for the Apple Blossom Festival in Wenatchee, Washington. Wenatchee is in the heart of the largest apple growing region in the world. For a week the city tries to accommodate multitudes who come from far and wide for the festivities. The last weekend of the party much of the downtown is blocked off and crowds roam the various attractions. It was always the first big ride of the year for hard core bikers.

The guys Will ended up riding with were genuine Hawg Ridin' Fools, but they didn't wear a patch. The most notorious color flying clubs are the Hell's Angels and the Banditos, and with good reason. They were hardened criminals who would not hesitate to take a life that hindered their interests. When someone puts a patch on their back, they are making themselves responsible for everything every other guy wearing that patch does, smart or stupid. Will figured he had his hands full staying out of his own trouble, much less being on the hook for whatever some other guy did. He liked the excitement, thrills, and danger. The drunken revelry to be sure. But he had no desire to challenge death just because of who his friends were. He would stand in there, but that patch was an open challenge to every other flag flying scooter tramp around.

One particular bar on the west end of town, The Icicle, served as a known gathering place for 1%ers, but was also accepted as a place where you didn't come looking for trouble. They always had their first beer east of the mountains there. Across the river, outside of East Wenatchee, was Drunken Acre. Even the cops didn't go in there without serious reason.

Will and the guys he rode with had already been escorted by law enforcement out of a few reputable camping areas between Wenatchee and Leavenworth, and were coming down from some full-blown partying at Drunken Acre. About 2:30 AM, it was still warm out when Will and Butter Dog decided a little putt was in order. Will was on his Norton, and Butt was riding a 1952 Harley Davidson Pan Head, fashioned after the Captain America bike in the movie Easy Rider.

They headed east toward Rock Island Dam, away from town. Will's Norton had a tach and speedo that topped out at 7,000 RPM and 110 MPH, and it could reach those limits quickly. Will was in the right-hand lane, and Butter Dog had drifted over to the left of the centerline. No one was around, and any headlights would be seen a long way off. Without looking at each other they began easing the bikes up, a little faster, and a little faster until they were haulin' ass down that country road.

Will looked down and his tach and speedo were both maxed out. His bike only weighed 320 pounds and was vibrating like mad, buzzing underneath him at that RPM. He hung on with both hands and both knees, hunkered down to lessen the impact of the onrushing air. Nobody with any style at all had a wind screen. Needless clutter was avoided at all cost.

He turned his head and looked over at Butter Dog. The frame on the old hard-tail had been cut to drop the rider's butt down near the ground, with his legs out and around the big V-Twin, rather than sitting up on top of the engine like Will's English bike. The front legs and neck had been cut and extended so the tank and triple-clamp – where the front forks and handlebars met – rose up in front of him, breaking the wind against his body, if not his head. His right hand was on the throttle, and his left hand rested in his lap, as casual as could be. Suddenly, he screwed it on and just pulled away, blasting up to speeds Will's Norton could never hope for. Will watched in awe as he thought, "I've GOT to have one of those!"

(1964)
Boldly Forward

Will and Gary left the lights on in the house to make it look like they were still home, slipped out the back door, and left the TV on in the living room. Gary was 14, and a year older than Will. They started the car and idled down the driveway with the headlights off. As they rounded the first corner Gary turned the lights on, and 10 blocks away he pulled over to pick up Eric and Peter, two guys Will had never met before.

Emboldened from the success of sharing Will's parents' Thunderbird, the boys saw no reason to limit themselves to one car. Gary was Will's buddy from church, and they each told their parents they were staying at the other one's house. Gary's dad was a fireman, and would be at work all night. Gary's mom was visiting her sister in Snohomish and Will's mom was not inclined to even suspect her son of sneaky things.

Gary's dad had a 1959 Ford Station Wagon with a luggage rack on top. He liked to go fishing as often as possible, and kept a small aluminum boat tied upside down to the rack on top of the car. The oars and his fishing tackle were in the back of the wagon so he could hit a local lake after work when he had a couple of days off.

On this particular night he had ridden to work with a friend, and the wagon was left at the house unattended. It was backed up into the driveway, alongside of the house, just outside the garage in the back yard. It wouldn't fit in the garage with the boat on top. It was dusk as they eased away, out to the street for a night on the town. They hadn't been able to get ahold of any beer. Gary steered the car toward Golden Gardens, north Seattle's only beach hang out. Maybe they could get lucky.

After a few passes through the parking lot it was obvious they didn't know anyone and saw no realistic prospects. Four teenagers in a station wagon with a fishing boat on top were not all that cool.

Heading back toward Market Street through Ballard, Will said, "I know some girls from school who are having a slumber party. Maybe we should go over there."

Gary turned to look at Will. His eyes were wide open, his brows arched up, and a grin was spreading over his face. He considered himself a real ladies' man.

"How many girls?" he asked.

"I don't know for sure," Will said, "But more than two, I think".

All four of them agreed it was a good idea.

They drove past the house a few times, scouting things out. The front porch light was on, and the glow of one lone light shown dimly through the closed curtains of the front room window.

"They're in the rec room down in the basement," Will said. "We'll go around back and tap on the door." He and Gary eyed each other.

They drove a block past the girl's house, parked at the curb around the corner and halfway down the street, got out and started walking. At the corner Will turned, stopped, and looked at Gary. "I don't know how many friends she has over, so it will probably be best if only one of you comes with me."

Gary nodded and turned to the other two, "You guys wait here. We'll let you know what's going on." He winked at Will and started walking away. Will didn't even give them a glance.

Out in front of the girl's house they looked up and down the street. No one. They climbed the steps up from the sidewalk, eased around the side of the house in the shadows, and crept down the steps to the basement door. They could hear The Beatles playing inside. Will smiled and nodded at Gary as he reached out and tapped on the door three times. The music was turned down a notch and Sarah opened the door halfway. She was tall with dark hair, developing womanly curves, and had a shy smile on her face. Long, dark lashes made her big brown eyes look deep.

"Hi," she said.

"Hi." He reached out and took her hand, turned his head to the right, and said, "This is my friend Gary."

Sarah smiled at Gary and opened the door fully. "Come on in."

The room was softly lit, with a couch, two armchairs, and a Hi-Fi with a TV. Two other girls stood up from the couch, and a third one sitting in one of the chairs raised her hand in greeting.

Sarah said, "Amy, Denise and Gail – this is my friend Will and his friend Gary."

Gary moved right over to meet Amy and Denise, ignoring Gail who was ignoring him. Will slipped his right hand around Sarah's waist and drew her closer, leaning in and giving her a light kiss.

Gary was talking freely with both Amy and Denise, when a strong knock at the door turned all of their heads. Gary looked irritated, Sarah looked stunned, and Gail marched right past them all and opened the door to someone no one else in the room recognized.

An older guy stepped in, wrapping both arms around Gail. She turned to Sarah and said, "I didn't know how this would all turn out, so I made plans of my own." As she walked back over to get her jacket and purse, the guy in the doorway scowled at them.

"My friends are in the car," he said.

Gail looked around at Amy and Denise, ignoring Sarah. They looked at Sarah, and then at each other.

"We'll stay," Amy said for both of them.

"Suit yourself," Gail said, stepped outside with her friend, and closed the door behind her.

They all looked around from one to another in bewilderment. "Can we talk?" Will asked Sarah, nodding toward the door.

"Sure," she said. "We'll be right back."

They stepped up into the back yard and walked over to the shadow at the corner of the garage. "What's going on?" Will asked.

"I have no idea," Sarah said. "I've never seen that guy before, and had no idea she was going to do this. He looks creepy to me, but she's on her own now."

Will pulled her close and locked his lips on hers in the kind of kiss he'd been thinking about since they planned this at school. She surrendered to his embrace.

Parting only their faces Will asked, "What do we do now? Gary picked up two of his buddies on the way. They're waiting for us back by the car."

"Well, I can't leave my friends here alone and there are four of you guys."

"Great!" Will blurted out, dropping their embrace and rubbing his hands through his hair.

"Well, it's not my fault," Sarah said.

He turned around, and melted in the face of her disappointed, but cute pouting. He walked over and gently pulled her toward him. She allowed it, but dropped her head and turned her face to his chest, making it impossible for him to kiss her.

Leaning back, he said, "Okay – let's figure this out. I need to talk with Gary."

When Will and Gary rounded the corner, Peter and Eric were not there. Halfway down the block, they stepped out from the darkness of the alley. "We saw one guy walk out of the house with a girl. Two other guys waited outside when he went in. Then they all got in a car and left. Who were those guys!?"

Will said, "We only saw one."

"There were three," Eric said. "The first guy was angry, and they looked like trouble. When they pulled up, we jumped into the alley and they didn't see us."

"Crap!" Will barked. "Damn it! Well, I've got to go talk to Sarah. I'll meet you guys back at the car in a few minutes."

As Will rounded the corner coming back from Sarah's house, all three of the others were running toward him. "Shit!" Gary

Without Malice

screamed. "They found my dad's car, and we're in real trouble!" They all took off running.

Will saw the first evidence from half a block away. All of the ropes holding Gary's dad's boat to the car were cut and hanging loose down the sides, and the hood was open. As they walked up beside the car, the streetlight revealed that all of the spark plug wires were gone.

"Oh, shit," was all Will could say.

"You have no idea how my dad will explode if we don't get this fixed," Gary moaned, "I'll be dead meat!"

No one spoke for what seemed like forever.

The XXX was a drive-in hamburger place about a mile from Sarah's house and open 24 hours a day. It was 2:30 in the morning, and the boys had walked around for hours before landing there. Sitting in a booth in the corner farthest from the counter, they must have looked as hopeless as they felt.

"Hey," a strong baritone voice said right beside them. They turned and looked up at two of the meanest looking huge guys they had ever seen. They must have been 25 or 30 years old.

"You guys look like shit," the one closest to them said. "What the hell's wrong?"

"You wouldn't believe us if we told you," Will said, hanging his head.

"Try me," the guy said, as he and the other guy wedged themselves into the booth beside them on the end of each bench.

Surprisingly, Will wasn't scared. It felt like these guys really cared. He looked over at Gary.

"What do we have to lose?" Gary said. "I don't see how it could get any worse."

The two rough looking guys didn't say anything else, but focused on Will, waiting for the story.

When Will finished telling them everything, from stealing Gary's dad's car to finding it vandalized by the older guys, the talkative one of the two said, "Let's have a look," and got up.

All four of the boys looked at the two big guys, and then around at each other. They nodded their heads, got up, and followed them out to their car.

They had a beautiful, turquois and white, 1956 Ford Crown Victoria two door. The guy who'd done all the talking got in behind the wheel while the other one held the passenger side seat-back forward so they could get in. A green tree shaped air freshener hanging from a radio nob masked the smell of cigarettes a little with the strong scent of pine. All four squeezed into the back seat together, shoulder to shoulder.

The driver started the engine and turned to them, "Where to?"

When they pulled to the curb behind Gary's dad's car the two guys up front got out, leaving the boys to themselves, and walked up to the station wagon. The silent one looked at each piece of cut rope, while the other one lifted the hood and leaned in over the engine.

Leaving the hood up, he walked back and opened the trunk of the Crown Vic. He closed the trunk, tossed a long, coiled length of rope to his buddy, and said as he walked off, "No problem. I'll be right back."

The big quiet guy began undoing the cut segments of rope, dropped them in the street and retied the boat down with their own well-worn rope. He had worked his way more than half way around the car while the boys sat on the curb watching. The first one reappeared out of the dark like an apparition. He walked up to the engine compartment and began rewiring the distributor cap and spark plugs with the wires from someone else's car.

When he finished, he closed the hood, walked over to the curb, and said, "Keys."

Gary stood up and fished around in his front pocket, pulled out the keys, and handed them to their benefactor. He eased himself into the driver's seat of the wagon, stuck the key in the ignition slot on the dashboard, turned it over, and VROOM, the faithful old wagon jumped to life.

Gary, Will, Peter, and Eric stood in speechless amazement as the two dark angels finished tying the boat down to the luggage rack. When they were done, the one who did all of the talking looked at Will and Gary, winked, and curled the index finger of his right hand as he turned and walked to his own car.

Opening the passenger-side door, he leaned in, reached under the front seat, and raised his muscled, heavily tattooed arm with a long, sharpened, baling hook in his hand.

His eyes took on a dark, sinister glow as he said, "Now let's go find the dirty bastards that did this to you."

His grin sent cold waves through the boy's veins.

It was 5:30 in the morning when Gary, Eric, and Will flopped down and sprawled out in Gary's bedroom. They had never known such relief. Peter asked to be dropped off on the way.

An hour earlier they were thankful to be driving away from the whole mess, having declined their rescuer's offer to find and maim the guys who had vandalized Gary's dad's car. These guys looked like they were capable of murder.

"It's already 4:30, and if we don't get this thing back in the driveway before my dad gets home, he'll do to me what you want to do to those guys," Gary said. Though the avenging angels looked genuinely displeased, they relented and stood by the Crown Vic as the boys drove off.

Backing the car up the driveway with the lights off was not easy, but they believed they had pulled it off and escaped the hell they were sure awaited them earlier.

"Those guys were crazy," Will said softly, eyes closed and hoping for some sleep.

Eric chuckled to himself, "What do you think we should do for the rest of the weekend?" He got a muffled laugh from them all.

BANG!!! The front door downstairs slammed open with such force it may have broken as it hit the hallway wall.

The boys were mid-air and coming bolt upright when Gary's dad bellowed, "GARY! Get your worthless ass down here, NOW!!!"

Will glanced over, just long enough to see the terror on his friend's face, as he and Eric shot across the room and dove out the upstairs bedroom window. They had each been out this window before, though never together, and always more slowly when slipping off while Gary's mom was asleep on the couch down stairs.

Will and Eric knew the back porch roof was just outside the window. With practiced agility, they were down the porch post, across the back yard, over the neighbor's fence, and away from danger as fast as their young legs could carry them. Gary's dad was not to be messed with.

Green Lake was several miles away, but they had walked to it casually, expecting to stall until later, showing up at Will's house as if nothing unusual had happened. Gary's dad had no idea they were supposed to be together, and none of the parents knew Peter and Eric were involved. Gary wouldn't squeal on them, no matter what his dad did to him. He was used to it by now.

It was about 7:45 as they walked past the entrance to the Aqua Theater, which was closed at this time of the morning. The lake was deserted, except for a few fishermen here and there. The two new friends walked along in the comfort that only comes in the aftermath of having been threatened and survived.

They were talking when Eric's eyes popped open wide, just before he took off running. Will heard a car pull to a stop beside him at the curb. Turning to his right, the passenger door of his parents' Cutlass swung open. His father's stern face was staring at him. He looked around as Eric was rounding the corner of the path beside the lake.

It was not a joyful encounter, but it would be the last time his father applied any physical punishment to him. Will knew their relationship had to change, but he had no idea how to go about it. A year later he would be thankful when his parents divorced. He loved his father, but it seemed his dad's primary purpose in his life was to make him miserable. Whenever Will was happy, it appeared to anger him. Will usually did his best to avoid him whenever he could, and outsmart him whenever he needed to. Even at this age, Will viewed most people as contestants in a battle of wits he expected to win. It would not always serve him well.

It turned out, the old lady next door to Gary had heard the car start up the night before. She was on the phone to the fire station where his dad worked before the boys rounded the corner. His dad had called his wife at her sister's, who told him Gary was over at Will's. The conversation with Will's mom exposed the ruse, and Gary's dad immediately called the police to report the car stolen. As a fireman, he knew a few cops.

The Seattle police had been out looking for the boys all night, and Gary's dad headed straight for home as soon as he checked out of the station house in the morning. Will's dad learned about it when he got home. Will's mom would probably have kept it all secret if she could have, but with Gary's dad involved, that wasn't going to happen. None of it deterred Will's appetite for driving cars without authorization. If anything, it stiffened his resolve to get better at getting away with it.

(1972)
Talk and Walk

Though he had been hauled into the Wallingford Precinct a few times for relatively minor issues, Will had never used or handled drugs in any way while still in school. Once he did start smoking pot after graduation the doors opened more gradually for him than most. When he started riding with The Boys a few years later there were no limits to what was readily available, and he steadily expanded his experiences.

By the summer of 1972 his job at the car dealership was gone, and he had begun augmenting his income with a little drug dealing to a select group of people he knew personally. For the most part, he simply sold enough to get all he needed for personal consumption at no cost. This also allowed him to be generous when socializing. His family was on the lower end of middle class growing up, but they were the first to help anyone in need. Will had been taught to be a giver, not a taker, and he took it seriously.

He would buy a kilo of weed and sell enough lids to recover his investment. Once done, he removed the remaining lumber and seeds, and sifted the leaf and buds to the consistency of rolling tobacco. The Pot Pot, a round red ceramic kettle with a matching lid and brass handle, was usually found on his kitchen table. When he was out and about, his pre-rolled joints were kept in an ever present flip-top Marlboro box. For getting a buzz at home with friends, he carried the Pot Pot out to the living room coffee table, lifted the lid and gave his guests a whiff, then slowly twisted up a joint with great care before admiring it, lighting it up, and passing it around. A few clever roach clips and an ash tray adorned the table.

Similarly, though less frequently, the far more costly Charis hashish was apportioned in foil-wrapped grams and sold until his coveted stash was on hand like Crown Royale whiskey, which he also shared less often. Gradually, he added several other items to the menu offered to trusted buyers. When an established customer requested something he did not currently carry, he would check his sources for availability. If it looked like a reasonable prospect, he would pick it up. As word of mouth increased demand, he would respond with increased supply. Simple market economics. What shifted his business from personal convenience to plain old profit making was speed.

Crisscross, small white tabs also known as speed beans, was flowing into town from Mexico like a river, and cheap. Will didn't use speed, except for the rare occasion when help staying awake was needed, such as a long drive to another state or some other unusual demand. He didn't like the anxious feeling it brought on. Some people jumped on it so hard they were rarely awake without it, sometimes for days on end. Will's workmate from the dealership, Dan, became so dependent he was dissolving them into a solution he injected directly into his body. When he crashed it was for days.

Will offered Dan words of caution, but he also knew he would buy it from someone anyway, so it might as well be among friends. Will knew he could trust Dan to never turn on him if he got caught. Will bought in quantities of 1,000 – known as a Jar. Most people were occasional, though regular users. A weekend of partying was typical.

Butch would actually use them to keep other, more powerful drugs – or combinations of various drugs and alcohol – from rendering him unconscious. Most people purchased 10, 20, or 25 hits at a time. Two to four was a typical dosage. Dan bought 50 or 100 at a time. He was Will's best customer. It was rare for Will to sell a whole Jar to anyone.

Will's car was a 1959 Austin Healey 100-6. Though he loved excessive power, he had a compelling affection for British sports cars. His American muscle car mantra was, "Any car that won't cause you to fear for your life in less than four seconds is underpowered," and the Healey could not do that. But it looked so good, and the sound was intoxicating. It would not be his only Austin Healey, and he went on to enjoy six British Sports Cars over the years. This particular Healey was a rolling drug store. He also wore a thigh length, light weight leather jacket with multiple pockets, inside and out. If he didn't have it on him when he walked into Our Place, it was out in the car. The place seemed safe after all those years.

Butch and Will were sitting in Will's Healey directly outside of the front door one warm summer night with the top down, nose to the curb. That curb had probably kept at least a few patrons from driving right in. The place was packed, as usual. They each had a fresh schooner, poured from a pitcher at a table of friends inside. Will was casually toking on a joint as they sipped and talked. Butch had never smoked anything of any kind… ever. His body was a temple he worked hard to keep as hard as a rock. Smoking could kill you. In the small space behind the seats Will had a bag of cherry bombs. He loved blowing stuff up, and almost always had explosives of some kind nearby.

He reached behind the seat, and brought the bag up into his lap. Butch looked over at him, curious.

"What's in the bag?"

Will only grinned at him.

"Come on, you dog. What're you grinning about?"

The glimmer in Will's eyes brightened. He turned his head to the bag, opened the top, and looked in. He turned back to Butch, smiling ear to ear.

"What!?" Butch almost yelled at him, Will's grin igniting one on Butch's face, too.

Will turned back toward the bag, sat his beer on the floor between his legs and reached in, feigning curiosity. With a look of startled surprise he lifted up a little bright red ball with a green fuse sticking out.

"What do we have here?" he asked. Butch couldn't help but smile as he shook his head.

Without Malice

"What do you think?" Will asked.

Butch looked at the open front door, then back at Will. "Are you crazy?" he asked, through his own laughter. They had set them off in public places before with dramatic effect.

Without a word, Will put the little surprise in his left hand and drew a lighter from his right front pocket.

Butch's face grew serious as Will flipped the lid of his Zippo open with his thumb and stroked the wheel, sparking the flame to life. Will had a bad habit of holding lighted explosives way too long for Butch, and it made him nervous.

Will's eyes narrowed as he switched hands with the lighter and the bomb.

"OK, then. Let's have some fun," he said as he lit it, held it long enough to be sure it was burning well, and tossed it over the windshield right in the front door.

Just inside the door to the left was a eight foot long waist high wall made of vertical peeler poles. It made a 90 degree turn to the right and ran about six feet further to a stool for whoever was working the door. That left plenty of space inside if a group of people were all coming in at once. Will looked first. The space was empty.

The cherry bomb bounced once off the floor, and again off the short wall before exploding – BOOM!! – concussing like a hand grenade inside the crowded tavern. An explosion of shrieks and screams followed immediately from the unsuspecting patrons. They came gushing out the front door in a torrent, wanting only to escape whatever was happening in their midst. Like enraged fans at a South American soccer match, they were so consumed in a stampede mentality they didn't even notice Will and Butch overwhelmed in fits of hilarity in the small car.

Once the nervous owner realized no harm or damage had been done, he scurried around, herding everyone back inside, and announced the next glass of beer was on the house. He quickly realized it would create a buzz among them that would draw even more people looking for an exciting night out with others their own age. As the bulk of the crowd began flowing back in to the promise of free beer, Butch and Will joined them and blended in.

About 30 minutes later, a guy named Nick, whom Will had known only peripherally, approached him. Seeing him coming they had eye contact.

"Hey," Nick said, extending his right hand. He was medium height with a slight build and wiry, out of control light brown hair. His intense, light blue eyes looked like they were straining to get out. He looked a little twitchy to Will.

Will reached out and shook hands. "How's it going? Nick, right?"

It had become Will's habit to keep himself acutely aware of his surroundings, especially after the unforeseen attack in this very place. He always chose a spot that gave him the broadest view of any room he was seated in.

"Yeah, Nick. And you're Will. Seen you around."

They both nodded and took a drink of their beer.

"So, what's up?" Will asked.

"Well," Nick said, "I heard I might be able to score a little speed from you," arching his eyebrows with an inviting inquiry.

Will had seen the guy around and knew they both knew some of the same people, but he didn't know anything about him and wasn't picking up any strong impressions one way or the other.

"Yeah? From who?" he asked.

Nick turned his head to the right and nodded over toward a table by the juke box near the front door. A guy Will knew, but not well, lifted his hand in a slight wave. "Jake," Nick said.

"Yeah," Will said. "Well… I could probably find some for you. How much you looking for?"

"Oh, just enough for me and a buddy for the weekend. 20 or 25, maybe."

They agreed on a price, though Will did not negotiate. You want to pay less, buy less.

Will had small baggies of different small quantities stored systematically in different pockets of his jacket. He was out of 20s. "I can do 25" he said. "Let's talk," and turned toward the back of the building.

The restrooms were near the back door, the Women's room was closest to the action, and the Men's was along the back wall. The door to the outside had a large back-lit sign that said clearly enough for the average drunk to read: EMERGENCY ONLY! ALARM WILL SOUND. Will had an agreement with the head bartender, and no alarm would sound.

"Take a leak, then meet me outside," Will said, and slipped out the door right in front of him. A few minutes later, Nick came around the outside corner of the building from the parking lot.

A bag of 25 formed a little tear drop in the corner of a baggie, twisted and tied tightly. There would be no questions of count when he turned loose of the pills in exchange for the offered cash.

"Have a good time," Will said as he turned and went back in through the forbidden door, leaving Nick in the parking lot. He would not see him again that night.

The next weekend they did business again for 25, and over the next few months Nick would tap Will almost weekly, usually for 25, sometimes 50. Once he was desperate and got only 10.

As they settled into a consistent working relationship, Will gave Nick his phone number. They didn't chat. Nick would occasionally call to ask Will if he was going to be at the tavern that night. A couple of times Will let Nick drop by his house, out in the alley, lights off. Will would slip out through the garage, and Nick would be off. Except for personal friends who were often at his house anyway, Will rarely did business out of his house. It was the exception, not the rule. He lived in a normal, middle class neighborhood and got along well enough with most of his neighbors.

Sometimes Will was a little loud and boisterous with his cars and bikes out in the street. There were occasional explosions, just for fun, but they knew he was not a threat, and crowds of unruly people didn't congregate at his house.

The Boys had a house for that, and Will felt genuinely sorry for the people who lived near them. Those poor people had to endure things typical Americans never dreamed of – dozens of scooters, kick stand to kick stand at the curb the length of the property, and dozens more on it, front and back, with more in the basement. Sometimes swarms of dangerous looking people roamed about. Combined with the really loud music, this contributed to an environment so potentially volatile that even the police just cruised by as a hopeful deterrent. The ones who did know where Will lived knew he would never tolerate that kind of action at his house. Some of these Scooter Tramps were in it for life. Will knew this was a season he was enjoying for the unparalleled thrills, but he fully expected to grow up and have a normal life someday… no rush.

After several months of what seemed like predictable business, Will expected the usual when he saw Nick coming his way at Our Place one Friday night.

"How's it going?" Will asked. "The usual?"

Nick dipped his head a bit as he said, "Well… actually, no. Um… I was hoping I could get quite a bit more. What do you think?"

Will was a little surprised, but he'd seen other people want to make a larger than expected buy from time to time. One reason he never planned to expand into larger quantities was he didn't want to become a larger target. The cops would arrest someone like him if they had to, but in the grand scheme of things, he was a small fish in a small pond and he fully intended to keep it that way. He liked to get high for free, and a little extra cash here and there wasn't bad. But he liked his freedom even more.

"I don't know," Will said. "How much are we talking about?"

Nick looked at his shoes again, then looked up and said, "Oh… how about a jar or two?"

Will didn't flinch, but he didn't have a jar or two. As soon as he bought one, he divided it up into smaller packages. He could get it, but wasn't sure he wanted to. At least he would know he would turn it right away, and he wouldn't have his money tied up, not knowing when his return would come. He wouldn't make much, but it wouldn't take long. He also had no intention of supplying his own competition, but if Nick had a brain in his head, he knew that.

"When were you thinking?" he asked. "I don't tote that much around."

"Oh, not tonight," Nick said. "Next week some time?"

"Let me see what I can do," Will said. "You going to be around tomorrow night?"

"Yeah," Nick said.

"OK. I'll let you know."

They shook hands, and went their separate ways for the rest of the night. They were often in the same place, but the only table they ever shared was a pool table.

The next Wednesday night they met in the parking lot of a steak house on Bothell Way. Will was driving a different car. They did the deal for two jars and left.

Saturday night at Our Place Will saw Jake when he walked in. "Hey... haven't seen Nick around this weekend."

"Oh, he split down to California. Him and another guy. Sun, fun, and sand, I guess. Hopefully some California girls," he said with a smile.

"Cool," Will said, and that was that.

Three weeks later Will was shooting a game of pool on one of the back tables and saw Jake coming his way. He took his shot, and then looked up to give him a nod. Jake motioned him over to the pay phone on the wall. It was set away from other stuff, as if that would make it easier for people to hear.

"Did you hear what happened to Nick?" Jake asked him.

"No," Will said.

"Him and his buddy got busted down in California with some speed."

"No, shit! So, what's happening to him?"

"Some small town. He went before a judge almost right away. He pleaded guilty and got 90 days in a county detention center. I guess they send 'em out picking up trash and shit. He says no big deal. At least he gets to go outside. You do 90 days inside and you come out looking like a ghost."

Will stood still, his face freeze framed. After a few moments of chewing on it he said slowly, "Yeah... Well, I guess that wouldn't be too hard to do. Let me know if you hear anything else, OK?"

"Yeah. You got it," Jake said, and turned toward the bar to get a beer.

Will didn't say anything else to anyone. As far as he knew, no one else knew he had sold Nick the two jars. He finished his game and left for home. Doing business didn't feel as safe as it had. A little later when his phone rang, he didn't answer. He didn't feel like talking to anyone. He was downstairs in his room. All the upstairs lights were off, inside and out.

Will wasn't back at Our Place all week. His only sale was to Dan from the car dealership. Toward the weekend, he wasn't feeling so nervous and walked into Our Place Friday night about 8:15 without a thing on him, or in the car. When asked for a lid, a gram or a dime bag he just said, "Sorry – got nothing with me."

Over the next week he fell back into his normal routine with his friends, but still kept nothing with him except personal stash, and that was in the car. Nothing looked or felt out of order, and the following week he eased back in business. He was more like a vending machine than a grocery store, anyway. He was certainly not a wholesaler. No reason to get jumpy.

Two weeks later, he was shooting pool on the front table about 9:30 when Nick strolled through the door. Because the front pool table was to the left of the door, and behind anyone turning to face the doorman, Nick didn't see him. As soon as Nick was out of sight in the crowd, Will leaned his stick against the wall and said, "Gotta take a leak." He walked around the waist wall, out the front door to his car, and drove straight home without another word. He stopped in the alley with his headlights off, got out and opened the garage door, drove in, shut the car off, closed the door, and went inside with all the house lights off.

Will sat on his bed in the dark, his mind racing. "That son of a bitch talked," he said to himself. "There is no way he gets out halfway through 90 days unless he talked. Shit!"

"Damn it!" he barked, and slammed his hand down on the bed. Did those two jars put him over some kind of threshold that would mean more time? He did NOT want to go to prison.

He didn't want to do any County time either, but a year or more? NO THANKYOU!

BRRIIINNNGG!!! His phone went off on his headboard and he almost jumped out of his skin. He reached over and picked it up, "Hello."

"Hey Man! Where the hell you been?" It was Dan. "Look, I ran out and I need something Right Now, Tonight!"

"You must have the wrong number," Will said, and hung up. He turned the phone base upside down and switched the ringer off. He hadn't even known that switch was there until he was telling a friend about the monster hangover he had a couple of years earlier.

Will was up on his feet, pacing in circles around his room. He raked his hands through his hair and slapped his palms against his thighs.

"Shit! Damn it!" he shouted. "That little weasel! I can't even touch his worthless little ass! You know he's being watched. Son Of A Bitch!!!"

When he went off like that around other people they just backed off and gave him space, except for his really close friends, who may give him a ration just to see if he would pop.

He sat back down on the bed, still and silent. What could he do? Get rid of everything, pronto... that was for sure. He had storage garages around north Seattle he kept cars in. He could stash it all in one of those, or several of them. But what if the cops were outside watching him right now? What the hell could he do? What should he do? His mind was not working real well.

There was not much in life he reacted more poorly to than feeling trapped. He usually handled it badly. When cornered by people trying to manipulate him, they usually didn't get what they were hoping for. He'd never felt so trapped in his life, and hopeless.

"Oh, I know," he said to himself, but didn't feel at all confident he could ask God to help him. God had been bugging him regularly lately. No one else knew. No one but his mom and his sister would even suspect he ever gave God a thought. He ridiculed phonies who turned for help to people they had ignored before things went bad. Real friends were there no matter what happened, and he had been telling God for several years, "Not Now," whenever he felt pressed by Him.

"Look, God... I know I haven't been right with you for a long time. I'm sorry. Please forgive me. But I'm in a real jam. I promise, if you keep me out of prison with this deal, I'll never sell drugs again."

There. He'd done it. He made a deal with God, and he meant it. Will was somebody who kept his word, ask anyone who knew him. He had stretched some lines to near what he thought must be the breaking point, but was genuinely fearful of crossing any that would close the door to God for good. He doubted anyone even noticed that though he could curse fluently, far better than most, he never spoke the name of Jesus as an exclamation or an expletive, and never, ever said God damn. He knew his lifestyle was unacceptable to God, but had no intention of personally insulting Him. He expected to turn back to God someday, but also expected that would require giving up much of what he enjoyed, and he just hadn't been ready. Not so far.

He sat in the darkness in silence. He didn't feel anything. When he was a kid on Vashon Island he knew God was right there. He knew God was certainly right there when He made him feel bad in the midst of doing stuff he knew he shouldn't be doing. But now... nothing. He wondered.

He waited a week. The hammer didn't fall. Then he discreetly moved his entire inventory to some of his garages, ones he rarely went to, and let it all sit for a month. When asked for anything at Our Place he said, "I'm not doing that anymore. Sorry, can't help you."

The first week Dan had jumped on him big time, "Man, what the hell's wrong with you!? You hang up on me when I'm in a jam like that?"

He told him what had happened, and sold all of his remaining speed to him at a bargain. He hoped Dan wouldn't kill himself with it. He offed the rest of his product to a few other guys who dealt, too. They were happy to get it. Will always had good stuff. When anyone called him at home and asked about anything related to drugs, his standard reply was, "You must have the wrong number," and hung up. If the cops were watching and listening they wouldn't get any fresh evidence, that's for sure. He still got high, but bought one day at a time from the personal stash of friends. He had always been generous, and they were accommodating. When asked why he got out he simply said, "It was time."

God kept his end of the bargain, and it was months before Will bought more that he needed that day. It was even longer before he did a friend a favor and edged his way back toward paying for his own stuff through simple commerce again. He just kept having the discussion with himself until he justified his rationale that no harm was being done. He wasn't going back into full dealing. The camel's nose was under the tent. Then he thought, "Okay… looks like there's no threat. Keep it small and safe." He was a little surprised that after he pushed his thoughts about God out of the way, He didn't bother him about it. Maybe it wasn't that bad.

(1964)
More In 64

Will had been taking classical piano lessons since he was five years old. He started playing the clarinet in the 5th grade, and in the 8th grade was playing in The Seattle Junior High School All City Band on clarinet and All City Orchestra on the bass clarinet, but he wanted more from music. In the fall of 1963 he persuaded his mother to let him begin taking piano lessons from a jazz teacher who had played at the Monterey Jazz Festival – Johnny Whitworth. His life began to change.

Johnny got him involved in a Rock-n-Roll band of young musicians sponsored by the music studio. By the summer of 1964, Will wanted his own band. He bought a small, portable organ and recruited a sax player and a guitar player through the studio. He ended up with a 23 year old bass player who was married with one child and another on the way. He had met a drummer on an Explorer Scouts mountain climbing expedition in the Olympic Mountains the summer before, but he was already in another band, and introduced Will to a friend of his, Allen, who was available. They hit it off and became close friends.

Will and Allen both loved British Sports cars. Allen had been working on a 1959 Austin Healey Bug Eye Sprite for almost a year, and finally he had it running. He had done some engine work and a few other performance enhancing upgrades, and they were eager to put it to the test.

Will parked up the street from Allen's house. Allen's family lived in an upper income neighborhood of mostly brick homes with multiple car garages. As Will walked down the driveway at Allen's house, the front end of the Sprite was raised up and he was bent over it fiddling with the side draft carburetor. He heard

Will's footsteps coming down the concrete driveway. He raised up from the car, grabbed a red shop rag from the inner fender, and wiped his hands.

"So, when do we light this sucker up and take it out for a test beating?" Will asked.

Alan grinned. He walked over, opened the small door to the sports car, and dropped down in the very minimal driver's bucket seat, a mere eight inches above the ground. Will saw and heard the carburetor throttle rods rotate three times as Allen pumped the gas pedal, then heard the mechanical choke cable pulled from the dashboard. Allen flashed him a smug, confident look as he turned the key.

VROOM... and the 948cc engine roared to life with the ferocious rasp of unmuffled exhaust. Allen let it idle roughly until the engine oil pressure needle moved above 30 pounds. When the water temperature gauge began its upward march, he eased the choke in and revved the engine mildly a few times. Once it was warmed up enough, he pushed the choke all the way in and let it lope along at a lazy 650 rpm. Not having run for months, the hot smells of oil and dust cooking off filled the garage. His eyes rested on the dashboard with a look of warmth and affection he never showed human beings.

He pulled down on the inside door cord, swung the door open, stepped out and raised himself to his feet. He joined Will at the front of the car as they both stood looking at the humming little beast with shared admiration.

"Shall we?" Allen asked.

"Oh, yeah," Will replied.

Allen reached up and grabbed the underside of the one piece nose of the Sprite, pulling it down until it rested on the center latch. He spread his hands and placed them on the curves of the rounded fenders and pushed down until he heard the latch click. He then reached under the nose and turned the T-handle, locking it in the closed position.

He looked at Will and said, "Let's do it."

They eased into the tiny cockpit and snugged the doors closed. Allen pushed the clutch pedal to the floor, and gave the engine just enough gas to engage things fully and propel the car out of the garage and up the drive onto the street. They coasted down the hill to the stop sign and drove off, shifting from 1st to 2nd and 2nd to 3rd at about 2,500 rpm. The car felt good. After a four or five mile moderate shakedown cruise, they rolled it back into the garage. No problems. "Alright then," Allen said.

"7:00 O'clock?" Will asked.

"That's it," Allen said, and Will headed up the hill as Allen went to work installing a muffler.

It had been a good night so far - top down, plenty of beer, and they had not been out of the Sprite except to put some gas in it once, and take a leak now and then as needed. The car felt good, and had not stumbled or faltered even once. The winding, twisting roads leading in and out of Carkeek Park and Golden Gardens Park were giving them greater and greater confidence in the nimble little sports car's ability at ever increasing speeds. As the boys got more well-oiled, it seemed there were no boundaries they could not explore that the Sprite's agility would not handle. The car deserved its name.

Just after midnight they passed through the green light at N.E. 75th, northbound on 15th Ave. N.E. at about 45 miles per hour. Allen leaned into the throttle a little more, and in a few blocks they were cruising steady at 60 mph. As they approached N.E. 82nd, Allen said, "We should swing by and see if Baldwin is up," and without notice he cranked the wheel hard to the left while stomping the gas pedal to the floor. He hoped to maintain as much speed as possible coming out of the corner, but pitched the little car into an unexpected slide.

When it appeared the tail-end may come all the way around, he turned the wheel back hard to the right and lifted off the gas pedal. His inexperience would be costly. If the car had had enough hoot to break the rear wheels loose with more power, it could have been driven through a power-slide and straightened out, assuming there was enough room. But his ill-advised combination of actions caused the rear end to bite, and the front end to whip back around to the right so hard it ripped the steering wheel from his hands. With a little more room the car may have just bounced up over the curb.

Unfortunately, there was a 1963 Pontiac four-door sedan parked at the right-hand curb about 100 feet down 82nd Street. At their speed that ground was covered quickly, and the front end came around just in time to slam into the back of the Pontiac so hard it knocked it into the car parked in front of it. Neither of the boys had seat belts on. Seat belts were not standard equipment for British cars built in 1959, and the car was intended for casual sports driving, not the race track.

Both of them may well have died, were it not for the unusual design of the Sprite's front end. Instead of typical separate fenders and a hood, held together with a radiator support and grill between them, the Sprite had a one-piece solid front end that hinged at the firewall, and lifted up from the front. The left-lower point of the Pontiac's rear bumper dug into the sheet metal of the Sprite's solid nose, and wrinkled it up in front of the windshield. That kept the tiny sports car from going under the much larger American family sedan. It also kept Will from going completely through the windshield. As they lurched forward on impact, Will instinctively lifted his right hand up in front of his forehead. When he hit the windshield the back of his hand was cut open badly, but it was his only injury. Allen suffered no visible damage at all. The Sprite was another matter.

The car popped out of gear and recoiled backward, rolling to a gentle stop in the middle of the street, steam spewing from the mangled radiator. Surprisingly, the engine was still running. As usual, Allen was drunker than Will, and the two of them got out and staggered around to survey the damage. The impact awakened people in the nearby houses. The owner of the Pontiac came out to investigate after he had looked out of his front room window to see his car banged into his wife's car, with its right front wheel up on the curb. He briefly assessed his cars, then approached the two young drunks.

"Are you boys Okay?" he asked cautiously.

Will looked back at him, dazed but sobering up fast. "Uh, yeah… I think I'm Okay," he said, unaware of his bleeding hand.

Will turned to ask Allen how he was doing, just as he was dropping into the driver's seat.

"What the hell are you doing?" Will shouted.

"We've gotta' get outta' here," Allen replied.

"Are you nuts!?" Will screamed. "We're not going anywhere in that thing."

"You might not be," he slurred, "But I sure as hell am."

That was immediately followed by the awful sound of spinning gears grinding against each other. Allen was attempting to put the transmission in gear, but the crash had caused the hydraulic clutch to fail.

Will turned back to the owner of the Pontiac.

"Is there anyone I can call for you boys?" the man asked. Will gave Allen's parents' phone number to him. The man didn't tell him he had called the police before he came out of his house.

Will turned around when he heard the car engine stop. Allen was wrestling with the gear shifter, hoping to restart it with the transmission in 1st gear, but the starter wasn't strong enough to move the car forward on its own.

The police pulled up just as Allen was attempting to push it away and try it on the roll. The officers tried diplomacy, but Allen's drunken belligerence was wearing them down quickly. When he repeatedly refused to sign the ticket, he was placed under arrest. He was sitting in the back seat of a squad car when his father pulled up. Allen's dad was a kind, intelligent, and highly accomplished man, but his son's fate was sealed for the night before he got there. After the unavoidable details were settled, he gave Will a ride home. A tow truck was hooking up Allen's car to haul it home, and Allen was on his way to jail.

Working Man

Will's first paycheck job at "The Stinker Station", Vic Green's Gas & Tire Mart on north 45th Street, had been a good fit. He'd left the house one summer morning with the declaration, "I'm not coming home until I have a job." He was tired of mowing lawns.

The station's huge, brightly lighted sign had a giant skunk painted on it. Ten gas pumps along with every petroleum distillate known to man, and a full-service tire shop. The rule was, "Get a hose in every tank." The place had not been closed for even one hour since it first opened in 1947, and every kid in north Seattle stopped in on Friday and Saturday night to put a couple of bucks of gas in mom and dad's car on the way home. Regular was 23.9 cents a gallon.

His second week on the job, he was running from car to car when a $1.00 customer started griping at him about checking all the tires. He told the guy it would be a few minutes. The customer was getting loud when the owner came out.

"What's going on here?" he asked.

"He got a dollar's worth of gas and wants all of his tires checked," Will said. "I've got all these other cars going, and I told him it'll be a few minutes before I can get to it."

The owner walked over to within ten feet of the irate customer. "You got a dollar's worth of gas?" he asked.

"Yes!" the guy said firmly.

"And you want all of your tires checked?" the owner asked.

"Yes," the guy said as he folded his arms across his chest.

"No problem," the owner said. He then pulled a large stick of yellow tire chalk from the breast pocket of his shirt. Walking briskly around the car he put a big yellow check mark on each of the car's four tires. That finished, he walked back up to within two feet of the confused looking customer, smiled wickedly, and said, "Now get the hell out of here!" He then turned and marched back into the office without a word. Will suppressed his laughter until his boss was inside.

Will started at the gas station the summer he was 14 and life at Stinker's was rarely dull. It was robbed a few times, though always between 2:00 and 6:00 AM, and never when he was working. After one hold up the owner mounted a double-barreled 12 gauge shotgun over the door inside the back room. During the most recent stickup the employee was locked in there.

A Seattle Police officer came and gave the employees instructions. If they were locked in the back room by a robber, they should first take the shotgun down, go to the breaker panel and turn the main power switch for the whole property off and on three times. Then aim the gun at the door. If it was opened by the robber, they were to point it at the center of his body and pull the trigger.

After working there two and a half years, he quit in protest half way through his senior year of high school over a deceitful manager. He was hired shortly afterward, down the hill at Dale's Texaco station, right across the street from Dick's Drive In.

Dale's was a high-class place where clean, starched and pressed, uniforms with the employee's name embroidered on them were provided every week. The rule there was "Never leave a car you are working on until you are completely finished with it." That meant cleaning all of the glass, checking all of the fluids under the hood, and filling them as needed, and checking the air pressure in all four tires. Employees were usually swarming like bees, so someone was running to a new customer when they pulled in.

As it worked out, one particular spring day everyone else was gone for one reason or another, except one of the two full-time mechanics, whose butt was hanging out of an engine compartment in a work-bay inside the building. The mechanics didn't pump gas. Will was on the pumps alone. He had just gotten started on a full service fill up, when another car pulled in on the other side of the pump island. The driver of the second car shut it off, got out, and stood beside his car.

Will nodded, waved to him and said, "I'll be right with you as soon as I finish this car," and smiled at the man. He did not smile back.

As Will hustled along servicing the first car, the other man walked to the end of the island and stood beside the gas pump glaring at him.

"I'll be right there," Will repeated, and kept working. The tank wasn't full yet and he wasn't quite done checking the fluids.

As he closed the hood, the other man pulled the hose handle from the pump and barked at him, "How do you turn this thing on!?"

Will stepped over, reached out and flipped the small lever on the side to clear the register, then swung the large pump handle up 90 degrees to turn the pump on. "Just about done over here," he said as he moved back to the first car.

As he stood up from checking the air pressure in the third tire, he saw the angry second customer standing beside the pump again with the hose handle in his hand. The man scowled at him and barked, "What the hell am I supposed to do with this thing now!?"

Will replied, "Buddy, you can shove it up your ass for all I care," though it didn't seem quite as funny as when the owner at Stinker's did it.

"Pompous Ass," Will muttered to himself as the man drove away in a huff. Will didn't care if he paid or not. He hadn't been there long enough to get much. The pump readings would show any discrepancy, and he would explain when asked.

Walking in to work the next day, the owner invited him into his office and closed the door behind them. Neither of them sat down. As the boss extended Will's check to him, he said with an understanding tone, "You know, Will… I don't know if you're cut out to work with the general public." It turns out the old buzzard was the owner's best friend.

Will looked down at the check, then reached out and took it. It was obvious there was nothing to discuss.

The owner concluded, "Just bring your uniforms back in the next few days. I'm not withholding any deposit for them." He smiled softly and reached out to shake his hand. Will obliged. "No hard feelings," the owner said. Will turned and left.

(1972)
A Change of Venue

Will's life was sailing along smoothly after the drug bust scare with Nick. "If I were going to be arrested from that whole mess," he thought, "it would have happened already." He was limiting his dealings to people he knew well, and for only enough to provide for his own needs. No more speed. He had a good job with a plumbing and mechanical contractor on the Eastside, and was working steady making decent money. Some of it was hard physical labor, but he was learning how plumbing went together and the hard work had him in great shape.

If a house needed a new water service that ran less than 75 feet from the meter, he did the digging. He kept track of the parts inventory in the warehouse, delivered parts and materials to construction job sites, picked up specialty supplies from wholesalers, and even did a little fitting from time to time.

Will was in the warehouse putting a shipment of parts in the proper bins one October afternoon when the secretary called him into the boss's office. He walked in and stood waiting while the owner finished something he was writing. Putting his pen down, he looked up at Will and smiled. "Hey, Will… how's it going today?"

"Looking good," he replied. "I'm just about done putting that shipment of parts away."

"OK, good. Say, you know that apartment building we started out on 158th?"

"Yeah," Will said. "I dropped off the soil pipe out there awhile back."

Without Malice

"All right," his boss continued. "They've stepped up the schedule. The framing is up, and they want us to start the rough in tomorrow. I'd like you to run out there and punch a hole through the foundation wall in the carport this afternoon so they can get going in the morning. Anything that would keep you from getting on that right away?"

"No. I'm good to go," Will said. He loved getting out of the warehouse, going somewhere in the shop truck, and doing some hands-on stuff. He liked working on his own, too. Talking it up with another employee on the way to a job, or at lunchtime was Okay. But blabbing on the job was not what he was being paid to do. And he hated to start something he couldn't finish. This would be a great way to finish the day, and he would get to take the shop truck home that night.

"There's a horse and a half roto-hammer out in the shop that will do the job," the boss said. "I had Hugh drop by and mark the spot to drill in blue chalk while he was on the way to another job a little earlier. Just call it a day when you're done there."

"I'm on it," he said. The boss winked and they both smiled.

Will walked out to get the hammer as the owner picked up the phone.

When Will pulled up to the jobsite, no other workmen were around. As he hopped out of the truck the only sound was evening traffic in the distance. He grabbed the roto-hammer from the back of the truck and walked around the corner of the foundation footing for the carport entry at the back, on the downhill slope of the property. The large blue chalk X was about five feet above the ground, toward the interior of the ceiling-height foundation wall. He put the power tool down, and went back to the truck for a ladder, an extension cord, and a drill-bit pack.

He figured he'd drill a ¾ inch pilot hole through the concrete wall, then punch in the 1 ½ inch hole they needed for the water service. They were going to be nice places, four apartments, two on each of two floors, each unit with its own off-street parking.

Will set the bit in the chuck, tightened it hard with the chuck-key, and squeezed the trigger. It torqued over in his hands with some serious force. He climbed up and braced his feet on the third and forth steps of the ladder, and grabbed the tool hard with his right hand on the rear handle grip, his left hand on the solid handlebar at the bottom of the motor. He raised it up with his right elbow at ear height, and pressed the bit against the center of the chalk mark.

When he squeezed the trigger the powerful tool began turning, twisting, and pulsating as it pounded away at the wall, bits and pieces of concrete flying off with the dry, gray dust, the bit sinking deeper and deeper into the wall. With a release of tension, the bit burst through to the other side, and he kept the power on as he eased it back and forth in the new hole a few times. He stopped, exhaled, and rested a moment with the heavy motor in his right hand, the bit in the hole bearing most of the weight.

He smiled to no one but himself. It felt good. The larger hole would be much easier now.

He climbed down and upended the tool on the ground, with the bit pointing straight up. Kneeling down, he loosened the chuck, reached in the bag, and exchanged the 1 ½ inch bit for the smaller one. He tightened the chuck with an extra cinch, blew out a breath, and went back up the ladder to finish the job. He squeezed the trigger one more time, and the powerful tool began pounding away at the wall, moving forward much more quickly than before.

When Will came to, things were a little foggy at first. As he opened his eyes he was on his back on the ground, looking up at the ladder beside him with no idea how long he had been there. The hefty drill motor was on the ground beside him and his jaw hurt like hell. He reached up and drew his hand across his bearded chin, and pulled it away a little bloody.

It was dusk and silent all around. The job site was in a newly cleared development with no dwellings on the adjacent properties. He slowly began to recall the bit grabbing something that stopped it hard, spinning the lower handlebar full force into his chin as he leaned into it, knocking him off of the ladder. He didn't know if the roto-hammer had knocked him out, or the ground when he hit. The back of his head hurt too, but he didn't remember landing.

He sat up and looked around. He looked up at the half-finished hole in the wall, sure he had struck a piece of rebar. He slowly got to his feet, packed up his stuff, and headed for home. It was getting dark, and he would come back early to finish the hole on the way to work in the morning. He didn't tell anyone at work about it, and his beard hid the evidence well.

That winter brought a long, hard freeze. The temperature had been in the low 20's for ten days and pipes were bursting all over. Old galvanized water supply lines were common, and froze easily when not buried deep enough. An arc welder was loaded in the back of the shop truck, and the boss sent Will out to see if the frozen lines could be thawed. He clamped one lead to the connection at the meter and the other at the connection nearest to the house. As the line heated up and the meter started turning, the flow rate revealed if the pipe was leaking or not. If the meter stopped moving, the line was probably good. It if kept turning the line was probably ruptured. Repair was not an option. A new trench would be dug with a Ditch Witch, and a new plastic replacement pipe installed. The other most common broken pipes occurred in inexpensive construction with kitchen and bathroom sinks on outside walls with no insulation. Those could be repaired.

The shop had been running at maximum capacity, 15 to 18 hours per day for a week. Will walked into the office at 6:30 one night as the owner said to a customer on the phone, "We'll see what we can do and call you back." Will didn't know if he was done for the night or not. He'd been there since 6:00 that morning. The boss was standing behind the counter with his head down and his eyes closed, breathing slowly.

"What's up?" Will asked.

He looked up at Will, his eyes expressionless, and said nothing.

"What?" Will asked again.

"Will," the owner said. "Do you think you could go out and fix a broken, leaking copper line under a kitchen sink in Kirkland? There's a mother with two toddlers and an infant who has water all over her kitchen. When she came in the room and saw water coming from the cabinet under the sink, she opened the cabinet doors and the spray hit her in the face. She closed the doors, left the room, and started making calls. We're the first one that answered the phone. Her husband is out of town, and she is at her wits end. We have every truck on a job already, and no one is likely to be freed up for quite a while. What do you think?"

Will thought about it. He knew he could do it. All the needed parts and materials were either already in the shop truck or in the warehouse.

After a moment's pause he said, "Yeah… I can do it. But it will be the company doing the job for her, and you'll be charging shop rates. Extra-hours rates, if I'm not mistaken. You charge shop rates, I want journeyman pay." Will didn't blink or smile. It was a simple computation.

The owner looked back at him, at first a little surprised, and then a slight smile emerged on his big, round face. "Get going," he said, and handed him the work order.

The big freeze finally broke more than a week later. Will hadn't slept much, but he'd made better money than he'd ever made in his life, and none of his repair jobs had had call backs. He was well pleased.

As summer turned to fall that year the settlement from his lawsuit for the bar attack came through and he was in the market for a house. On his mother's advice, he called a few banks that did mortgage lending and asked for a list of repossessed houses for sale. He made a list of addresses, and began driving by to look at them after work a few nights every week. Most were unoccupied.

Washington Mutual Savings and Loan advertised their mortgage services as "The Friend of The Family." More skeptical former clients called them The Repo Depot.

By the time Will was in the market, most mortgages were made with a deed of trust. Older, earlier loans had often been made by way of a traditional real estate contract. With a deed of trust, failure to make scheduled payments could result in eviction in as few as 90 days. With an old school real estate contract it could take 18 months or longer. Free rent for the troubled buyer, and lost revenue for the lender.

One night on the way home, after several fruitless investigations so far, Will pulled up in front of an unlit, unoccupied little house in the Lake City neighborhood of north Seattle. It was small with a mostly above ground basement on a large 60' X 120' lot. A dozen wood steps led up to the small, covered front porch. It was modest, post-WWII construction on a well-worn asphalt two lane street with no sidewalks, and gravel parking strips between the road and the front yards. He had a flashlight in his car, but didn't want to go snooping around in the dark.

He called the bank from the shop while he was on his lunch break the next day. He was told the house was completely empty and the back door was unlocked. He was free to go in and look around, which he would do the coming weekend.

Will parked his 1962 Impala out front about 10:00 AM Saturday morning, stepped out and looked up and down the street. Quiet and sedate. No one in sight. He walked down the short gravel driveway and up the steps to the front door. It was locked, just as he expected. He cupped his right hand over his eyes and leaned against the front room window to look inside. The morning sun at his back produced a glaring reflection. Empty, as expected. He walked back down the steps and headed around to the back of the house.

There were half again as many steps leading up to the back door, the ground dropping gently from the street and leveling out from the house to the back of the property. He climbed the stairs and looked into the kitchen through the window in the door. His brow furrowed involuntarily as he reached out and twisted the doorknob. The door opened, as expected. His first sensory impact was a foul stench. Disgustingly foul, almost overwhelming. Stepping inside, the source was immediately obvious. Cat feces lay in mounds on the kitchen counters. Rotten garbage mingled with more animal sewage and spilled from an overflowing sink onto the floor. He left the door open and cautiously entered, stepping carefully, passing through the mess into the living room.

More animal crap was piled in the corners of the floor and along the walls. Some of it was larger, and most probably from dogs. Stepping even more carefully into the hallway, he could see the worst of it. Human excrement was heaped to a peak in the lidless toilet. Resisting the urge to vomit, he glanced around quickly, and briskly made his way through the house and out the back door again, gulping in fresh air as he bounded down the steps two and three at a time. He walked out into the back yard, almost staggering, and holding his head as he looked back up at the house. "How could anyone live like that?" he said out loud. He was an admitted neat freak. His friends playfully razzed him about his spotless cars and meticulously organized toolbox.

He was living in the basement of his mother and step-dad's house at the time, south of Woodland Park between Green Lake and Lake Union, 15 or 20 minutes south of the place he was looking at. Not even half way there, the itching began around his ankles. With a few miles to go, the intense biting was moving up his legs and increasing from irritation to pain. By the time he pulled onto their street it was crawling beyond his butt and hips onto his torso. He realized he was being eaten by more fleas than he had ever imagined. He had no idea how long the house had been unoccupied, but he was obviously the first meal these starving parasites had had in too long. He was having a hard time keeping his attention on his driving.

Pulling to the curb, facing the wrong way in front of his parents' house, he burst from the driver's seat, ripping his clothes off as he ran for the front door with the car door left hanging open. His pants, shirt, jacket and T-shirt were scattered between his car and the house, his boots and socks ripped off and dumped on the front porch. No one else was there to see him sprint through the house for the shower in his undershorts. He did not want to bring the flesh eating plague in with his clothes.

Stepping from the shower after a long, hot, soapy rinse, he hoped to find some soothing lotion to calm his flaming skin. He would never see that filthy dump again.

Mid-morning Monday, Will was out in the shop at work, checking a list of parts to be delivered to a job at an I-5 rest stop, south of Seattle down in Federal Way. The secretary leaned through the door from the office and called out, "Will."

"Yeah... I'm out here," he returned.

"Phone. Guy says he's your mortgage banker. Line three," she said, and let the door swing shut.

He didn't have a mortgage banker, and had anyone seen him he would have looked as puzzled as he felt. He would never be a poker player.

The shop phone was above a bench on the wall nearest the office. Will lifted the handset and brought it to his ear, then punched the lighted #3 button on the base unit. "This is Will."

"Will, this is Jack Morgan at Washington Mutual. Did you look at that house on 37th N.E.?"

Will paused, closed his eyes and exhaled. "Not interested."

"Not even if the price was right?" the banker asked.

"The price would have to be Really right," he said, disgust evident in his tone.

"How does $7,500.00 sound?" the banker said matter of factly.

Will extended the handset at arm's length and looked at it. Returning it he said, "You looked at it, didn't you?"

After a moment the banker said, "Yes, I did. So... what do you think?"

"Did you go in?" Will asked.

"Uh, no... I didn't. I did look in the back door. I'm pretty sure that was enough, though. I take it you went by there."

"As a matter of fact, I did. Saturday morning."

"OK, then," banker Morgan said. "That probably explains the open back door."

"Well, at least you got a good whiff of it," Will said. "To call that place a dump would be a huge understatement. I didn't have the stomach to go back up the stairs and close the door. I only wanted to get away from that shit hole, and I hope I never see it again. I doubt I'd be willing to buy a house on the same street!" Will blurted out.

"I understand, Will. If that place were in good shape, it would be $13,000.00 or $14,000.00. $7,500.00, twenty percent down, and 6 percent on the balance. That's a great deal, Will. A little sweat equity and you'll double your money in no time."

"You just want to get rid of that rat hole, don't you?"

"Yes, we do. So, how does $7,500.00 sound?"

"I'll call you back," Will said. "That place is the farthest thing from my mind, but your offer surprises me, even for that dump."

"Okay. You've got my number. I'll be here till 4:00 O'clock."

"Okay," Will said, and hung up. "Shit," he said to himself, and stood there leaning against the bench. Not exactly what he had in mind for his first house. He was familiar with basket case bikes and cars, but had never thought of a basket case house.

Living in the basement of his mother and step-dad's home, he frequently ate dinner with them. His mother enjoyed having him there, and his step-dad was a sports junkie, so they always had something to talk about. Having enough food at a meal with them was never an issue.

Will's mom had grown up in the Great Depression, and food was scarce. A day without a meal was not uncommon. During the war that followed, everything was rationed and people learned to get by on as little as possible. Her reaction to it all was that no one would ever go hungry if she had anything to say about it. For any meal, no matter how many were expected, she prepared at least twice as much food as people could eat. She figured that if there was always more than enough on hand, everyone would eat as much as they wanted. Leftovers were a good thing in Will's childhood. That's what snacks and lunches were made of. Growing up he ate non-stop. Meals were only larger portions. His mother made sure he was involved in every sport he was interested in, and the Boy's Club was his second home. If he wasn't playing sports, in school or sleeping, he was eating something.

At dinner that night he said, "I found a house to buy."

His mother paused, lowered her fork, looked at him and asked, "Which one, Will?" He had told her about all the ones he had looked at, and she wasn't aware any were up for consideration.

His eyes flicked over to his step-dad, who didn't stop eating but was obviously tuned in. He looked back to his Mom, who had not looked away.

"The little crap and flea dump out on 37th N.E. in Lake City," he said, a slight smirk on his face.

She set her fork down on her plate, and picked up her napkin. "Why, Will? You said you never wanted to see that place again."

"$7,500.00 is why. It will take some time, effort, and money, but if I can still live here while I work on it, I can afford it," he said.

His mother looked over at his step-dad, who glanced back his approval.

"Of course you can live here, Will. It will take a little time to put the deal together, and then you'll probably be working on it for several months to get it livable and pass inspection."

It had been condemned as the only way to get the former resident out. "Winter will be here in a few months," she continued, "and you're going to need every dollar you can spare."

Will's mother was a strong-willed person. Trying to dissuade her when she was committed to something was wasted effort, and she was completely committed to her son's betterment in life. She fully expected he would grow out of this wild exuberance one day, and she didn't mind saying so to anyone. She also boasted he would serve God. No one believed her.

When he came home a little late from work Friday night, they had eaten and things were already put away. His mother and step-dad were watching TV in the living room. After warming up some leftover ham and potatoes, he cleaned everything up as if he'd never been there. Pull your own weight could have been the family motto. Even as a teenager, his employers knew that he may be a little frisky, but he worked hard. So far he had only been fired from one job, and he thought that was understandable.

    Walking in the front door and past his parents that Friday night, he just waved a hand as he disappeared down the hallway to the kitchen. He didn't want to interrupt them. His step-dad was always riveted to whatever he was watching, and did not care to be drawn away. No problem. Will had places to be. He bounded down the basement stairs after eating, and flung his work jacket on his bed, which he made up crisply every morning before he left for work. He sat down and pulled off his boots.

    Looking around his room after showering, he couldn't find his riding pants. Will lived, worked, and played in button up Levi jeans, but the pants he rode in had an identity all their own. Freshly cleaned clothes were folded in his dresser drawers. Clothes to be laundered were placed out by the washer and dryer in the corner of the big basement room with the pool table. His riding pants were laid across the chair in the corner of his room with his snorting stash kept in the watch pocket; his riding jacket was draped over the back of the chair. Friday night was time to ride.

    His scooter was in the garage, just through the door from the big room. A 1948 Pan Head 74 on a 1957 Straight Leg frame, it was one inch short of nine feet long. The 1937 Indian frontend was extended 27 inches; the neck and rear legs were stretched and lowered, putting the skinny little seat 20 inches off the ground. The wire wheels, front legs, and every possible engine and linkage part were all beautifully chrome plated. The bike had a sprocket ratio that could take it to 140 mph. Unmuffled exhaust pipes made it impossible to go unnoticed, whether it was seen or not. Will loved that bike. He was careful to get it away from the house before most people went to bed and shut it off at the end of the alley when coming home late.

His drug use had escalated to include almost everything except opiates. He would never inject anything directly into his body. He swallowed, sniffed or smoked his illegal stimulants. He, and many of the boys, had become fond of a drug they called Jet Fuel. It came in white powdered form and Will snorted it. Some guys sprinkled it in joints they called Dusters. In reality, it was horse tranquilizer, and extremely potent.

They were usually drunk and high on other drugs when they used it. Too much Jet Fuel could prompt bizarre behavior, along with almost total disorientation. Will bought his in tiny collector stamp baggies for $25 or $50 a pop. The smaller portion would get one person and a few friends through a good party. The larger size would last for a weekend. It was Friday night. He didn't throw it in his parents' faces in their house, but he was also going to do as he pleased, regardless of what anyone else thought of it.

Will leaned out his bedroom door and shouted up the stairwell, "MOTHER! I can't find my jeans!"

In only a moment she was looking down the stairs at him. "Which jeans, Will?"

"My riding jeans. They were hanging across my chair."

"Oh, I washed them," she said with a smile.

"WHAT!?" he exploded, and sprinted across the big room in his underwear, ripped open the lid of the washing machine, and pulled out the only pair of Levis in the soggy load. Standing back, he shook them hard before digging his fingers into the watch-pocket. Lifting the little baggie, he held it up to the light. Empty.

His face contorted into an angry scowl, reddening as his eyes filled with explosive fire. He turned toward his mother, who had descended half way down the stairs to see what all the commotion was about. Extending his arm as he walked toward her with the empty, little baggie in his hand, he stormed at her, "DO YOU SEE THAT!? There was $50 worth of drugs in that bag, and YOU'VE RUINED IT!"

An easy, pleasant smile spread over her face and she said cheerily, "Good. That's what you get for wasting your money on that stuff". She turned and walked back up the stairs without the slightest concern over his anger.

Will stood there quaking, working to get control over his raging emotions. What was he going to do? She was his mother.

The Makeover

Three weeks later the deal was done, and Will was a home owner of sorts. After his 20% down and other related costs, his payments would be $107.00 per month. Cheaper than rent, but now there was some serious work to be done. Will met the fumigator at the house at 8:00 in the morning on the first Saturday after closing.

"Spray every square inch of the place with enough chemicals to kill a heard of Rhino," he said. Even though he had been told on the phone their most powerful stuff would take care of eggs too, he reaffirmed his instructions to the guy with the truck. "Then come back in two weeks and do it again. I don't want a live flea or bug within 50 yards of this house."

"You've got it," the guy said. They shook hands, and Will drove away.

He had driven by only twice during the next two weeks. He called the day before the next spraying to confirm it was going to happen as scheduled.

One week after the second treatment, Will pulled down the street and parked behind a beat up old Chevy pickup truck with two teenagers in it. Their newspaper ad led him to call and make the appointment. "Hard working teens will do any job. Have truck." They all got out, did the introductions and shook hands. Will was in his standard Levis and plaid flannel shirt and riding boots, but these boys looked like they'd just left a barn. He tried to discreetly sniff, but didn't smell anything cow-like.

"So, what's the job?" the driver asked.

"Follow me," Will replied, and started toward the house.

Opening the front door, what a difference! All the human and animal excrement remained, but the only scent was the strong smell of chemicals. Will left them standing in the living room, staring in amazement, while he went and opened the back door and all of the windows. They were still looking stunned when he returned.

"Yup... shit" he said. "Lots and lots of shit... everywhere. Floors, counters... prepare yourself for the toilet. But... you'll notice it doesn't smell like shit anymore. You should have smelled it the first time I came here. Unbelievable!"

They looked at each other, and then back at him with blank stares.

"Anyway... I've had this place completely saturated with the strongest kill everything chemical known to man... twice. You won't smell anything but the death juice. The next strongest thing was NAPALM! But I intend to live here. So... your job? Make it all go away. Everything!"

The two boys looked at each other again and shrugged their shoulders.

"You guys said anything," Will reminded them.

The driver turned to him and asked, "What's everything mean?"

"All of the fixtures, the cabinets, the flooring, of course all the shit and garbage... everything but the wallboard, ceilings, doors, hinges and windows. Everything! Make it all go away. Are you guys up for it?"

The two boys looked at each other and grinned. The driver looked back at Will and asked, "How much are you paying?"

"How much are you asking?" Will responded.

The two boys looked at each other again. The big one hadn't spoken a word so far. "$100.00," he said with a firm glint in his eye.

"You boys got yourself a deal," Will said. "You need any tools?"

They both grinned. "Nope," they said in unison.

"When can you start?" Will asked.

"How about now?" the driver said.

"Get to it," Will said, as he extended $50.00 cash to the one closest to him. "The rest when you're done."

"You care if we work tomorrow, too?" the driver asked.

"You can work round the clock, seven days a week for all I care," Will replied. "I'll check back tonight and see how it's going. Don't bother locking up," he said as they walked out together. "I doubt anyone's going to steal anything".

Getting in his car, he saw them lifting sledge hammers and crow bars from the back of their truck.

When Will pulled to a stop behind their truck again about dusk, it was heaped full and tied down, ready to be hauled to the dump first thing in the morning. He walked up and eyed the load. Smashed and broken up cabinets from the kitchen took up most of the space, well fit together to fill as much space as possible in the pickup bed. He could hear them still working inside as he climbed the front steps to look in the front door. They were pealing up flooring in the bedrooms.

"Hey, guys!" he shouted.

"Back here!" came the reply from the rear bedroom. They had long handled crowbars and big flat-blade shovels that looked well used. Obviously not their first experience.

"Wow. You guys have got a lot done!" Will said.

The smaller one, who did most of the talking said, "Time is money, and this ain't our first rodeo," while leaning against his shovel handle.

"Cowboys," Will thought. Okay. "Looks like you'll have it finished up tomorrow before noon," he said.

"I expect so," the little guy said.

"So… how'd you boys like to round out the day with a little more?" Will asked.

They looked at each other, then back at Will. "What?"

"Take a breather," Will said and motioned for them to follow him as he turned and started toward the back door.

Stepping out onto the elevated back porch, he turned to make eye contact with them. He turned his head toward the very back of the property, and swept his left arm, palm open, in an arc from the right side to the left. "Blackberries," he said.

Spanning the width of the 60 foot wide lot was an impenetrable mass of blackberry bushes, standing six to seven feet high and about 18 to 20 feet deep. Typical to western

Washington, left unchecked, blackberries grew into thick, tightly woven masses of brambles with huge, sharp thorns. Without heavy protective clothing a person could not reach more than a foot into a swath like this without risking some severe cuts and heavy bleeding. Bushes that reached this height had stems ¾ of an inch thick coming out of the ground. The berries would grow thick, plump and juicy, but most were impossible to harvest. There was no way to reach them.

"Make 'em go away," he said. He turned back to them with a smile.

Once again, the two boys looked at each other, and then back at him.

"How much?" the big one asked.

"You're at $100.00 for the house," he said. "I'll give you another $50.00 to take that whole mess to the dirt."

"Done," the big guy said without pause, and the two of them grinned broadly.

When Will stopped back Sunday afternoon, they had finished off the house and already hacked the main body of the blackberries down to ankle level. The truck was piled high again, and several huge mounds of blackberry vines stood waiting to be loaded and hauled off. Over on the side of the yard sat five of the ugliest, most beat looking old rotary lawn mowers Will had ever seen.

The big guy followed Will's gaze to the old mowers and began walking toward them. Reaching for the handle of the first one, he said, "Two of these we paid $3 apiece for. The other three were $10 for the bunch. Watch," he said, and pulled the starter cord, firing the scary looking old thing to life. Smoke billowed from the rusted out muffler.

He started off straight across the back yard toward the blackberry stumps, some as big around as Will's thumb, and several inches tall. With no bag or chute, rocks and debris flew out like scatter shot across the yard. Will jerked his head around and quickly decided his house and the neighbor's house were probably too far away for most of it, and it was fun to watch. He hoped for the best.

Will had staked a heavy orange twine across the back property line, from the other side of where a fence once stood. His young workman began marching out a grid over the berry stumps, not only hacking them down but leveling the ground as he plowed through it. WHAM! The mower was stopped cold by a rock the size of a grapefruit. The big guy picked it up and tossed it like a shot put ball out into the yard.

"There's plenty more where these came from," he proudly stated as he strode past Will to grab the next one.

The following Saturday morning Will pulled up out front of his house with two five gallon industrial pails of Pine-Sol, some pans, paint rollers with long handles, and a couple of large brushes. For household cleaning, Pine-Sol could be mixed high strength at about one cup per gallon of water. He intended to apply it generously, undiluted. When he drove away all of the windows were wide open, and he could smell the disinfectant 30 feet from the house. He was glad it was winter, with the temperature in the mid 40's. It was two weeks before the smell faded enough for him to be comfortable working inside.

His buddy Ted's brother-in-law was a cabinet maker and would be out to measure for new kitchen and bathroom cabinets on Monday night. Will had already scoped out some fixtures and appliances from an appliance shop that resold second hand stuff removed from remodels. He needed functional, not fancy. He would paint the whole place, and the carpeting would be new. Because the house had been condemned, all of his work would need to be inspected and approved by the city. He would also need a fence.

Once the electricity was turned on he was able to work inside at night. Heating oil was cheap, and he was looking forward to getting the furnace brought up to snuff and warming the place up. That would also help to fully dry things out and get rid of the Pine-Sol smell. He didn't realize he was just used to it until a friend dropped by for the first time one night.

"Hey man… it smells worse than a hospital in here."

"Yeah? If you'd have smelled it before you'd think this was a field of flowers."

"Well, I didn't, and it doesn't"

Will twisted up a reefer. The subject and the smell changed.

By the time March arrived, the days were longer and warmer and he'd had the heat on every night he was working there. The disinfectant smell was becoming so faint some people didn't mention it at all. He hoped to move in the next month, and figured that cooking some food in the place would make it homier. Both of Will's parents were handy around the kitchen. His Father was a baker, and Will could cook far better than the majority of single guys.

He had met some of the neighbors, and they all seemed reasonably nice. All of them were interested in what he was doing to the place. Knowing what it was like before he bought it, he suspected anyone but a mass murderer would be a welcomed improvement.

The back yard ran 80 feet from the house to the rear property line. Closing it all in had taken 255 feet of fencing, six feet high, and made of 1x6 cedar planking in eight foot sections between 4x4 posts. Treated lumber was just coming out, and too expensive for his budget. He poured used motor oil around each post to stave off rot. The primary purpose was to keep dogs in and curious neighbors out, so each vertical plank was pounded down into the ground as far as possible. The top line of the fence was not level, but strength trumped beauty. He was so tired of it all when it was completed, he never gave a serious thought to going back and trimming the tops off to a uniform height.

Will's dog at the time was a black Afghan hound named Pasha he had raised from an eight week old puppy. The mutt could be as quick and silent as a snake, and was absolutely fearless. He wasn't shy about people he didn't like, either. Will had trained him, with great difficulty, to almost robot-like obedience.

With the house finished, he was ready for his first roommate. Carl had a Great Dane named Duke, who liked people well enough, but took no lip from other dogs. Fortunately, they were both present when the two dogs went at each other, and an enforced truce was established.

Will's bladder woke him about 2:30 in the morning one week night. He had slept in the buff since he was a teenager, and there was no need to slip his robe on since he and Carl were the only ones there as far as he knew. Carl was not in the habit of bringing girls home when he had to be to work in the morning.

In the hallway, just before he turned right into the bathroom, he noticed The Duke dancing around the living room and figured his bladder was full too. So he walked past him through the living room and into the kitchen to let him out the back door. Halfway across the kitchen floor his right foot almost slipped out from under him on something soft and mushy, unseen in the darkness. With both arms propellering like windmills, he regained his balance and didn't fall.

Awakening from half-sleep and being suddenly startled, he realized he was standing ankle deep in a pool of fresh, hot, runny dog poop. He exploded into a bellowing full blast string of profanities that jolted Carl awake. Turning on the kitchen lights, his roommate burst into laughter as hard as Will's cursing.

"You dirty, rotten son of a bitch!" Will screamed, causing Carl to double over laughing harder until he was crying and red in the face.

The two young guys were their own version of the Odd Couple, Will, the fastidious biker, and Carl, the slightly sloppy corporate type. But they both liked to party.

Party Crasher

Summer. What better way to inaugurate Will's first house than to throw a party? Carl had taken off to hike around Europe for a couple of months and would miss the bash, but it wouldn't be his crowd anyway. The Duke didn't even miss him.

Once a week Will dropped into the butcher shop at the Morningside Market in Wedgewood and bought five pounds of pet-meat. It was frozen one pound packages of the ground up scraps from everything in the shop – beef, pork, chicken, fish, fat, guts, gristle… everything that couldn't be sold to people as food. Every other day he set out a pound to thaw in the morning. At night when he fed the dogs, he stirred one-fourth of a pound into Pasha's dry food, which he ate in the kitchen. When the Duke was finished with his bowl of kibble on the back porch, he just opened the door and tossed him the remaining three-fourth pound lump. The giant dog's mouth opened up like a suitcase. He caught it and pitched it once for position, and then swallowed it whole. His equally huge tongue made a complete right to left wipe of his face, and he was done.

When Will put the word out that he was throwing a party on a Saturday afternoon, the news spread like wild fire. Kegs of free beer were the main draw. Everything else was peripheral. Mid July, sunny and warm, and light out until after 9:00 PM… if things went as usual for one of these bashes, some people would still be at it Sunday morning. Though this would not become a regular occurrence for his house, he owned this place, and any fallout would be his own. It was supposed to get started around 3:00, but the first scooters rolled down 37th N.E. about 1:45. Some were just getting going from a party somewhere else the night before.

The fenced in back yard was 60'x 90', and by 4:30 it was jammed with more than 20 scooters. About 100 boisterous people were milling about, drinking thirstily. Music louder than the neighbors had ever experienced before was blaring from every open window of the house.

As the back yard, driveway, front-yard, and nearby street filled up with bikes, cars, trucks, and people, the other neighborhood residents were feeling a little overwhelmed. They had never seen anything like this, or these people before. It looked and sounded like Woodstock had come to Lake City. Though there was plenty of free-flowing beer, it was BYOD, bring your own drugs, and drugs they did bring. You might have been able to get high from the yard next door. You name it, and it was being used, and often washed down with whiskey or wine straight from the bottle.

Will's childhood buddy, Ted, had recently returned to Seattle from Minneapolis and had said to him, "I hear you're part of the

Too High crowd now." Will introduced him to Jet Fuel, which Ted didn't particularly care for.

Will didn't plan on going anywhere and was well lit from a good measure of everything on his personal menu. A little before 5:00 PM the first squad cars showed up. A little after 5:00 two cars were positioned at each end of the block, and a police helicopter was hovering over the back yard. They didn't approach. A crowd like this could be volatile, and if they weren't actually troubling anyone but each other, let it ride and see what turned up.

Someone had notified Will when the first cop car appeared, so he was paying attention, as best he could, as the police presence continued to increase. But there was no putting this toothpaste back in the tube. Things were off and running and had taken on a life of their own. By 5:30 he was convinced the police just wanted everyone, partiers and neighbors alike, to know they were there. The helicopter was hard to miss. Hopefully that would be enough to prevent any emergency intervention.

Will took his last toke off the butt of a joint, handed it to someone else, and went into the house to take a leak and make sure the music was staged to keep playing. Most of the male clientele didn't require the use of the toilet, definitely a minor code violation in light of the other activities. He went on through the house and out the front door to check on things out on the street. Early on he had waved to a few neighbors, but now he just wanted to be sure none of the partiers were getting out of hand outside of the back yard. He walked a few houses each way up the street and back, and waved at the cops in the cars pointing nose first toward his place. They didn't wave back.

Things were pretty quiet out front, and he walked back down his driveway. He stood alone, taking it all in before rejoining the fray. He was blitzed. Then INSTANTLY, without warning, he was stone cold sober, and he knew without a doubt he was standing eyeball to eyeball with God Himself. Though he couldn't hear words in his ears, his mind knew as clearly as if the words were spoken out loud that God was saying to him, "Look at yourself! If you die like this today you're going to hell!" He had never been so stunned in his life. It didn't matter what he thought or wanted. There it was, and he couldn't push it aside. Neither could he fight back like he did when that big goon had crushed the beer pitcher over his head. He was completely powerless... and speechless.

And then, just as suddenly, he was all alone, without God, but still sober. He heard the cacophony pulsating from the back yard, mixed with the whump, whump, whump of the helicopter blades, and the deafening throb of the music. It sounded like hell, and he was no longer having a good time. In fact, he was extremely irritated.

He turned and stomped up his front steps, through the front door, and across the living room to the beautiful stereo rack Ted had built for him. Without touching any other equipment, he switched the power amp off and everything went silent. In the short time it took him to reach the porch above the back yard, every face was turned toward him in befuddlement. In a blast loud enough to be heard half a block away he bellowed, "PARTY'S OVER! GET THE HELL OUT OF HERE!!!"

As the first complaints started to erupt, he let them have it again. "I'M NOT KIDDING. GET OUT OR I'LL TURN THESE COPS ON YOU MYSELF."

He turned and walked back inside, and it began to sink in for everyone. Slowly at first, then in a measured, purposeful flow, they started walking out of his yard. Scooters were kicked over and fired, a little sod was thrown as tires spun and curses were uttered, but the police presence kept things more quiet and orderly than might be expected otherwise.

Twenty minutes later he was on his back on his couch, looking up at the ceiling. What the hell was he supposed to do with this? No demands had been made, no ultimatums issued. The only sound was the wind moving through the open windows and doors. He got up and closed the doors and went down to let the dogs out of the basement bedrooms. The basement had been off limits during the party. His tools were down there, and the doors to the inside stairs and the yard out back were solidly locked.

Will told no one about the confrontation, and God didn't get in his face again anytime soon. But neither could he escape the gripping reality of what had happened. What was he going to do? Was he willing to shut his lifestyle down as abruptly as he had the party? What would he do, and who would he do it with? He was enjoying himself… until this. God might not be happy, but Will was having a good time. What was he supposed to do, go to church? He had tried it once with his mom and step-dad when he was 19. It was plain to everyone he didn't belong.

But this encounter haunted him unexpectedly, lurking around like a stalker he couldn't see or hear. When faced with the memory of it as he was entering a party or a drug buy, he would forge ahead, determined to not be forced off his chosen course. He was going to do what he was going to do.

As summer wore on and Carl returned from Europe, Will was completely captivated by an extreme '64 Corvette that was available. He decided he had to have it, and sold his beloved '48 Pan Head to get it. Other changes were looming just over the horizon that would permanently change his life.

(1966)
A New Set of Wheels

Will's parents had divorced in the fall of 1965, a few months after he went to work at Stinker's, and his sister graduated from high school in the spring of 1966. Their mother wanted her to have a nice car, so she put a down payment on a 1965 Mustang, 2+2, 289 V8, 4-speed and co-signed for the loan. It was the first 2+2 Mustang ever sold out of West Seattle Ford, and one year later his sister got it with only 2,400 miles on it.

At 10:00 AM, the morning of his 16th birthday, Will took his driver's license test in the Mustang. It had a very short back end and was easy to parallel park. His Mom had kept the 64 'Cutlass in the divorce.

The next summer his sister married. When she and her husband moved to Alaska their mom bought the Mustang back and gave the Cutlass to Will. At the start of his senior year of high school, he had a three year old car that ran very strong. One month later he tore the engine apart to do some performance upgrades and help it run even stronger.

Every waking hour he wasn't at work, at school, or football practice he was working on his car. Grease and dirt were a consistent part of his daily attire. He didn't realize he smelled like a garage most of the time. After two years at Stinker's he had picked up a sizeable collection of increasingly rare coins and bills. He had buffalo nickels, Mercury dimes, and Kennedy halves along with several Silver Certificate ones, fives, and tens, and even a Gold Certificate twenty. He spent every last one of them, and sold his old upright piano to buy speed equipment and a 4-speed transmission. He would not fail to put it all to use.

After the upgrades to the Cutlass were complete, with a fresh cylinder hone, rings, bearings, valve train, intake, and headers, it was off and running hard. Some impressive wheels and tires and suspension work made the makeover complete. This was not his father's Oldsmobile.

Dick's on Friday and Saturday nights was crawling with young street racers eager for an opportunity to demonstrate what their cars could do. The nearest launch site for a couple of short runs up into 3rd gear was north on Roosevelt Way from N.E. 50th. If it wasn't decisive at that length, they would need to go a little further out where they could get into 4th gear.

Mr. Baker was the regular rent-a-cop for the N.E. 45th Street Dick's. Everyone knew what was going on, and he only worked the parking lot, but he'd make sure things were orderly while they were there.

Will's buddy Pete had a 1964 Pontiac GTO, and the two of them squared off every weekend. Stock, the GTO would have naturally edged out the Cutlass. Will's work paid off, however, and they went back and forth from week to week, always uncertain who would win.

Will had come to know the Searcy brothers down at Golden Gardens, where some racing took place later at night from time to time. It never lasted too long before the police came. The twins had a '55 Chevy two door wagon with a punched out 283 that ran well, and Will's car had gained a bit of a reputation. A few bull sessions turned into a challenge. Their first faceoff was on a Saturday night a little before 1:00 AM, north on Greenwood Avenue between 110th and 130th.

They were running hard, wheel to wheel at 100 MPH, about a half block from the light at 130th when it turned orange. Will hesitated, and Searcy didn't, so he slammed on the brakes as the Chevy pulled away. Drum brakes all around locked up and Will went through the intersection sideways with smoke pouring off of all four tires. When they pulled over together in a parking lot at 145th, the Searcys were cackling. There would be a rematch.

Without Malice

On the appointed night they were delayed because Will had opened his headers before pulling into Dick's. He was backed into a spot on the quieter side of the parking lot. When he and the Searcys decided to go for it, Will casually strolled over to his car and got in. As soon as he turned the key and the engine fired, Mr. Baker stepped out from around the car beside him and almost smiled. Will shut it off immediately.

Officer Baker walked in between the cars and leaned down to Will's open window with his elbow on the door. "Sounds a little loud tonight, son. Are you having exhaust problems?"

"No, sir," Will said.

"Oh..." the cop continued, "it must be loud on purpose then."

Will didn't say anything. It was obvious this was going to go wherever Baker wanted it to, and he wouldn't need any help getting it there.

"Well," Officer Baker said, "you were just going somewhere, weren't you?"

"No... I think I'll just stick around awhile," Will said.

"I know," the cop said. "You'll need to cap those headers before you leave. If you drive out of this lot with those things open, I'll have you pulled over and your car impounded. Is that what you want?"

"No sir," Will replied.

"Uh huh," Baker grunted. Will thought he still might be safe.

"Start it up," Officer Baker said, as he stepped out from between the cars and stood by Will's left front bumper.

"What the hell," Will thought. He turned the key, and as soon as the engine ignited, he pushed the gas pedal to the floor. The noise from the open four inch collector tubes exploded like open warfare as the tach bounced off of 5,000 RPM before Will let off. Every head in sight was turned toward the source – Will's Cutlass.

"Might as well get something for my money," Will said to himself. Officer Baker had a little smirk of his own.

A decent sized crowd had gathered around as Office Baker wrote out Will's defective exhaust ticket on the hood of his car.

After having Will sign it, he tore off Will's copy and handed it to him with a smile. Will was still seated behind the wheel.

"You take care of that now," Officer Baker said as he tipped his hat and walked away.

When Will got out of his car several guys stepped forward to offer commentary. Will tried to shrug it off, wearing it like a badge of honor. That would cap his record of three tickets in one day. A couple of friends handed him things after he got the caps and bolts out of the trunk and crawled under the car to put them on. The whole car was jacked up so high there was plenty of clearance. The giant rear tires justified it.

When he and the Searcys pulled into the parking lot of a closed restaurant about an hour later, the twins were a regular comedy team, razzing him mercilessly about his encounter with Officer Baker. Will just worked quietly under the car while they did their song and dance.

He put the caps, bolts and tools in the trunk. Closing it, he walked to his driver's door, put his left hand on the door handle, looked them in the eye, and said, "Speed talks, bullshit walks." He grinned, nodded, and got in. They started both cars and pulled out onto Roosevelt Way. Will was at the right-hand curb, and the Searcy brothers were at the left one. Roosevelt was one-way northbound. When no cars were coming from behind them, they nodded to each other, pulled into the driving lanes, and stopped at the nearest intersection, waiting for the light to turn red. Both cars were rumbling like wild animals eager to spring forward.

As the opposite light switched from green to orange, both drivers brought their RPM up to launch point. Though they had done this before, it took forever for the light facing them to flash green.

The Chevy had wilder gears and leaped ahead by a fender in first gear. Will fell back to their rear tire. But Will's car had more grunt, and pulled even when the Chevy grabbed 2nd. When Will banged 2nd, he dropped back to their front wheel, but his greater power, cubic inches, and torque pulled him even with them, and then he began to crawl further forward. They were at his door when he slammed the Muncie into 3rd and began to pull away even more. When he went to 4th gear they were at his back bumper.

They were a little less than a block away from the light at N.E. 65th and coming up on it fast at 110 MPH when, once again, the light turned orange. This time Will didn't flinch. He thought, "The faster we're going the faster we'll be by any problem." They both stayed in it, building speed as they bore down on the intersection. With the headers open, the screaming Olds could probably be heard a mile away. Close at hand it was deafening.

About 100 feet from the intersection Will saw a man run out onto 65th from his side of the street. He stopped in the middle of the street, frantically waving his arms and urging an approaching car to stop. It did, and the intercessor turned his head and looked at the two cars as they sped by. Everyone knew he had averted what would almost certainly have been a horrible collision.

As they shot through the intersection Will was sure the noise from his open exhaust had alerted the man who was just out for a walk. He wished he could have thanked him.

He and the Searcys were even.

(1973)
A New Way of Life

The Corvette was more fun than Will had ever had. He had never lost a race in it. It was instantly life threatening and capable of getting away from him at any time in 1st and 2nd gear. Revving freely beyond 8,000 RPM, it was a thrilling ride. Even so, as summer transitioned into fall, he wanted more. He wanted the car to be show quality.

That summer a confrontation with the foreman at work led to him being fired for the second time in his life. He had become a skilled shear operator and was hired at Boeing within a week.

Just after Thanksgiving he took his car to a buddy's shop in West Seattle and stripped it down to the bare body. His friend was a custom painter, and Will was excited about what they could do with it. When it rolled out on its way to the Custom Auto Hot Boat & Speed Show at the Seattle Center in February, he had sanded the entire car five times, in primer, color, graphics and clear. It was as smooth as glass, and looked as good as it ran. In exchange for his use of the shop, tools, and materials, and his friend's expert skills, he put in several hours each day working on customer cars. He went straight from Boeing to the auto shop every day and left there between 9:00 and 10:00 at night.

That fall he and Carl had taken in another roommate to cut down on expenses. His new roommate, Grant, was a bartender at a place that served good food, so on the way home most nights he stopped in for a couple of drinks and something to eat. Usually he sat and ate alone. It was a trendy, popular spot, the first known tavern in a shopping mall and not his typical style. Mall workers and shoppers crammed the place in the evenings and on weekends. When Will showed up he was filthy from working with metal and body shop dust all day. Weeknights at 10:00 or 10:30 it was lightly populated, pretty laid back, and felt relaxing. Grant took care of him.

One night he sat down at the bar, as usual, and Grant slid a draft beer in front of him without a word. As he walked away to grab a food order for someone else, Will turned to scan the room. He was thankful the swivel stools had well-padded seats and backs. His were both tired. He'd been on his feet since clocking in at Boeing in the morning. Lowering his glass, he almost came to a stop, and then slowly placed it on the bar as he stared at one of the most gorgeous women he had ever seen. On the far side of the room she wouldn't notice him. She was focused on her work.

She was tall, maybe 5'8", and wearing heels. Her long legs were showing very nicely below a skirt that stopped a little more than midway up her thighs. It contoured her rounded hips to a small waist where a well fitted, but not too tight sweater revealed her tapered torso. From his vantage point her long, straight dark brown hair hung to just below her shoulder blades. He saw her just as she turned to give him a view of her well-proportioned bust-line and her beautiful face. Then she smiled as she spoke to someone. Wow. How could any man not look at her?

His gaze followed her as she walked to the other end of the bar and offloaded some glasses to be run through the conveyer belt washer. She started walking in his direction, stopping to place an order with Grant not 15 feet from where he sat. She moved with graceful, feminine elegance. She didn't strut like a runway model, but walked like an everyday person who happened to have extraordinarily good looks. She was just being herself. He was glad she didn't look in his direction. He felt he was probably gawking at her. He was. If she did look at him, he would turn away. But wow…

Grant must have seen him staring, because he was smiling slyly as he placed another beer in front of him.

"WHO on earth is that?" Will asked, turning to his friend.

Grant's eyes lit up. "Eva," he said.

"No kidding," Will stammered. "It makes sense. Any woman who looks like that should have a name like that. When did she start working here?"

"A couple of weeks ago. You just haven't been here when she's on. She's being worked into the schedule."

"I'll bet she gets good tips," Will said.

Grant winked at him and walked off, then turned around and asked, "You want anything to eat?"

"Yeah," Will said… "a Rueben."

Saturday morning about 10:00 Grant walked out into the living room at home rubbing his eyes.

"Coffee?" he muttered.

Will raised his mug in his right hand and pointed to the kitchen with his left.

The bar closed at 2:00 AM, and if Grant cleaned up and left quickly, he was out by 2:30. If someone stayed there with him for a while, or he went elsewhere before coming home, he may not show up until sunrise. It was 10:00 in the morning, so he must have stayed there after closing to enjoy some privacy with someone.

"I didn't see you last night," Grant offered, sipping his coffee as he sat on the small couch across the coffee table from Will. "I thought you might be back in to check out Eva again."

Though Will came across as confident in most situations, he never felt more vulnerable than when he was around beautiful women… except for the arrogant ones. Arrogance was ugly no matter who was wearing it.

"Yeah," Will exhaled… "There's no doubt I'd like to meet her, but… I'll be back in. We'll see."

"Well, she saw you," Grant said matter-of-factly.

"What!?" Will blurted out. "How do you know that?"

"She told me. After you left she asked me, 'Who was that guy?' I told her you were my roommate and came in almost every night after working on your car."

"What else did she say?" Will was now sitting upright, leaning forward in Grant's direction.

"She said, "Oh. I'd like to get to know him." She kind of smiled and walked away. We didn't talk about it anymore."

Will sat back and said nothing.

Will came in Monday night, and Eva wasn't working. Tuesday night she was. When he sat down, Grant poured a schooner and set it on the bar. Eva walked up and put it on her tray, then came over and placed it on the bar in front of him. She smelled as good as she looked - elegant.

"Hi," she said and smiled softly. "Nice to see you again. I'm Eva."

"Nice to see you, too," Will replied, more smoothly than he expected. "I'm Will."

"Yeah... Grant told me. Nice to meet you, Will. See ya," she said, smiled again, turned and walked away. Coming or going, from any angle she was a pleasure to watch. And her face... what a face! Those big brown eyes and her unassuming manner. She wasn't flirting, just being real. If she was, she was better at it than anyone he'd met before.

Will took a big drink of his beer. It tasted especially good.

It was busier than usual that night, and they didn't get a chance to talk any more before Will left about 11:00. He needed to be up at 5:15 in the morning, and Grant told him she wasn't off until 2:00. She came up to place an order just as he was standing from his seat at the bar. He smiled and gave a slight shoulder high wave of his right hand. She smiled warmly back to him, and he turned toward the exit. The warmth of her smile glowed like embers in his chest, and he felt good about the future.

Wednesday morning Grant was just getting home as Will was packing his lunch before leaving for work. "Hey, man... I don't know what you said to Eva, but she's very interested in you, my friend."

"We barely talked at all," Will said.

"Well, whatever it is, keep doing it. It's working," and Grant gave him a knowing wink as he headed for the bathroom.

Will paused over his sandwich, pleased and puzzled. "She could date anyone she wanted," he thought. He'd never been real pleased with his own looks. Unless a girl showed interest in him, he was hesitant, unlike Grant who considered any girl lucky to have his attention. The guy spent 30 minutes brushing his hair and admiring himself in the mirror before leaving for work.

Will closed his food and thermos up in his black workman's lunchbox and headed out the door for a job he loathed.

The procedure in Boeing Shop 2143 at Plant II, down on the Duwamish Waterway, often left him with substantial gaps in the workday. A skid of raw material with a set of plans would be dropped at his work station by an expeditor with a pallet jack. After doing the layout and setup, then making and measuring the parts, it was all put back on the same skid. It sat there until an inspector came by, examined it, and tagged it for transport to the next station in the manufacturing process. If a new skid had arrived before the one he and his partner were working on was completed, they moved on to the next job. All too often there were no other plans and materials in place yet, and they were left waiting for something to arrive. Boring! The company was affectionately referred to as "The Lazy B". The older guys would stand around and shoot the bull.

At the private shop he came from he could go to dispatch and pick up a new set of plans when a job was completed. He would then jump on a forklift, an internal crane, or whatever it took to get the needed material to his work area. He was never left without anything to do. At Boeing he was prohibited from operating any machine other than his own. It was a good thing he loved to read. He devoured many good books while waiting for plans and material. In the dead time that Wednesday he thought about Eva.

Wednesday and Thursday night his painter buddy, Chip, wanted to stay late at the shop, so Will grabbed a couple of tacos from the Jack-n-the Box on the way home, sucked down a beer, smoked a joint and crashed. Given their weekday schedules, it was not uncommon for him and Grant to not see each other unless Will came into the bar on the way home.

When Will came into the shop Friday after leaving Boeing, Chip said, "Hey – I'm going out with my wife tonight, so let's hit it hard. I want to be outta' here by 6:30."

"No problem," Will said, and got busy on the customer car they wanted to deliver Monday morning.

"What's with you, man?" Chip asked. "Who lit you up? You're usually draggin' ass after leaving the Lazy B on Friday night."

"I might have a little female companionship myself tonight," he replied.

"Really? Who? That hot chick at your roommate's place?"

Will turned to him with a smile on his face. "We'll see."

"OK, then. Good luck," his friend wished him.

Will had time to go home and clean up. He hoped not looking like a shop rat would make a good impression on Eva. She always looked fabulous, and he was always filthy when he came in on the way home.

Will got to the bar about 9:00, sat down, had a beer, and ordered something to eat. It was busier than any time he had ever seen it before, and Eva was working in a section on the other side of the place. So far they hadn't even made eye contact. Over the next half hour she smiled and waved a few times while placing or picking up an order. It was jammed and she, Grant, and one other waitress were running.

Finally, around 11:00, she caught a breather and sat down at the stool next to him with a cup of coffee.

He smiled slightly at her and said, "You're earning your pay tonight."

She said, "Friday night… it will stay strong until closing."

He wasn't much for beating around the bush in any situation, so he just popped it out, "Would you like to go out for breakfast when you get off?"

He was excited about getting to know her, and Grant had him enthused and confident that she felt the same way.

When she said, "Oh, I'm sorry… I already have plans," he felt deflated, like a balloon with the air leaking out of a small hole.

"Oh… OK. No problem," he said.

"Eva!" Grant called from behind the bar. They both looked over and Grant spun the index finger of his right hand around in a tight circle and nodded sharply to her.

She smiled weakly as she stood, deposited her coffee cup down by the dish washer at the other end of the bar, picked up her tray, and strode off into the crowd. The next time she came up to the register he was gone.

Will always did what he could to set himself up to win. He didn't abuse people or force them to do anything against their own will, but he almost always took steps ahead of time to make sure things would come out his way. He liked his surprises to be good ones, and he expected to be in charge of his own affairs. He never asked a girl out a second time when she'd turned him down once.

About 3:00 AM Sunday, Grant and Will both drove up to the house at the same time. Grant parked out at the street, and Will pulled down into the driveway, right next to the front steps. He got out of his car and waited for his roommate at the bottom of the stairs. They were both pretty well lit.

"Hey… didn't see you tonight," Grant boomed to him. "Eva was disappointed."

"I'm sure she was," Will replied cynically. "Not exactly my regular environment. I was down at The Scoop," the nickname the regulars had given Our Place. "Carl should be here in a minute. I think he was lining up a sucker to fleece."

Carl could count cards, and very few people, much less drunk ones, could best him in any game that used a deck of playing cards. Hearts, spades, or any brand of poker would do. His favorite movie line was W.C. Fields from the film The Hotel. Sitting at a table alone in the hotel lobby while shuffling a deck of cards, a local hick walks up and says, "Oh, a friendly little game of chance."

"Not the way I play it," Fields replies.

Sunday while watching TV, Grant tried to reassure Will that Eva really did want to see him again.

"Uh huh," Will grunted cynically… "We'll see."

Without Malice

Will worked late on his car every night and didn't stop into Grant's bar all week long. They hadn't both been home and awake at the same time and hadn't spoken at all.

Saturday night Will left Our Place about 1:00 AM and went over to the bar at the mall before going home. Most people had already left for the night. As he sat down at the end of the bar nearest the entrance, Grant slid a beer in front of him with a wink and a nod. He was about half way through that first glass when Eva came over and sat down next to him.

"Hi," she said easily, without much expression.

"Hi," Will responded, probably just as expressionless.

"I'm not doing anything tonight," she said matter-of-factly, looking him straight in the eye.

Will woke up Sunday morning about 9:00. He rolled over in his bed and looked at her, still asleep next to him. "Wow, she is beautiful!" he thought. On any other day his feet hit the floor shortly after he realized he was awake. This day he continued to lie there. After looking at her for a while he turned onto his back, thinking. It was 30 minutes before she began to stir. She awakened slowly and turned her head to look at him. Then she moved over next to him, snuggled up close, and put her head on his chest. Her warm, soft skin felt better than anything he could remember, ever.

He exhaled long and slow, and then said to her, "You are an angel sent from God."

After a few moments he told her he was probably the best omelet maker she had ever met, and he would be glad to make them breakfast. She offered to do the coffee and toast, and they talked about what ingredients his fridge held. Unlike most single guys, Will kept real food in the house and fed himself well. Some of Carl's married buddies who dropped by as he was eating looked on in amazement.

"My wife can't cook like that," one guy said. Will just grinned, lifted the next forkful into his mouth, and chewed slowly, while making mock sighs of satisfaction.

When he and Eva came out of the bedroom Grant was watching TV in the living room. Carl could sleep until noon, no problem.

Grant smiled, winked at them and said, "I see you two are getting to know each other better."

"You want an omelet?" Will called from the kitchen.

"Why not?" Grant shouted back. He appreciated a good home cooked meal once every few months. "Thanks."

Eva left in the afternoon after they watched a Sunday movie together. She spent less time getting ready than Grant did. Will walked her out onto the front porch and stood watching as she got into her car and drove away.

Monday was a holiday of some sort for Will. Carl was at his retail job, and Grant hadn't come home the night before. Will played with the dogs out back and fussed with his car a little. He was cleaning up the house when he heard someone walking up the front steps, followed by a light knock on the door. Grant never left any evidence of even being there but Carl was often less than tidy. Will didn't mind straightening things up because they really got along well, and he never had to hassle him for his share of rent and utilities.

They didn't get a lot of drop by visitors, and most of Will's friends could be heard coming down the street. He walked over to the front door, thinking it may be one of Carl's softball buddies and was surprised to find Eva smiling at him when he opened it.

"Hi," she said. "I don't work tonight, and Grant said you weren't working today either, so I thought I'd stop by and see what you're doing."

"Cleaning up a little," he said, and swung the door open with a smile. "Come on in."

Will got up Tuesday morning at 5:15 and when he left for work at 6:00 she was still sleeping. One week later she moved into an apartment she had been on a waiting list to get for months. One month after that she moved in with Will.

(1974)
Redefined

Eva was almost too good to be true… someone who went out of her way to make him happy. Maybe she was an angel. Will was 23 and she had just turned 26.

Eva's two year old Beagle, Gabe, moved in before she did since her apartment allowed no dogs. Three months later Carl, Grant and The Duke moved elsewhere, and Eva and Will came home to each other every day. Eva had been married for a short time in her early 20's, but living with a woman was a first for Will. He also now dropped into the Mall Pub more often, whether Grant was working or not.

One month before they made their connection exclusive, Will put his Corvette on display in the annual Custom Auto Hot Boat & Speed Show. He and the boys had displayed some scooters there in previous shows. His car had a good spot right next to the reviewing platform, and he posted the obligatory "For Sale" sign at the bottom of his display easel. He priced it so high that if anyone was willing to pay his asking price he wouldn't be able to turn them down.

Will's car was assigned the "Street Racer" category, and the final night of the show he was called up to receive the second place trophy. It took all the self-control he could muster to not smash it on the platform, knowing which car was about to win first place in the class. He knew the car and the owner.

He waited until the trophy presentations were concluded, the general public had left the building, and car owners were packing up their stuff. Will travelled pretty light and was ready to go in short order. The two best times of a car show are the day before it opens and just after it's all said and done. The cars that run, street legal and full race, are fired up and driven in at the start, then out the door to either trailers or the road home at the end. The smell of high octane fuel and burned rubber were almost as good as at the race track.

As Will walked up to the other car, five or six people were standing around shooting the breeze, none of them too eager for the whole experience to end.

"Arnie," Will said to the owner.

Arnie was with his wife and a few people Will didn't know. "Hey, Will. You really should have won the class, man. Sorry about that," he said apologetically.

"I know," Will said. "But what the hell does a trophy mean anyway… especially for cars like ours, huh?" Arnie looked a little puzzled.

"So," Will continued… "Our class is street racer, and the street is right outside. Let's get out there and settle it where it matters – right now. What do you say?" his eyes blazing with intensity.

"Oh, man," Arnie said, apologetically again… "I'm a quart low on oil, and I can't risk running it hard."

"No problem," Will replied. "I've got a quart of Racing 40 I'll give you. Let's get to it."

"Yeah… my wife's riding home with me, and I've got so much crap to take along it just won't work tonight."

"Uh huh," Will snorted dismissively. "You look me up when you're ready," he said as he turned and walked away.

Will stored his Corvette in a rented garage in Ballard, miles from his house out in Lake City. On the way there from The Seattle Center the rear tires suffered greatly. His favorite launch was to set the front brake Line Lock, release the rear brakes and then stand on the gas pedal. When the tachometer needle swept past 6,000 RPM he would side-step the clutch and hold the Line Lock button down. Once the huge rear tires were billowing smoke, he would lift the Line Lock button and let the car gain traction before shooting forward at multiple G forces, then bang the next gear every time the tach needle reached 8,000. It was therapeutic.

Two weeks later he heard the spindle bearing in the right rear suspension groaning and pulled that assembly apart. The car had been sitting up on jack stands for about a week before the new bearing came into Bill's Auto Parts by Green Lake. Will bought the parts for his first car there and never went anywhere else, though he now lived miles away. He liked doing business with people he knew. His plan was to put the car back together Saturday. Thursday night about 8:00 o'clock the phone rang.

Will picked up the receiver… "Will."

"Is this the guy who had the 64 Corvette in the car show?" an unfamiliar voice asked.

"That's me," Will said. "What can I do for ya?"

"I want the car," the guy said. "I have cash. When can I drive it?"

"I've got it apart for some minor repairs right now, but I'll have it running Saturday afternoon," Will said, matter-of-factly.

"I want to drive it tonight," the caller said dryly.

"Well," Will snorted, "that's not likely to happen. The car is over in Ballard and I'm out in Lake City."

"How long would it take you to put it back together?" the guy asked.

"45 minutes to 2 hours, depending on how it goes," Will replied, thinking that would put him off for the night.

"I'll wait," he said.

"What?" Will asked.

"I'll pick you up, drive you over, and wait while you put it back together… tonight."

"Seriously?" Will asked.

"I want the car," the guy said.

"You haven't asked how much I want for it," Will said.

"I know," the guy said. "We can talk about that after I drive it."

The caller had never once asked if he was willing to do it.

Will lowered the receiver and covered it with his other hand. Eva had come to stand near him and listen as the conversation went on. He said to her softly, "A guy on the phone wants me to put the Corvette together right now so he can drive it tonight. He saw it in the car show and says he wants it."

He had quit the Lazy B the day after the car show. Mid-morning that Monday he realized, "I don't have to be here anymore". He had suffered there to get the car finished. He put down the part he was working on, put on his jacket, punched out his time card, and went over to the supervisor's shack. Walking in and handing the boss his time card he said, "Mail me my check. I'm never coming back," walked out, and never drove into the parking lot again. He went to work for Chip and could come in late if he needed to.

Eva shrugged her shoulders and arched her eyebrows. "If you want to, why not?" she asked.

Lifting the receiver back to his head, he said, "Okay. Pick me up. Got a pencil?"

After writing down the address the guy said, "I'll be there in 20 minutes".

"Alright," Will said. "I'll look for you," and hung up.

Fifteen minutes later a black Lincoln Continental Town Car pulled up in front of Will's house. He walked out onto the front porch, turned and kissed Eva, and walked down the steps to the driveway. An Asian man got out from behind the wheel of the Lincoln and waited for him. As he approached, the man took a step in his direction, extended his right hand and said, "Matthew Lee."

"Will," Will said, and shook his hand.

"Hop in," the man said, and pointed to the front passenger seat. When Will walked around he saw a woman sitting in the back seat.

As he drove toward Ballard, Matthew Lee introduced the young woman in the back. She looked to be in her mid-twenties. Mr. Lee looked like he was in his mid-thirties, but Will knew he was not very good at recognizing people's ages anywhere between young and old.

Matthew Lee went on to explain, with no small measure of pride, that he was the cousin of Bruce Lee, the karate master. Bruce Lee's original studio was in the U-district, and Will had seen him at a school assembly ten years earlier, so the cousin story was believable.

Will had an old overstuffed armchair in his roomy garage, and Matthew Lee sat in it while Will bolted the Corvette back together. His girlfriend stood the whole time. Things went well, and Will put the car back on the garage floor about 40 minutes later. The girlfriend went to wait in the Lincoln while Will took Lee out for a demonstration.

He had learned years earlier that people were much more highly motivated to buy if he gave them a real good scare right away. Lee had been poker faced from the moment they met in front of his house, but as Will took the car beyond reasonable limits, the man's face and body became so animated he was almost bouncing up and down in the passenger seat.

"I want to drive it," he said, probably a little louder and faster than he usually spoke. "When can I drive it?"

They were cruising southbound on Greenwood Avenue, north of 87th Street at the 35 mph posted speed limit. Will said, "I'll let you drive it, but I haven't seen any money yet. You can have a little taste, but this car can get away from you, so you'll have to take it easy. If you get out of hand I'll pull the keys out while you sit there." Will was not negotiating... not about pulling the keys anyway. He was serious about not risking his car. He turned right on 85th, and pulled into the Bartell Drugs parking lot one block down the street.

Matthew Lee settled himself into the driver's seat, put the beast in 1st gear, and pulled very cautiously out onto 85th Street, westbound. Three blocks later he came to a stop for the red light at 3rd Ave. NW. He turned to Will and asked, "Can I get on it a little?"

"After you're rolling," Will said. "But be careful."

Lee eased away from the light, and just across the intersection he stabbed the gas pedal to the floor. The engine RPM exploded and the car jumped forward like a rifle shot. The rear tires went up in smoke, and the rear end began to bend hard to the right. It gave the novice driver far more than he expected, and startled him so badly he immediately lifted his foot off the gas. The gear ratio was so radical that the car nosedived and Lee stomped the brakes as they jerked to a stop almost as violently as they had leapt forward.

Will was about to say, I told you so, when the siren and flashing lights pulled up right behind them. "Just shut it off," he said.

Their windows were both down, and they sat as the patrol officer slowly exited his car, switched his flashlight on, and began to approach. He walked up to the driver's side window and shined the light in both of their faces, Lee's first. When the light hit Will's face he said, "It's my car officer. Mr. Lee is hoping to buy it and was taking it for a test drive."

"Licenses and registration," the officer responded.

He returned to his patrol car for several minutes. When he came back to the Corvette he began to circle the car slowly, bending down almost to his knees as he looked underneath, front and back. Will had the feeling the cop just wanted to check out the car. Returning to the driver's window, he handed Will's license and registration back to him. As he offered Matthew Lee's license to him he said, "I don't know, Mr. Lee. I think this car might be a little too much for you."

Turning his attention to Will he said, "I think you should drive the car from here, Mr. Wilson. Mr. Lee has had about enough for tonight."

"Thank you, officer," Will said, and they waited for the cop to get back in his car before they switched seats. Neither of them spoke on the short drive back to Will's storage garage.

Will pulled into the driveway, shut the Corvette off, and they sat in silence for a moment. Lee's girlfriend remained in the Lincoln.

"I want the car," Lee said, then said nothing more.

"Okay," Will replied. "The price is $3,200.00. I don't negotiate."

Will had paid $1,900.00 for it before transforming it into show condition. Average 64 Corvettes could be found any day for $1,400-$1,500. The nicest available were $2,200-$2,500. New ones were $6,000-$6,500. Will's car was far above average before he'd sweat blood getting it ready for the show.

"I want it tonight," Lee said with a flat stare. "I have cash."

"We can do that," Will said. Matthew Lee extended his right hand across the cockpit and they shook firmly, each man with a faint smile on his face.

"You must come to my house for dinner," Lee said. "We can pick up your girl on the way."

Will had a phone line in the garage and called Eva. She didn't work until the next evening, and was ready when the Lincoln pulled up in front of the house behind the Corvette about 11:00 PM.

Matthew Lee's house was 15 minutes north of Will's, around the end of Lake Washington in the community of Mount Lake Terrace. A very typical middle class looking house in a modest middle class neighborhood, nothing distinguished it from the other well-kept homes on the street except for the black Lincoln Town Car in the driveway. A waist-high white picket fence surrounded the nicely maintained front yard of an average size, box shaped, post-WWII house.

Will pulled the Corvette in the driveway behind the Lincoln, and Eva parked her Ford on the street out front. They joined each other on the sidewalk, opened the latched gate of the fence, and walked up to the five step concrete front porch hand in hand. Lee and his girlfriend had gone ahead to prepare. Will reached out and knocked three times.

The door was answered by Lee's girlfriend, who smiled as she swung it open wide and gestured for them to come in. The small entryway had a coat closet and opened into a spacious living room with thick carpet and large overstuffed furniture. A high archway connected to a dining room with a well-set elegant table of old, dark wood.

"Welcome," Lee boomed with a broad smile as he came through the door from the kitchen. Walking toward them and extending his right hand to shake Will's, he kept moving into the living room and said, "Sit, please," as he pointed to the couch opposite the coffee table.

"Let me take your coats," his girlfriend said.

After handing her their coats, they sat down on the couch. Lee was already seated in one of the big armchairs at the end of the coffee table nearest the fireplace. Before them on the table sat a display unlike anything either of them had ever seen. A 1 ½ inch high stack of what turned out to be crisp $100 bills, was placed neatly beside a 6 inch square mirror with a small, pearl handled, antique folding straight razor. Across the mirror from the pile of money was a crystal dessert bowl, ¾ full of what Will was sure had to be cocaine. The other end of the oval table was occupied by a crystal decanter of brown beverage that looked to be either bourbon or brandy. Matching cut-crystal tumblers filled out the extravagant display.

Will looked from the table before them to Lee, whose eyes were gleaming. "We have some filet mignon ready to broil in the kitchen, but let's sharpen our appetites first," he suggested brightly.

Will turned his head and looked to Eva, who was looking back in only slightly suppressed amazement.

Will looked back to Lee who said, "Pure, uncut cocaine… only the very best for the occasion."

With that, he lifted the silver sugar spoon from the bowl and spilled it onto the mirror. Replacing the spoon, he picked up and opened the razor and began lightly chopping at the powder while deftly dividing it into 4 equal lines, in almost perfect order, side by side on the mirror. His preparation held his undivided attention.

Satisfied all was properly arranged, he smiled briefly at Will, took the $100 bill from the top on the stack, and rolled it into a tube the diameter of a drinking straw. He slid forward to the edge of his chair, leaned out over the mirror, bent down, and with one uninterrupted swoosh, sniffed the line nearest him up into his right nostril as he held his left nostril closed with his left forefinger. He closed his eyes briefly, let out a sigh of satisfaction, and tossed the rolled bill into a small wicker basket beside the bowl of coke.

Grinning slyly, he looked to Will and gestured to the stack of pristine Federal Reserve notes. Ben Franklin seemed to be looking back knowingly. Will had snorted some coke before, but not much, and wasn't entirely confident of what he would be putting almost directly into his blood stream very near his brain. Not that he had been all that careful, having inhaled more than his share of Jet Fuel.

When he looked from the table back to Lee, his host assured him, "You have nothing to fear, unless you don't do cocaine. This is as close to perfection as the steaks waiting for us in the kitchen."

Will took the top bill, rolled it, and sniffed the glass clean of the line before him with the skill of an old pro. He too closed his eyes for a moment and snorted back a tiny bit. It didn't burn, but this was obviously some potent stuff. He tossed the used bill in the basket as Lee had done.

Lee then gestured toward Eva and said, "Your lady next."

Will rolled up the next new bill, and as he handed it to Eva and said, "I don't know if you want the whole line or not. Take what you're comfortable with."

She took the rolled bill in her hand, leaned forward, and sniffed up half of the next line. She paused briefly with her eyes closed, and then opened them and finished the line. She sat back into the thick, pillowed couch while extending the bill toward Will with her left hand. He took it and pitched it into the little basket with the others.

Lee glanced to his girlfriend, and she stepped from her chair at the other end of the low table near the decanter, knelt beside the table, and made the last line disappear immediately. It was clearly not their first dose of the night.

"Whiskey?" Lee asked.

"I'm good," Will replied. He looked at Eva and she shook her head. "How about some water?" he asked.

"Of course," Lee said. As his girlfriend rose he added, "Let's get those steaks going." She brought out a pitcher of water and disappeared into the kitchen.

As Lee's girlfriend cleared the dishes from the dining room table he brought the cocaine supplies from the living room. "One more to settle things," he said as he spread out four slightly smaller lines than the ones they started with.

After everyone had partaken, he asked Will, "Did you bring the title?"

Will nodded, "I did."

Lee stood and walked over to the buffet table at the end of the room. He slid open a drawer, lifted something out, returned to his place, and sat down. He reached out and plopped a tightly wrapped plastic bag down on the table in front of Will. Looking him straight in the eye without wavering, he said, "Four ounces of what we've enjoyed tonight. The supply cost is slightly less than your price for the car. Divide and sell three ounces, get more than twice what you're asking for the car, and keep an ounce for yourself." He withdrew his hand and sat back in his chair without expression.

Will had never faced such a proposition in his life. This was no jar of speed. As all the variables ran through his mind, something deep inside him said, "Take the money."

His thoughts kept bouncing back and forth between the cash and the much larger amount the coke could turn into. Then he remembered sitting on his bed with the dread of going to jail after the relatively minor speed bust in California. "Take the money" repeated like the resonance of timpani beneath everything else. He closed his eyes, paused, and breathed out slowly.

He opened his eyes, looked at Lee and said resolutely, "I'll take the cash."

Ten days later Will and Eva had just finished dinner when the phone rang. The kitchen phone was a wall mount with an extra-long cord between the kitchen table and the window looking out onto the driveway.

Will picked it up. "Will," he said.

"Mr. Wilson?" the strong male voice said on the other end.

"Yes," Will replied.

"This is detective Johnson of the Mount Lake Terrace police department. There is a certain undesirable in our community who has had your Corvette parked in his driveway for the last several days. Does it belong there?"

"It's not my car anymore," Will said. "I sold it to Matthew Lee, and it's his car now."

"All right, then," detective Johnson said. "Just checking. Thank you."

"No problem," Will said, and they both hung up.

"Wow," Will said to Eva. He told her what the detective said, and said to her, "Right now, I'm thinking I should be real glad I didn't take the coke from that guy."

Two weeks later Will walked out onto the front porch and picked up the Sunday morning Seattle P.I. He tossed it onto the couch and walked into the kitchen for a cup of coffee. After his first sip, he slipped the A section from around the outside of the bundle and opened the front page in his lap. Large, bold headline type shouted at him, MAJOR DRUG BUST IN BELLEVUE!

The third paragraph told the story of seven men sitting in a hotel room with several kilos of cocaine. One of them was a DEA agent who got his gun out first. Three paragraphs further he read the names of those arrested and charged in a two year investigation. Matthew Lee's name stood out as if it were neon, and Will's armpits became wet.

"Eva!" he called out. After reading the important details to her, he said, "They knew every time that guy wiped his butt for the last two years. If I'd have taken that dope, they'd have been knocking on my door before the paper hit the porch this morning."

Eyes wide, they stared at each other, and Will was thankful. He had never spoken a word about God to her, but he knew He had intervened and spared his life again.

1974

With the Corvette gone, Will needed another hawg. His search produced a 1950 Pan Head, another chopper, not as radical as his 48', but a beautiful scooter none the less.

When Eva and Will began their life together she had never been on the back of a motorcycle. He began taking her on short rides around town to get used to it. The Apple Blossom Festival was a month away… plenty of time. He also needed to introduce her to The Boys before the first big ride, and what better introduction than a party at the house on Roosevelt, party central for Will's scooter tramp buddies.

Given how he knew things could turn out at one of these blow outs, he decided he wouldn't subject her to a ride home on the bike. There had been times when he was incapable of standing on his own two feet, so his buddies would start his scooter and hold it up while a few others carried him out and put him on it. He hadn't died yet, and his only crashes on such occasions were minor, a broken part or two for the bike but no serious bodily injuries. They drove to the party in his car.

Things were well under way when they arrived, and the closest parking spot on the street was more than a block away. He had told her about it, but knew there was no substitute for the experience. The festivities could be clearly heard when they got out of the car around the corner on a side street. It wouldn't be long before some of the guys began to razz him for always walking around the car and opening the door for her. When he was finally asked why he did it he replied, "Because I was raised well."

As they came close and walked into the fray, Eva could only have stood out more if she was naked, though naked women were not entirely uncommon in this crowd. Just being her usually elegant self, it was obvious she was not a regular. It wasn't just that men looked at her. In any environment, women looked at her too.

A few of Will's buddies came up to say hi, anticipating an introduction. Hairwood just said, "Hey, Will. Who's this?"

Will looked to her and said, "Eva... this is John."

His buddy smiled large and said, "Nice to meet you, darlin" with a southern gentleman affectation, though he bore little resemblance to one.

After a brief walk around and showing her where the bathroom was on the main floor he said, "Well, I'm going down to check on things in the basement. I'm pretty sure the action down there will not interest you. Walk around and check the place out for yourself. The beer is just about everywhere, and booze is in the kitchen. If anyone makes you uncomfortable, tell them you're with me. If you need to, find John, the guy you met when we showed up, and tell him I asked you to stick with him until I show up. Or you can ask him to bring you to me. Who knows, maybe you'll meet someone you know already." He smiled and gave her a peck on the lips, then disappeared into the crowd.

Coming back up the basement stairs 20 minutes later, Wild Willy, also known as RBH, hustled up to him and said, "Geeze, Will, that new old lady of yours sure ain't very friendly!"

"Sorry, Willy, I don't think you're her type."

When he found Eva, she was talking casually with a nice looking young woman.

"Hey," he said. "You two know each other?"

Eva smiled and said, "We went to school together. This is Gail."

They both nodded and Will reached out to shake her hand. "Seen you around," he said.

Eva continued, "We never knew each other back then, but we recognized each other. She asked how I ended up here, and your name came up." She smiled and reached out to take his arm.

They left a short time later. Eva would come to know most of Will's friends from this crowd, and be easily accepted by them, but she didn't come around with him too often. Her real initiation would come on the ride to Apple Blossom. The full meal deal would be the annual "You Shoulda' Been There" summer time blow out. Nothing could prepare the uninitiated for that monstrous three day party, with 50 kegs of beer, live bands, mountains of food and hundreds of bikers. And drugs, lots of drugs. Most people didn't sleep, they passed out.

None of Will's biker buddies ever came down to the Mall Pub where Eva worked. It was much too sedate for their taste, but Ted joined him there once in a while.

Two weeks after the party on Roosevelt, Eva came home from work one night obviously upset. Will was mellowing out to some James Gang. He got up, turned the music down and wrapped her in a hug.

"What's up Babe?"

She grabbed him around the neck with both arms, "Oh, Will! I was walking down the stairs to work tonight, and some guy I've never seen was walking up. As we passed each other he reached out and grabbed my boob. I jumped back against the wall and was about to scream, but he turned and ran up the stairs and out into the parking lot."

The Pub entrance was outside the main body of the mall, the tavern itself in the basement beneath a family restaurant and the J.C. Penny store. The double doors were carved, dark wood, and the enclosed carpeted indoor stairway was wide enough for four people.

He stepped back and held her at arms-length, looking at her intently. "Who was tending bar?" he asked.

"Julie," she said.

"Did you tell anyone?"

"Yes. She called mall security, and we ran up there, but he was gone. Julie remembered him being there, but had never seen him before either. She let me sit and have a drink to settle down before going to work, but there was no one else available, so I just stayed and worked my shift."

"Did you call the cops?" he asked.

"No," she said. "Mall security wanted us to, but that would have just messed up the whole night. I wasn't hurt, but if he would have come back, we would have. We closed up and walked out to our cars together. We didn't see him again, but I was nervous driving home until I got here."

She wasn't crying, but wasn't far from it.

"CRAP!" Will barked. "I hate this! I'd like to find that creep." He hugged her tightly, and peeled her coat off. He sat her down on the love seat while he went to the kitchen and poured her a glass of white wine. She didn't like weed or beer. He had a little more of both as they tried to relax to some Blood Sweat and Tears before going to bed.

Will figured he'd spend a little more time around the place and hope he was there if the creep came back. The next Friday night he and Ted were sitting at the end of the bar soaking up the suds when three guys walked by on their way out. Will thought he heard what sounded like an off color remark about Eva.

He jerked bolt upright and grabbed Ted's arm. "Hey! Did you hear that?"

"What? Ted asked.

"What those guys said about Eva" he said as he spun his buddy around and pointed at their backs as they rounded the corner to the stairs.

"No. What was it?"

"I'm not sure, but I think they insulted her."

"Well, we'd better take care of that," Ted said as they shot from their seats and trotted after them.

They didn't have a plan, but even drunk they knew that mixing it up on the stairs was a bad idea. They passed them by as the three unsuspecting men slowly made their way up toward the parking lot.

Outside they slowed down eight or ten feet from the doors and turned to confront them as they came out. Will intended to demand an account of what they had said, when Ted bent down as if to tie his shoe. He was blocking their path, and they all looked down at him as he did. Then he exploded from his crouch and caught the closest guy right on the chin with an overhand right. The guy staggered backward into the other two, and Ted launched himself right into the middle of them.

As Will moved in, one of them came straight at him, and they squared off. Things went Will's way quickly, and when he turned back toward the others, Ted was on his back with two guys on top of him.

He ran to his friend, jerked the top guy off, and threw him aside. Just as he grabbed the second guy, one of them jumped on his back. Will was staggering around trying to get the guy off. Finally he reached up and grabbed a hand full of the man's hair on both sides of his head. With a good grip he suddenly bent forward hard and pulled down violently with all his might. The man was launched forward onto the pavement in front of him, hit the ground, and came up running. Will had two hands full of hair. He turned around, and the other two were running after their friend.

People were streaming out of the bar, and Will ran over to Ted, who lay on the ground badly beaten. As he lifted him to help him to the car, Eva ran up shouting, "Will... what are you guys doing!?"

Expecting the police to show up, he said, "I'll tell you later," and hustled Ted over to his car.

When Eva got home after closing for the night, Ted's pain had been soothed with plenty of whiskey and weed, but he did not look good. The area all around his left eye was purple and red, and the eye was swollen shut. His nose was bent to one side, the right side of his mouth and jaw was discolored and puffed up, his split lip was fat and bulging. When he coughed, he winced, clutching his right side. When Eva asked him, he admitted it felt like his ribs were cracked; it hurt even when he breathed.

"He needs to see a doctor," she said passionately, turning to Will.

'Yeah, well... he doesn't have any insurance or money, and the police are liable to have the word out to any local hospital emergency rooms. He's not going to die, so let's see how things look in the morning."

"Will, what happened?" she asked.

He turned to face her. "Well, we were sitting at the bar having a few beers when those guys walked by, and I thought they said something bad about you. So, we went out to discuss it with them, and it didn't go well," he said sheepishly.

"Will, those guys are good guys. They came back in later to apologize for anything they may have said or done to cause any trouble. One of them has two big bald spots on his head. None of them look as bad as Ted, but they're a little beat up." She paused, took in a deep breath and looked down.

"Shit," he said softly. "I'm sorry. I guess we could be in some trouble, huh?"

She looked back up, "No. They said they weren't going to call the police and weren't interested in pressing any charges. But you owe those guys an apology. They didn't do anything wrong," she said with conviction.

She stepped toward him, reaching out to take both of his elbows in her hands. He looked up at her, and her big brown eyes were open wide, beaming sincerity.

"Will… you can't suspect every guy who gets near me because of the guy who grabbed me that night. We haven't seen him again, and it's over. Okay?"

He sighed. "Okay."

He had tried to teach her how to spread her fingers and jam her hand into someone's face, telling her that at least one finger would find its way into an eye and she would have time to run while screaming her head off. But she was incapable of aggression and could never pull it off, so he'd given up.

In the morning Ted looked even worse and was sober. He hurt like hell.

"Okay" Will said. "I've got it. You take my Group Health card and go in to the Northgate Clinic. It's members only, no public E.R. The card has no picture I.D., and you know my address, phone number and personal stuff. They'll fix you up like it was me, and no one will ever know. I pay my monthly membership fee, and that's that. What do you think?"

Ted looked back at him with his one good eye and muttered through his swollen mouth, "Okay, if you say so. I don't have any other options."

Will dropped him off at the far side of the clinic parking lot and handed him a quarter.

"There's a pay phone in the waiting room. Give me a call when you get out. I'll be at home, Okay?"

"Deal," Ted said, and got out of the car.

Only an hour and a half later Ted called, ready to be picked up. Fifteen minutes after that, Will pulled into the parking lot where he had dropped him off. He thought Ted looked like he was walking a little better as he came across the lot to the car.

Ted opened the door and eased himself down in the seat carefully, pharmacy bag in hand. He closed his eyes without looking toward Will, and gave out a slow sigh.

"So, how'd it go?" Will asked eagerly.

Ted slid his good eye open slowly and said, "Fine. In spite of how bad my face looks, nothing is broken. They cleaned, and swabbed, and prodded here and there. I even had x-rays. Ribs aren't broken. One is cracked. Nothing to do for it but take it easy and wait for it to get better. I've got a few pain pills I had enough on me to cover. I suppose things are better than expected, but..."

"What?" Will blurted out.

"After the intake and being examined by a nurse, a doctor checked me out. Not too busy in there on a Saturday. A lot better than a public hospital, that's for sure. X-rays didn't take long either. Then the doctor came back. After explaining the film and a few questions, he asked me how my knees are. I said, fine. Then he said, 'I know. Will's aren't.'"

He turned and looked at Will's puzzled face for the first time. "His name is Dr. Vander Haven."

Will's eyes closed, and his chin sank to his chest. "Shit," was all he said.

"Yeah," Ted agreed. "After explaining that he's your doctor, he calmly told me this was a bad idea, that I could be in legal trouble, and you could lose your insurance. But he also admitted that as his patient he cares about you, and doesn't want any trouble for either one of us. So… a bill for services rendered will be mailed to me at your address, and I'll have 30 days to pay it. Nice guy, really."

"Yeah, he is," Will agreed. "Wow. What are the chances?"

"Well, it could have gone a lot worse," Ted said.

Will started the car and they drove back to his place without talking.

The Ride

When the end of April rolled around Eva was as ready as she could be without having been on a long ride. Apple Blossom Festival was upon them, and it was time to ride. Fifteen or twenty scooters rolling down the road, two to a lane, may look like a precision effort, but getting them gathered up and on the road at the same time was no military exercise. This was not a scrappy looking version of a motorcycle drill team. Most of these guys were genuine non-conformists, anytime, anywhere. Some are early, some are late. Some are focused and ready to go, while others are still drunk from the night before. A few have had their gear sorted and packed since hitting the sack that night, and one or two are just now trying to mooch a sleeping bag to strap to their chicken bar for the trip.

Eventually Eva would gain a well-deserved reputation, and a few nick-names, but her make up essentials were on board, and she would not be coming out of the tent in the morning until she considered herself presentable. Will's reply to wise cracks was, "Eat your heart out." There was always an assortment of cars, trucks, and vans travelling with them on a major ride like this, and she had a bag in one of them. There are limits to what can be strapped to a chopper, and Will was not going to have saddle bags cluttering up his perfect, chrome rear wheel. He could tie his sleeping bag in front of his handlebars and move his pack to the back side of the chick-bar with her riding behind him.

Of course, anything and everything that could be swallowed, smoked, snorted, or absorbed into the bloodstream in any way was being consumed in abundance as soon as the first of the group arrived at the house on Roosevelt. Will was the early and ready type, and he and Eva had been there almost two hours before he kicked his bike over to fire it up. She could see he was already drunk and high enough to be unfit to operate any motor vehicle, but had also learned that how much of a buzz he chose to get was not open for discussion.

They had made it through the gauntlet of traffic lights around the north end of Lake Washington and were just sweeping through a big curve onto Hwy 2 between Bothell and Woodinville, cracking the throttles open to get up to freeway speed. Will liked the surge of acceleration and pulled ahead of Wild Willy, who was riding beside him on his left. Willy had a throttle lock, so when he came up beside Will, he set his speed to match, reached back into his right hip pocket, and pulled out a pint of brandy he had for sipping along the way. Will looked over just as Willy extended it toward him and swerved to his left to grab it as Willy swerved to his right to make the handoff. If Eva screamed, neither of them could hear her over the roar of the bikes, their helmets, and the drunken fog that shrouded them both.

The two motorcycles clanged together and ricocheted away from each other without any parts getting tangled up. Willy let out a big HOOT, Will grabbed the brandy, and they both laughed as if it were the best thing they'd seen all day. Eva closed her eyes and tried to avoid thinking the worst. Will handed the bottled over his shoulder to her to take the cap off. He took a big pull and held it in his lap with his left hand awhile before taking another one. They were coming to a few more stop lights that would require using the clutch, so she held onto it until the next time they pulled over.

Shutting the bikes off beside each other in the parking lot of a tavern in Monroe, Willy shouted, "Damn, Boy! That was some

FINE ridin' back there!" Both of them grinned as Will reached back to Eva for the bottle, and with one long pull each, he and Willy drained what was left of it.

Eva closed her eyes, dropped her head, and sighed as the others pulled in and they all headed into the tavern for a beer. She would soon learn it was their custom to have a drink in every town they passed through on the way over Stevens Pass to Wenatchee.

After leaving Monroe and tasting their way through Gold Bar, Start Up, Index, and Skykomish, the boys were storming down the two lane highway on the eastern side of Stevens Pass toward the Alpine town of Leavenworth in the pre-dusk of late afternoon. Will was often out front, but had fallen off the pace when a guy named Rob blasted past him on a Limey. By the time his drug and alcohol addled brain processed the insult, the Triumph had rounded the next corner out of sight. Will stomped the old Harley down into 3rd gear, and cracked the throttle open, taking Eva completely by surprise. If it weren't for the chicken bar, she would have gone off the back.

Getting up to 75 or 80 mph, he backed off a bit going into a long, left-hand curve. Looking ahead from the middle of the corner, he didn't see the other bike in front of him, and he turned his head to glance at an old country store and gas station across the road when he realized Rob was pulling up to the gas pumps. Without a thought, he slammed his foot down on the old mechanical, drum rear brakes. The rear tire locked up and came around hard to the right as he jerked the handlebars sharply and laid it down on the left side at about 60 mph. Eva reflexively clamped down for all she was worth, with her knees in his sides, her arms around his chest, and her face buried against his neck. The old scooter hit the ground with a loud crash and slid through the lot, past the pumps, and out into the graveled side lot before coming to rest.

A dust cloud billowed around them as they lay on their side, Eva clinging to him tightly with her eyes closed. Will relaxed against the ground with the weight of the motorcycle resting on the primary cover and foot pegs, and the front wheel pointed at the sky. "You Okay?" he stammered.

Before she could answer, a swarm of the other bikes poured into the lot all around them and erupted into cheers. "YEAH! WILL!! Good job, Man!!!"

Someone took Eva by the arm and helped lift her up as she wiggled free. Will rolled over onto his back and started laughing while a few guys picked his bike up. He stood up, brushed himself off, and looked at Eva, gaping as he realized she didn't have a scratch on her. He hadn't faired quite so well.

Much of his jeans were gone away, revealing a sizeable patch of road rash on his left knee and hip. His left elbow didn't look too good either, but nothing was broken. The old Harley came through none the worse for wear. The rubber was chewed off the end of the left handle grip, the primary cover was pretty well scarred up, but the old hawg took it like a tank.

"Somebody get that man a beer!" Willy shouted.

Will slowly began to look around, wondering where he was. Things were hazy, sounds were fuzzy. He began to recognize some of what was being said in the chatter around him. He was sitting. He looked down and saw half a glass of beer on the table. He turned his head to the left and recognized Eva beside him, facing away while she carried on a conversation with someone. Things were clearing up. Looking around the room he recognized they were at the Icicle. "Okay," he thought, "how did I get here?"

Willy and Butt were across the table from him, and the other guys were spread out around the room not far away. He picked up the beer in front of him and lifted it for a swallow. "Alright… we're here." He sat listening.

Suddenly Eva said, "Hey… you're back with us!" She slipped her right hand inside of his left arm, leaned over, and gave him a peck on the cheek.

"Sure," he said. "Having a hell of a time," then looked over and gave Willy a nod.

He learned later that after they had gotten him, Eva, and his bike off the ground up on the pass, he had dropped it on her attempting to get going after gassing up. It had hit her on the left ankle and put her on the ground, pinned under the weight of it. She was feeling no pain at the moment, but when her boots came off around the campfire later that night, her ankle swelled up to the size of a grapefruit with a rainbow array of colors.

Though they had covered more than 40 miles, Will was so bombed he had no recollection of anything between the time his scooter hit the ground in the mountain parking lot and waking up in a fog at the Icicle. It sounded like they'd had a pretty good time. They rode up into Canyon Two, southwest of town, to camp for the night. No normal people to bother out that far.

They stayed stupid for the rest of the weekend and pointed themselves back up over the pass Sunday afternoon in the midst of an endless migration of cars, trucks, campers, boats, trailers, and motorhomes crawling at a snail's pace. The two lane road snaked its way along the edge of the river through the forest until it turned upward more sharply into the mountains. Just before leaving the river, they pulled over one last time at a place called The Cable Car, where decades earlier just such a vehicle carried people over the river. The boys wanted to fill their snoots with a good blast of Jet Fuel for the last leg of the journey.

With her bad ankle, Eva had traveled around in one the cars for most of the festival, but she wanted to finish the ride with Will on the back of his bike. Once again, she ignored how blasted he was.

After about two miles of chugging along with the wagon train in the bottom end of 3rd gear, Will had had enough. He kicked it down into 2nd, cracked the throttle wide open, and swung out into the oncoming lane. Eva gasped and gripped him around the chest like her life depended on it. There was some traffic coming down the mountain, so Will just planted his front tire on the center line and screwed it on. Eva clamped her eyes closed and prayed silently as they sped past rearview mirrors, no more than two feet away on both sides. He didn't have time for this crap.

Two weeks later the primary chain on Will's scooter began to chug and lurch when maintaining a slow, steady speed. Time to replace it. He had lost a primary chain at freeway speed on his first hawg while riding home from California a few years earlier. Fortunately, it had exploded right out of the primary cover and wrapped itself around the mouse trap. His last 20 miles of that trip was in the back of a truck, so this bike sat until he picked up a new chain.

It was a warm, sunny Sunday afternoon, and the boys had a pretty good party cooking at Hawk's place in Ballard. As everybody got more and more well-oiled, Will began to take some serious heat for being too much of a sissy to bring his bike out. Finally, he caved and grabbed a ride with someone to get it. Back at the party they all continued to get tuned up. As the afternoon was sliding into evening, Will, Al, and Butt decided to head for the house on Roosevelt.

80th Street is an East-West arterial in north Seattle that runs all the way from the bluff above Golden Gardens in Ballard to Bothell Way, east of Aurora and I-5. Roosevelt intersects 80th near the freeway.

The boys were eastbound on 80th between Aurora and the freeway, crawling along behind a string of cars stacked up behind a bus. Butterdog and Will were side by side with Big Al right behind them. Slow gets too long fast, and when Butt saw what looked like a good opportunity he cranked it open into the oncoming lane to get past the mess. Will followed suit immediately with Al right behind him. They were blasting past these Sunday drivers up toward the top of 3rd gear at 60 or 70 miles per hour, when Will's rear wheel locked up.

In his usual obstructed state of mind, he realized what had happened just before he hit the ground. The primary chain had broken and locked up around the clutch hub, bringing everything to a screeching and very sudden halt. Will went down sideways in the oncoming lane. The stretched-out chopper left Big Al with no place to go. He was still accelerating and hit Will without backing off of the throttle.

Al's bike smashed into the front legs of Will's scooter between the triple-clamps and the front wheel, snapping both tubes off of his Wide Glide completely. When they collided, Will let go of his bike and found himself on his butt as the two scooters and Al flew through the air in front of him. He skidded along until he slowed down enough to get up on his feet.

Al's motorcycle, a nine-foot long virtual twin to Will's first hawg, went up in the air in what looked like slow motion to Will. The rear wheel gained elevation until the whole thing was vertical and his buddy was flying through the air head first out in front of it all. Al landed on the right temple of his head just as his bike landed upside down on the concrete and turned into a thousand pieces, scattering in all directions. If Al hadn't been wearing a helmet, he probably would have died on the spot.

Still conscious, he stretched out lengthwise with his arms at his sides and spun up the street like a rolling pin. Adding interest to an already fascinating scene, Al had just sold his drag boat at the party and had more than $2,000 in $10 and $20 bills stuffed in his pockets. As his jeans shredded, the money came spilling out, blowing around the street like pixy dust.

The explosion of motorcycle parts were coming to rest in a 30-50 yard radius, and Will was on his feet running toward his friend who had gotten up and staggered over to someone's lawn, where he collapsed. Will ran up to him as he lay on his back looking up, stunned. There was a huge scuff mark on the crown of his helmet.

"Hey, man! Are you Okay!?"

Al didn't speak, but slowly looked at Will and nodded his head. Will turned around and began to assess the situation. All of the traffic had come to a stop, and people were getting out of their cars. It must have been loud, because even more people were pouring out the houses on both sides of the street. Given what slice of society these two represented, with the street ankle deep in cash, it must have looked like these scooter tramps had just pulled off a robbery or some other crime.

Convinced his friend was not in danger, Will began picking up the money. He didn't have two handfuls yet when one of the neighbors began handing out a few paper bags and people started gathering up the cash shifting around in the breeze. Before any police or fire arrived, all the money was bagged and returned. The count later that day revealed that not a dollar was missing.

Eight blocks up the street, where it widens to four lanes, Butter Dog had just stopped at a red light when a guy in a pickup truck pulled up and said, "Your buddies are spread out over about three blocks back there."

By the time he got off of his bike back down at the crash scene, Al and Will were walking around with onlookers, picking up pieces of their motorcycles and piling them on the parking strip. Will gave him the 30 second version of what happened, and he joined them.

A few minutes later Will felt someone tap him on the shoulder. He didn't expect anyone in particular. When he turned around he found a Seattle fireman looking him in the eye. "How're you doing?" the man asked him.

"I'm fine, I think," Will replied.

"Really?" the fire fighter asked. "When's the last time you looked at your butt?"

He had slowed to maybe 50 mph before the seat of his jeans had disappeared. From then on it was his hide and the street. Face down in the back of a fire department rescue truck, the EMT spread some salve on him and bandaged him up. Will had declined a trip to the hospital, and as he stepped from the truck to resume the recovery effort, the medic encouraged him to see a doctor. Will nodded and walked away.

Later that evening a crowd had assembled at his house. Calls had been made and his mother was also there. Will sobered up to the realization that this was more than just a scratch. He was now face down on his own bed, exposed to whoever found their way into his room. Carl was a softball fanatic and always had some aerosol cans of stuff he sprayed on the abrasions from sliding into a base while wearing shorts.

"Carl, spray that stuff on my butt."

"No! Not a good idea," he objected. "That stuff burns like hell on scrapes. You're down to raw meat. You need to see a doctor."

"Spray it on, man! It's my ass."

They went back and forth a few times, everyone urging Will to get medical attention. Finally, he prevailed, and Carl brought out the dreaded spray can. "Trust me… you're going to hate this, and it's not my fault."

"Yeah, yeah, yeah… spray it on."

Carl reached out and flooded Will's raw backside with a heavy blast.

He cut loose with a high volume string of obscenities few had ever heard, rawer than his bloody behind.

"Will!" his mother spouted.

"Then leave!" he barked back. "You don't have to be here!"

His mother and Eva exchanged a knowing glance.

The next afternoon Will was face down on a metal, rolling gurney in the Group Health Northgate Clinic. Eva was at his side when Medex Phillips walked into the room. A retired Army Medic, Phillips wasn't overflowing with warmth and sympathy. He introduced himself as he stepped up beside Will's prone body and bent down to examine the wound.

"What happened to you?" he asked.

Will gave him a brief but descriptive account of the incident and Phillips grunted, "Uh huh," and walked out. A few minutes later he came back with a stainless steel bowl of warm, soapy water and a scrub brush.

"There are little pieces of street embedded in your hide and this is going to hurt like hell, but there's nothing I can do about that," he said, and got down to business. He was right.

Ten days later Will was in the office of an orthopedic surgeon. Something was seriously wrong in his back. After a thorough examination he was sent home with a massive shot of cortisone in his lower back and instructed to lie down with an ice pack on it for 30 to 45 minutes. Almost miraculously, he felt like a new man three days later. After the maximum allowed two subsequent shots, three months apart, he wore a back brace indefinitely, wanting nothing to do with surgery.

Eva emptied her bank account to help him put his bike back together. She was a keeper.

Will's mom and stepdad parked out front of Will's house. Eva opened the door when they knocked and gave his mother a big hug as she stepped into the living room. Eva was 16 years old when her own mother died, and Will's mom filled a void she had suffered from for ten years. The two of them hit it off from the first time they met. (Will's mom was the first to reveal to her that his name was actually Mark Wilson. His buddies had called him Will since they were kids, and it was the only name she had ever heard.) Eva was eager to have them over for dinner. Her feminine touch was becoming evident throughout the house.

She wasn't just good looking. Among her many other attributes, she could cook and loved preparing meals Will loved to eat. He was even more drawn to her because of her genuineness. She appeared to be almost incapable of deception. He would learn she couldn't even be relied on to pull off a lie to set up a surprise birthday party. It wasn't that she couldn't keep a confidence, but her attempts to deceive were so transparent no one believed her. Tonight she was bubbling over with excitement to feed them all well.

Will and his stepdad sat down in the living room as the two women walked past them into the kitchen.

"What can I help you with?" his mom asked.

The table was already set with a proper tablecloth, napkins, and silverware. The pasta and sauce were simmering on the stove.

Eva returned to cutting up salad ingredients and said, "You can get some bowls out for the sauce and salad from the lower cabinets over there," pointing toward them. "And there should be a colander for the pasta in the next one over. Thanks."

Will pushed his plate away, too full to heap it up for the third time. Scratch spaghetti meat sauce with mushrooms and black olives, garlic bread, and salad. He didn't know how soon he would be able to get at a slice of fresh, hot apple pie. No better way to help things along than to sharpen his appetite with some of his best from the Pot Pot.

As Eva expertly cleared their dinner dishes, Will slid the little red kettle from its place against the kitchen wall out to the center of the table and drew a pack of rolling papers from his shirt pocket. His stepdad's eyes widened and shifted to his mom. She rarely registered the shock he intended and didn't even flinch. She knew her son's attitude about what went on in his home. "If you don't like it, there's the door," was a direct quote.

Will lit the joint, sat back in his chair, and inhaled a long, slow drag. Exhaling just as slowly, he flicked the thin, fragile ash off into the ashtray to his right.

As smooth as silk, his mother said, "That's fine, Will, but you're going to serve God one day," and smiled sweetly. He didn't reveal any surprise either.

After his next drag he said matter-of-factly, "I intend to get right with God one day, Mother, but I'll never be a preacher, so you can forget that." He had never spoken to Eva about God, though no one was surprised to hear his mother speak of Him. He was as much a normal part of her life as any of them.

A New Line of Work

Back on his feet, but not back to work, Will had more time on his hands than usual. While maintaining what he considered to be safe limits, he kept some cash-flow going with his customary, low level drug dealing. He also spent more evening time at The Mall Pub. It was way more crowded than he was willing to endure at 7:30 Friday night, so he went back up to walk around the mall for a while.

Ambling past one of the nicer Women's Clothing stores his eye was drawn to a particularly well dressed mannequin, built almost exactly like Eva with long legs, the proper waist and hips, and long brown hair. He stopped, turned, and walked up closer to the display window to examine the details of the outfit.

Made of a luscious, silky black fabric with tiny white squares well-spaced to highlight the stunning pants suit, it was perfect for her. She liked to wear black and would look fabulous in it. The buttons down the front of the jacket were a tasteful dark red, much like one of the lipsticks she wore. The lapels closed a few inches below her collar-bone with enough space to display a necklace, but high enough to be worn without a blouse. Her shape couldn't go unnoticed. She didn't need to dress to draw attention to it. The jacket was tapered to fit her perfectly formed torso, but cut loose enough to lay gently over her wonderfully rounded hips.

She liked her pants long, just brushing the floor while wearing high heeled, wedge, or platform shoes, and these were appropriately wide at the bottom, flaring all the way down to the one-inch cuff. He could see her elegant stride with these pant-legs swooshing gracefully.

Walking out the door with the suit beautifully wrapped in fluffy tissue paper inside the white, embossed box with the shop's own designer ribbon holding it together, he couldn't wait to present it to her. "She's going to love it," he thought. Both of his parents were gift givers and it had taken root in him. He loved giving gifts to people he loved. He also liked setting up surprise blessings.

He would drop down for a couple of drinks, have a few casual words with her as her work allowed, then tell her he'd see her at home as he left a few hours before her shift was over.

The gift box was resting on the coffee table when she came through the front door about 2:45. She had stayed to help Grant clean up, and then sat down to have a drink and unwind with the matchmaker who had guided her and Will toward each other. As she came through the door at home, not a word about work escaped her mouth.

Stepping inside she stopped at the end of the couch, her eyes locked on the box. She tilted her head and looked at Will, who was smiling slightly.

"Close the door," he said gently.

She reached behind for the doorknob without looking and closed it softly. She was beginning to smile and blushed as she shifted her gaze from Will to the box and back to him.

"What's in the box?" she asked.

"A gift," he replied brightly.

"For who?" she asked next.

"For me, I thought. Didn't you send it?" he said playfully, faking bewilderment.

"Will," she said, as she sluffed her purse off on the couch, walked around the coffee table, and sat down beside him. Her eyes followed his hands as he leaned forward, reached out to take the beautiful package, and placed it in her lap.

"Open it," he said, and sat back.

Her long delicate fingers reached to touch the satin ribbon, and she stroked it with pleasure. Ever so gently she pulled one end of it as the neatly tied bow began to slide apart. She stopped. Turning to him she said, "I almost don't want to disturb it, it's so beautiful."

When he said nothing, but kept his gaze fixed on her, she resumed, folding the ribbon carefully before she laid it aside to hold the box in her hands. She recognized the store logo embossed on the textured surface of the elegant box.

She looked at him again, then slowly lifted the lid only to reveal an abundance of fluffy tissue paper. She loved tissue paper, and gently folded it before placing it with the ribbon beside her.

The suit was positioned with the front of the jacket facing up to greet her; the rounded tips of the lapels, rich looking red buttons, and silky black fabric with the tiny white squares proclaimed the understated style and class. She lifted the jacket and held it up. When she turned to look at him, he was blushing slightly behind his widening grin.

"Will," she said. She wanted to hug him but didn't want to let go of it.

"Can I try it on?" she asked.

"Of course, Silly," he laughed, and gave her a gentle boost off the couch.

No one had ever given her anything like this before, and when she came out of the bedroom it looked like it was tailor made for her. They needed dinner reservations as soon as possible.

Will was sitting at the end of the bar half way through his first beer when Grant walked over and leaned on the bar with his left elbow, his back to the taps and the cash register. Will perked up as his friend tilted his head closer and said, "We're going to need another bar tender by the end of next week," and gave him a wink.

The same owner ran Our Place and The Pub. A year earlier Will had actually come to an agreement to begin tending bar at Our Place. But he proceeded to get drunk, rowdy, and destructive that night, and the owner thought better of it.

"What about my little scuffle with those guys outside here last spring?" Will asked.

"I've talked with him, and I'm pretty sure that's smoothed over. You've got the inside track. If you want it, I think the job is yours for the taking." He winked, nodded, and walked away.

Two weeks later Will was standing behind the bar in the most stylish clothes he had owned in years. His back brace wouldn't fit under them, and he sure wasn't going to wear it over them in this place. Diligent exercises he'd received from the physical therapist, pain pills, and determination would get him through a shift. He liked the place and enjoyed the work much more than an auto-body or sheet metal shop. He would not be scheduled to work with Eva until the owner saw how it would all work out.

Will was loading the conveyer-belt dish washer at the end of the bar to capacity as fast as he could. Three waitresses on the floor were stacking the used glassware on the bar above the washer faster than he could run them through, while he also tended to the 13 customers seated at the bar. One week after Thanksgiving, the very trendy food and beverage emporium had three times its legal occupancy standing and sitting at this very moment.

Customers were three deep on the other side of the bar, waiting for either a seat to open up or a fresh drink to enjoy on their feet. Three pool tables were busy, and the conversational buzz made it necessary to lean close to someone just to hear what they were saying. Music from the juke box only added to the flavor.

Will had never been so busy in his life, and it felt good. This was maximum productivity, and the crew working tonight knew how to function as a team. If Will was occupied, one of the girls would step down and pour an order of beers from the taps. If they were hammered beyond their ability to keep up, Will would hustle out into their section and clear a table for other customers eagerly waiting for a seat.

When he turned back from loading the dishwasher again, he saw two fresh faces side by side down at the curve of the bar; the woman had a welcoming smile on her face, and the man wore a scowl. As he approached them he was taken by not only how attractive she was, but he wondered if she was old enough to be there. He'd wait to see what she ordered.

He picked up the used glasses from in front of them, set them on the back bar below, and wiped the surface clean with a bar towel as he asked, "What'll you have?"

Her smile broadened and she said, "White wine for me and a draft beer for him, please."

Maybe a little too friendly, eager to speak, and "please"? he thought.

"May I see your I.D., please?" he responded.

"Hey!" the guy beside her barked. "We've been waiting 15 minutes for these seats!"

"Oh, no you don't!" she said to him. "Not this time."

She opened her purse, pulled out her wallet, and slipped her driver's license from the card slot. As she extended it to Will, her eyes danced with a fresh sparkle.

Will looked down at the card and back at her face to compare the picture. It was her, alright. Then he looked at the birthdate. He had always been good with numbers.

"Yes, Ma'am," he said with a smile, and handed the 34-year-old woman's license back to her.

An hour later they had moved to a table and he'd forgotten about them as the break-neck pace continued without letting up, when he saw her approaching the bar. She smiled that beautiful smile again and extended her hand with a $5 bill in it. "For service above and beyond the call of duty," she said.

Will smiled and nodded, "Thanks. Have a nice evening."

"I already have," she said as she turned to leave. Will was learning what tipping was really about.

Eva loved flowers and always had some on display around the house. He had learned from observing his Dad that giving flowers was always a good thing to do. He had been giving flowers to girls since junior high, and more so since he started dating. One of The Pub's more popular white wines came in a painted ceramic bottle Eva wanted to use as a flower vase.

The Pub had become a regular watering hole for many mall employees, and several of them would often gather after work to have a drink and unwind before going home for the night. Tuesday night, the week before Christmas, the after work rush was just fading before the after dinner shopping surge filled the place again. Will poured the last of the wine from one of the bottles Eva wanted, sat it on the back bar to take home to her, and then opened a fresh one. Eva wasn't working that night and he brought it to her as a little surprise at the end of the night.

Will didn't work Thursday night, and when Grant finished closing up at 2:30, he called Will at home, suspecting he would be up.

"Will," was his standard phone greeting.

"Hey. Grant," his former roommate said. "I've got some bad news, man. Sorry to be the one to tell you, but the owner wasn't willing to do a face to face. You've been let go. No need to come in tomorrow. Sorry, man."

"What!?" Will blurted out. "What's this all about?"

"Don't know, man. No reason given, just that you've been replaced. I'm sure I'll find out sooner or later, but for right now… that's it. That's all I know. Sorry, man. See, ya."

"Yeah. I'm sure you will, but not down there, I guess. Tell him to not worry his sorry ass. I'm not going to come down looking for him. It's just too bad he doesn't have the balls to take care of his own business. Thanks, anyway. I'd rather hear it from you."

Will wasted no time and hit the bricks Friday. He liked tending bar and set himself on a course to apply at every place in town until he had a job. He would work as hard at getting a job as he expected to work once he had one. It served him well as a fourteen-year-old and it would again now.

(1975)
The District

Will's first day on his new job, December 31, 1974, was unlike any before. The listed seating capacity of this establishment was 375, but there were more than 600 people crammed into the place for New Year's Eve. A ticketed cover charge and the most formidable door man in the state provided a reasonably accurate count. His first night would add valuable perspective when he began learning the hands-on administrative requirements of the job the next day.

The stage had more than enough room to accommodate the nine-piece band with a horn section. The transparent dance floor, two feet lower than the main seating area, was lit from beneath with multi-colored, shifting lights. But other than the glow shining up through the throng of happy dancers, it could not be seen - too many people. Disco was out, Funk was in, and The Bump was the hottest dance craze. Good thing, because you couldn't dance on this floor without bumping into someone. The clientele was also a bit different than Will was accustomed to.

"The District" was one of Seattle's largest and most happening Metropolitan night clubs. In 1975 that was intended to mean urban, mixed race, and there was no doubt they were mixing. From Will's point of view, it was a meat market. Hot music, plenty of your favorite adult beverages, and an open invitation to connect with other young adults looking for fun with no strings attached. Will had just been hired to run the place. Whatever the owners were looking for in a manager, the interviews had gone well.

Will walked through the front door only four days earlier looking for another job as a bartender. The club wasn't really open for business until evenings, but deliveries happened during typical workweek hours, and the doors were unlocked. Since it didn't close until 2:00 AM, janitorial was also done during daylight hours. As it happened, one of the three ownership partners was sitting at the bar going over some paperwork when Will walked up and introduced himself. Phone calls the next day, an interview in their downtown Seattle offices the day after that (which also housed the city's Number One black radio stations) and his OJT came out of the shoot like a race horse.

A warm up act got things started at 7:00, transition time for those who came straight from work. The band that would own the stage for the night started at 8:30, following a half-hour lull between them and the warm-up solo piano player, singer. By the time things got rolling at 10:00 o'clock, it was an active nonstop explosion, with 15 minute breaks for the band every 45-60 minutes. Three enormous ventilation fans on the roof sucked out the thick fog of cigarette smoke and body heat. Three extra large cigarette vending machines kept the patrons supplied with nicotine. Other smoking and sniffing substance was available in abundance, but not offered by management. Discretion and mild enforcement kept things at an acceptable level. When intervention was required, the doormen were not there to negotiate.

An OSHA inspection later in the year would reveal sound levels above that of a 747 taking off. Conversation was shouted at close range. There were 18 waiters and waitresses and 5 bartenders on the payroll, rotated, part-time throughout a regular weekly schedule. Twelve of the servers and four of the bartenders were working the New Year's Eve crowd, and they had no planned breaks, though some grabbed a smoke now and then.

All three owners were present for the biggest night of the year and took turns walking Will around, pointing out various aspects they thought important to the club's operation. Two were successful white businessmen and investors in the club and radio stations. One was a tall black man, predominant presence on the team, unquestioned boss of the radio stations, and rising personality on the Seattle business and political scenes. Will was clean shaven, except for his mustache, and outfitted in the sharpest, most stylish clothes available at Bernie's Fine Men's Wear. He was unrecognizable from the scooter tramp who had crashed his Pan Head twice in the previous year.

The Pub was also hopping that night, and Eva got home a little before 3:00 AM. The owners of The District were excited about the monster night they had just had, their first New Year's Eve since buying it, and Will stuck around to soak up all he could. He pulled down the driveway about 3:20. Eva had much to tell him about the night, but she had never been to The District, and Will's description of the club and the night took far longer. He would be back at noon to begin learning about deliveries.

Glenda was 26 years old, 5'4", and slightly built with streaked blond hair pulled back into a loose ponytail. If she did smile, Will hadn't seen her do it yet. She was the head waitress, all business, and as far as she was concerned her business was the wait staff. Prior to Will taking over management of the club, the owners had relied on her to hire, supervise, and schedule the waiters and waitresses. She was not dictatorial, but considered their requests for scheduling and worked her shifts on the floor alongside them.

Will was now responsible for all aspects of all the employees, including the bands who rotated through on a weekly basis. He too relied on Glenda to continue in her responsibilities while he gained a firm grasp of daily bookkeeping, product ordering, and the other mundane, behind the scenes practices that kept the place running smoothly and at a profit.

As January gave way to February, things were clicking along fairly well with Valentine Day on the horizon. It was evident from the start that Glenda was slightly resentful of Will's authority, though he had never exercised it to counter any of her decisions. She clearly didn't like reporting to him, and little by

Without Malice

little various challenges began to creep into their interactions. Will was not confused about who was in charge, neither did he want to deal with any needless disruptions while he was getting his sea legs.

The first Friday night in February, he was at the door and on the floor when the band kicked things off for the weekend at 8:30. This was a hot locally based band that was popular up and down the west coast, and he had been looking forward to having them. Their first three songs of the first set jumped off well, and people were on the dance floor when he headed upstairs to his office.

Twenty minutes later when he came down, the place had filled quickly and everyone was running to keep up. His two bartenders were keeping pace, but they were obviously shorthanded on the floor. In the competitive Seattle night club scene, if you wanted to keep customers for the night you had to keep them happy early. Disappointment would too easily send them to another club. Waiting for service on the floor did not contribute to a happy evening for anyone.

Will saw one of his more unstable waitresses pouring out her frustrations to a bartender while he poured as many drinks as her tray could handle. The size of the crowd was obvious and he walked over to the door where cover charges were paid to get the count. Unusually high for 9:15.

From there he walked along the mezzanine level overlooking the main seating floor across the radius of the fan shaped room: bar, restrooms, pool tables, front door and coat check room at the back – stage and dance floor at the front, mezzanine side seating above the main floor on both sides. The floor was seriously understaffed. Bottom line - lost money now and more as people left unhappy. He stood out of sight next to a cigarette machine watching for several minutes.

Glenda had just finished switching her best servers to the most demanding sections. Will walked up beside her at the bar while her own orders were being filled.

"How's it going?" he asked.

She gave him a dismissive look and said, "What does it look like?"

In any other environment she would have known immediately that was the wrong answer. He was actually proud of himself for not responding according to his first impulse, which would have been caustic and cut like a razor.

"I'm looking for something more specific," he said sharply.

"We didn't expect this size of a crowd," she said. "We're a little shorthanded."

"I did," he said. "Get on the phone and get some more people in here right away."

"I don't know who is available, and I'd have to leave the floor to do it. That would put us in even worse shape," she answered as if it were a trump card.

"Do it now," he said. "I'll pay a $10 bonus to the first two who arrive in the next 30 minutes." He held her gaze for a split second then turned and walked away toward the door.

Walking up to the doorman, he said, "When this song ends tell the band leader that all their drinks for the next break are on me if they play for another 20 minutes. I'll cover the door." Pulling hot, thirsty people off of the dance floor would be the worst thing he could do right now.

Will usually came in at 10:00 in the morning to begin deliveries and his daily paper shuffling. He'd already learned that moisturizer was vital to prevent cracked and bleeding fingers from counting the cash taken in on a busy night. Glenda was waiting in the parking lot when he pulled in. She got out of her car when he got out of his, and joined him at the back door as he slipped his key in the lock.

"You're here early," he said.

"We need to talk," she replied.

"Yes, we do," he said back, swung the door open, and walked in down the hallway without giving her another look. He stopped in the hall and removed the weekly schedule sheet from the wall. Stepping into the back room that led to the stairs up to his office he said, "Come on up."

At the top of the stairs, he crossed the private break room for the band and unlocked his office door. He left it open as he went in, hung his jacket on the coat tree, and sat down at his desk. Glenda walked in behind him and remained standing.

After looking over the schedule sheet for a moment, he swiveled his chair around to face her, holding it in his hands.

"Why did you take over my staff last night?" she demanded.

"Because you didn't," he replied. Neither of them looked away.

"You embarrassed me in from of my crew," she said.

"You were costing us money, and doing nothing was going to cost us even more. And just in case you don't understand… they're my crew. Everyone is here to make this club run well, and we were driving it into a ditch last night. Poor service has lasting implications. Why weren't more people scheduled?"

"Because I didn't think we would need them," she shot back.

"You were wrong," he said firmly. "An extra server costs me $2.25 an hour. Not having enough of them can cost $100 per hour each. They pay for themselves in the first two orders. We staff to win. If the crowd is light, buy someone a drink and send them home. They're here for the club, not the other way around."

"That's not fair to them," she said.

"This is not about fair," he said, "It's about profit and loss, supply and demand. If customers demand and we don't supply, we lose. We're not here to lose."

"Well, I think…" and he cut her off midsentence.

"When you're thinking is wrong, I don't give a damn what you think. That's why I'm here. If you can't take being corrected…" and she cut him off.

"I'll go to Jerry."

"Well," he said, "When you do, go with this knowledge; I still work here and you don't."

She stood speechless as he turned his chair back to his desk. "Be sure your time card is accurate before you leave. Your check will be ready Friday, just like everyone else's."

Word didn't take long to spread, and Will noticed an obvious deference replaced the initial curiosity toward him from the entire staff. Do your job, and you would be rewarded. Don't, and it would no longer be a problem.

Will's doormen were an interesting breed. None of them were small or timid, some were openly engaging, and others all business, but they were all prepared to take absolute authority over any situation that required intervention. Because most folks knew this, it didn't happen often.

Bobby was not only Will's best doorman, he was also known as the baddest doorman in the state. At 6'1" and 285 pounds, it would be a huge mistake to think he was a fat man. Bobby ran five miles every morning with a 2 pound weight in each hand, throwing punches as he went. He was as quick as a cat, and strong as an ox. He also had a heart of gold, but if you put him in the wrong situation, it may turn out to be the worst day of your life.

Two months after becoming the manager, Will brought Eva on staff. Though it was not her kind of place, she was the most skilled waitress he knew. Most people could not do the job well. To hear, remember, fill and return multiple, complex orders without error was a rare ability she performed with skill and grace. She made it look easy.

Her warm, genuine desire to serve customers well, along with her complete absence of any aggressive nature, could have made her vulnerable in the wild environment of the floor on a busy night, were it not for Bobby. Everyone knew that if you gave Eva a hard time, Bobby would break your back. Will and Eva both treated Bobby with respect and honor, and he embraced them as family.

Bobby had grown up in the roughest of circumstances and spent time in prison more than once. He became enforcement muscle, even on the inside. He was not to be trifled with, but if he was in your corner, you were as safe as another human being could make you.

Without Malice

Walking around the corner from the back room behind the bar one night, Will was almost run over by DeBorah, a club regular who felt like one of the crew.

"Oh, Will!" she shouted right in his face. "There's an out of control black chick beating up white chicks in the women's rest room!"

Will quickened his pace past her toward the problem. The women's rest room was just inside the front door, across the entryway from the cashier and coat check room. It was a busy Saturday night with two doormen on duty; Dan was on the door and Bobby was on the floor. Women were pouring out of the rest room and the screaming and scuffling could be heard from inside.

Dan took a few steps toward Will and told the cashier, "Hold the door."

Will turned to Dan and said, "Get Bobby."

When Bobby came jogging up, Will understood there were only three people left inside the rest room: the assailant, one active victim and another one locked in a stall. He told Bobby as much and said, "Get her out of there."

Bobby gave him a grim nod and stepped boldly into the outer entry of the women's room. He pushed open the outer door and held it while he shouted, "All Right! All you bitches get decent, cause' I'm comin' in!"

With that he walked through the inner door prepared for battle. Stepping to the back wall, he grabbed the attacker by both upper arms and jerked her backward with such force that her feet came off the ground. He spun her around with her right arm in the vice-like grip on his powerful left hand. He was just clearing the outer rest room door when her sister, unknown to be in the room too, leaped onto his back. Without breaking stride, he reached behind with his right hand, grabbed her by one arm, and flung her across several feet of space where she slammed into the wall. Dan immediately held her in place where she would not interfere again.

As Bobby dragged the troublemaker past the cashier and customers waiting to get in, down the steps, out the door, and into the parking lot, he tossed her out onto the pavement with more force than he had used on her sister.

She landed about eight feet from him and sprang off the ground like a coiled snake, with an open straight razor in her hand. She leaped at him and raised it to strike as she fearlessly rushed at him. She would have been better served by fear.

Bobby's eyes were blazing, and he tightened his focus on the charging woman. Her blade was half way forward when he took one long stride, and hit her so hard on the chin with his overhand right that her whole body reversed course, head first like a rag doll. She landed on her back four feet from him. She was out cold with her wig a few feet beyond her body.

Bobby stood ready for another assault, but a few seconds made it clear she was not moving. A moment later Dan unceremoniously deposited her sister next to her. No warnings were offered, but neither of them were seen again.

Transition

Will's private line rang. His desk at work had two phones, one for public business and a private line the owners could call him on. It even had a fancy new message recorder. He also shared it with his personal circle of contacts. It was 5:30 in the evening and the club was technically open for business with one bartender on the clock.

"Will here." He had added the "here" to his phone greeting for the sake of enhanced business propriety.

"Will, you old dog. Haven't seen you around much these days," his buddy Butter Dog greeted him. "What'd you do, dump us for the hip set?"

"Right," he replied. "Like this crowd could compete. Look man, this job doesn't live in a time clock. I'm getting the hang of it, and things are running pretty smooth, but it's high demand, and I'm responsible for everything every person who works here does. I'm just putting in what I need to to make it work. This is an unexpected opportunity, and I want to make the most of it. I'll be able to make more time when ridin' weather shows up."

Without Malice

"Yeah, well... now that you mention it, that's why I called. Apple Bosom is only two months away, and the boys are wondering if you're gonna' pussy out on us. I told 'em hell no! You know Will better than that. When's the last time you kicked your scooter over, anyway?"

"Shit... you know I started this gig New Year's Eve. I haven't even touched my bike this year," Will admitted.

"Well... you're in luck, then. You've got plenty of time to get things squared away and be ready to ride back over the pass. Haven't missed one in years. And I'm sure after last year, Eva is just dying to get back on that thing with you," he said, cackling in the background.

"Right," Will chortled. "She doesn't begrudge me the bike, and believe it or not, she likes you boys well enough, too. But no, she's not too eager to hop on that hawg again any time soon."

"As long as we're talking, I haven't seen any of you boys down here since I've been running the place. What's it gonna' take?"

"Come on, Will. You know that's not exactly our kinda' place. I don't think your regular clientele would be any too happy to see a bunch of us pull up, either."

"Well," Will answered... "I just might have something in the works for you. Nothing settled yet, but I'll let you know. Hey, I have to move along. Things start happening around here pretty soon and I'm more than a casual observer. I'll get back to you."

"Okay. Get that scooter going and we'll hit the road."

"Yup. I'll see ya."

Gabriel had just started the first song of their third set for the night. They were one of Will's favorite bands who performed at the club, one of three he booked regularly at proper intervals throughout the year. He had been waiting since the first set, and they knew it. There were five musicians, four of them talented singers who could harmonize like angels. Will thought they were as good as "Eagles" and could be as big if they caught the right break with the right people. They played up and down the west coast and farther inland as their popularity spread.

One of the Top 40 songs they covered was "Mighty Clouds of Joy" by B.J. Thomas. In spite of his active, unyielding resistance to God's involvement in his life, he loved that song and was excited about them performing it every time they came. Occasionally they would consent to closing the night with it for him even if they had done it earlier. Hearing Thomas's testimony in the music made him feel good about who God is.

When he came out the back door into the alley behind the club, Will was all alone, the last one to leave. Directly across the alley was the used car lot for University Porsche. It sometimes surprised him what types of cars people apparently traded in for a Porsche. But tonight he looked through the chain-link fence surrounding the car lot at the stunning hind-quarters of a 1971 Corvette T-Top. He stood still under the street light admiring it, an automotive work of art. His '64 had been extreme. This car could be a daily driver. He walked back and forth, from the back of the car to the front of it, then twice more before walking to the rear parking lot and heading for home.

When he came through the front door, Eva was sitting on the couch listening to her favorite Joni Mitchell album. She turned his way and their eyes met as he closed the door behind him. "Hey," he said. "How're you doing?"

"I'm doing good," she said. "Just waiting for you," she offered him a soft smile. She hadn't worked at the club that night. She really didn't like the place, so he didn't schedule her for anything but Friday and Saturday nights unless he was short-handed. She could serve on the floor or tend bar.

"Did you go anywhere?" he asked.

"No. Everyone was working or doing something already. I don't like going anywhere alone, so me and the dogs just sat around, watched some TV, then turned the music on. How about you? How was tonight?" she asked.

He reached around the corner and pitched his jacket onto the couch in the TV room. It was a bedroom when Carl and Grant lived there, but now served as a separate place for them to hang out and watch the tube. He was smiling as he walked over and sat down beside her on the living room couch.

"I saw a car," he said. It had been four weeks since his talk with Butter Dog about the ride to Apple Blossom, and two weeks until it was time to hit the road. It was ten days since he had sent his hawg off with a new owner on it. Eva was a keeper, and he thought the job might be, too. He knew that if he owned the scooter when it was time to ride, he would be gone. Eva would wait, but the job wouldn't, and he had a sense like never before he wasn't supposed to kiss it off just to have a hot time for a few days. He hadn't told the boys yet.

Her eye brows arched slightly. "What is it?" she asked. They had a beautiful black over black 1973 Monte Carlo with all of the options and Will liked the car, but his announcement didn't surprise her. Nice wasn't good enough.

His smile broadened. "A '71 Corvette," he said with obvious pleasure.

They looked at each other for a moment. It made sense, she thought. Style and power. Something distinctive. She reached out and took his hand. "Tell me about it."

Will drove it home to show her the next evening before the club opened.

Will pulled to the curb in front of the house on Roosevelt, Saturday afternoon. A few of the boys were sitting around the front room when he walked through the door. "Will... nice ride, man. Is that thing yours?"

"It is, indeed," he replied.

"All right then. Traveling in style." They started slowly getting up to go out and give it the once over.

Circling it with the usual questions, hood up, someone finally asked "What did you have to give for this thing?"

"My scooter," he said. They all stopped still, and every head turned toward him.

"What the hell's wrong with you?" Knuckle Head Dan asked. "Live to ride, ride to live, man. Are you dead?"

"I sold a bike for a Corvette before, and I wasn't crazy then," Will responded.

"Well, yeah… but not two weeks before Apple Blossom. What the hell are you going to do, roll over there in a cage?"

Will shrugged and raised his eye brows, hands out with palms up. Actually, he had a very popular band scheduled for that weekend, and he wouldn't be going. This was not the time to break that news to them. After a couple of short demo rides they wandered back into the house, questioning his sanity as he drove away.

Spring rolled into summer. Will's life revolved around the club, and he saw the boys less and less frequently. Usually on a Saturday or Sunday afternoon he'd drop by at the house on Roosevelt. His previous jobs were about doing his job. This job was about everybody else's jobs, and people who didn't do theirs well were getting under his skin.

Eva walked through the living room to the kitchen for a cup of coffee one Saturday morning. She came out and sat down next to him on the couch. The couch and love seat were along the two walls in the front corner of the living room and they usually each sat on one or the other, facing each other. After a peck on the cheek and a few sips she said, "We need to talk."

"Okay," he said.

After a few more sips she said, "I need to leave," as she turned to look him in the face.

"What?" he asked, startled and instantly feeling off balance.

"The club," she said. "I can't work there anymore. I don't know if you know it, but you're getting grouchy and barking at people, and me more than anyone. I need to get out of there before it causes us problems."

He was surprised to be taken by surprise, took a sip of his coffee, sank back into the couch, and sat in silence for a few moments. He was usually one step ahead of his employees and didn't realize he was taking her for granted.

"OK. How long?"

"As soon as possible, please. By next weekend if you can, but if you're in a bind I'll do one more week."

Will reached out and put his left arm around her shoulder, pulled her a little closer, leaned in and gave her a kiss on the forehead. "You've got it," he said. "Done."

Will usually came home after the last deliveries of the day, when the first bartender came on duty. He'd be back before the opening piano guy finished his 45 minutes. He was changing clothes Wednesday evening when he heard her come through the front door.

"Hey!" he called out from the bedroom. "I'll be out in a couple of minutes."

He saw her purse and jacket on the couch in the living room as he walked into the kitchen. She had just poured a glass of wine and turned to greet him with a bright smile.

"My, my… you look good," he said.

"I feel good," she said, and set her glass down on the counter. They both paused. Then she said, "I have a job!"

"Wow!" he said. "That didn't take long," and started toward her. "Where?"

"Claire's Pantry," she said. "It's a big, really nice family kind of place down in Lake City, in the bank building right by 125th and Lake City Way." She was bubbling with enthusiasm. "They serve breakfast, lunch, and dinner and they're open from 6:00 in the morning until the bar closes at 2:00 AM. It's a really nice place, and I know I'm going to like working there."

She hugged him around the waist. He was happy she was happy and glad she was gone from the club. Already she was bringing something happy home with her. It would be a relief for them both.

Just one month earlier he was stunned when counting the income from a busy Saturday night. The door receipts should have been much more. The next weekend was the end of a pay period and he scheduled the same front doorman and coat-check, entrance cashier for Saturday. Larry was an appropriately imposing, burly ex-con, and Linda was a pretty, sweet young woman in her mid-twenties. He also hired an undercover guy to sit quietly in an out of the way corner with a counter. Every person who paid the cover charge and was given an entrance ticket was clicked on the little device his undercover friend held below the table in his lap.

Cover charge ended at 1:00 AM, and the coatroom was open until all customers had left the building. Will always picked up the door receipts at 1:00 and usually locked them in the safe until the next morning when they would be counted along with the money from the bar. This night he took them to his office to count, along with the tally from his spy. Sure enough, it was $250 light. There had been 125 paying customers pocketed by the door. The dead giveaway the week before was the bar receipts. He always calculated how much per paying customer was spent at the bar, and last week was off the charts.

Just as the last customers were gathering their stuff to leave, Will told Bobby, "After Larry and Linda come up to my office, quietly come up and wait outside my door."

Bobby's eyes flickered a subtle glint of recognition as he gave a firm nod and said, "You got it."

Bobby hung back as Will walked over to the door. "Larry...Linda, when the front door is locked come on up to my office." He turned and walked away before either of them could say anything.

As they stepped into his office upstairs a few minutes later, Will said to them, "Close the door."

Larry closed it and they remained standing as Will turned his chair to face them directly. "You stole $250 from me tonight. I don't know how much you took last weekend, but it's over. Give me the money right now, and that will be the end of it."

Larry burst out, "I don't know what the hell you're talking about!"

"Come on, man... do you think I'm stupid? I hired a counter tonight because of last week. The bar tab per ticket was insane. Tonight you handed out 125 more tickets than I got money for. You scrounged tickets off the floor and reissued them. You think I don't know most of them get tossed because people don't plan to leave?" Sequential numbers were the advantage of tickets over a stamp.

"I'm giving you one more chance. Give me the money right now or you're done."

"Screw you!" Larry spouted.

"Okay" Will said softly. "Your paychecks are mine. It's not exact, but it'll do. Get out."

"You can't do that!" Larry protested.

"Yeah? Stop by on payday and see if there's anything for you," Will sneered.

"That's illegal. I'll report you," Larry shot back.

"Really?" Will asked. "Bobby is right outside the door. If I tell him to keep you here, you won't be leaving. Then I'll call the police, and tell them there is a convicted felon in my employ with a loaded .45 under the driver seat of his car. How do you think that's going to play out?"

Larry stood silently contemplating what he'd been told. He looked at Linda, who looked like she didn't really comprehend what was going on. Will nodded toward the door, and Larry turned to Linda. "Come on," he said, and opened the door into the deadly gaze of Bobby, who followed them down and escorted them out without a word.

Firepower

Will picked up the house phone. "Yeah." It was either the front door or the bar.

"Hey," Bobby said. "There's a dude down here with a gun for sale. I don't want it. You interested?"

"What kind of gun?" Will asked.

"A .38," he said.

"Sure. I'll take a look. I'll be right down."

It was early, and as Will approached the door no one was around except a slightly disheveled looking guy staring at the floor at the bottom of the steps. Bobby nodded his head in the guy's direction as he extended a folded dish towel to Will.

He reached out and took it, lifted the top of the towel, and concealed his immediate reaction. Bringing the weapon up close and examining it from every angle, he folded the towel over it again and looked at Bobby, who nodded back toward the guy who brought it in.

Will walked down the four steps to the stranger as he turned to look at him. "How much?" Will asked.

"$50," the man said.

"Deal," Will replied. He took his money clip from his pocket, peeled off a crisp $50 bill, and handed it to him. He hated ugly money. Every bill in his clip was straight, flat, clean, and crisp. He gave the ugly money to Eva. She didn't discriminate. These days he felt vulnerable if he had less than $200 in his pocket. The guy reached out and took the money almost reflexively, and turned to leave.

"Thanks," Will said to the man as he walked through the door and out into the parking lot, never to be seen again.

Will turned and started back up the steps toward Bobby, who asked him, "Man, why did you pay $50 for that old thing?"

Will held it up and said, "This is no .38, my friend. It's a Ruger Old Style single action .357 revolver with a 4 5/8 inch barrel and a half-cock safety, maybe my favorite gun in the whole world."

"Man," Bobby said. "If I'd known it was a .357, I would have bought it."

"I expect the western style threw you off," Will smirked. "You ain't no cowboy."

"Thanks," Will said as he walked away toward his office to admire his new acquisition.

"Damn!" Bobby said.

Guns were not uncommon in the club.

Early Friday evening the club was open for business, the solo act piano man was crooning away on stage, and a relative handful of people were sprinkled around the various sections of the floor; a small group clustered in the sunken area off of the mezzanine occupied by the pool tables. No door man would be on duty until the cover charge started a half hour before the band lit up the first set of the night. Will's office door flew open and the club's primary owner burst through it out of breath.

"Will!" he shouted. "There's a guy down there with a gun. Call the police!"

"What!?" Will asked as he stood to his feet. He hadn't been upstairs very long and didn't even know the owner was there.

"Some wiry little drunk just stuck a gun in my face and threatened me! Me!" he screamed.

The man claimed to have come from the mean streets of Philadelphia, but looked like a banker and lived on Mercer Island, one of the Seattle area's more wealthy and exclusive enclaves located half way across Lake Washington, and connected to the main land by bridges on both sides. He was a tall, handsome black man who didn't appear to buy his clothes off of the rack at department stores.

"Hold on a minute," Will said. "I was just down there. Let me go down and check it out. Have a seat," he said, pointing to his office chair. "Just sit tight a minute, please. We don't need cops crawling all over the place before opening. It won't be good for business. I'll be right back." He headed downstairs with more curiosity than fear.

Coming around the end of the bar he saw a patron he knew, Elmore, who was screaming and waving a gun around in his right hand. Two other regulars were standing about 10 feet away from him, telling him to put the gun away.

About 20 feet from him Will called out forcefully, "Elmore! What the hell's going on?!"

Elmore turned to face him and paused for a moment. Will kept walking toward him.

"Well?" Will repeated.

Elmore lowered the gun halfway to his side and screamed as he took a few steps toward Will, "Who the hell does that rich son of a bitch think he is?! Fuck him! I pay my money in here and I ain't taking no shit from that asshole! Fuck him!"

Will kept moving closer and reached out to take hold of the agitated Elmore's right wrist. "Hey man, he sure as hell ain't worth going to jail for. Give me the damn gun and get the hell out of here. Give it a few hours, come back sober, and I'll give you your gun back. Come on, man," Will said passionately. "Give it up."

Elmore relaxed enough for Will to reach out and take the gun from him with his other hand. The man looked up at him with alcohol sodden, watery eyes. "I ain't takin no shit from him," he repeated.

"I know," Will said. "But you got in his face big time, and if you don't get out of here, you're going to jail. I can smooth this over, but you've got to go. Now go on, get outta' here."

"Go on, man," one of the other guys said. "It'll be fine later."

Elmore looked at each of them, then turned and slowly started toward the front door. After he walked out, Will turned to the other guys. "What the hell happened?" he asked.

"Shit," Eddie said. "Big ass owner comes struttin' in here singin' opera or some shit. Elmore told him to shut the fuck up, and the dumb ass comes over barkin' and growlin', askin' him does he know who he is? Elmore tells him he don't give a rat's ass who he is and to shut up. The big dude was puffin' out his chest until Elmore stuck that gun in his face. Then he started huffin' and puffin' and took off toward your office."

Eddie shrugged.

"Okay" Will said. "Do me a favor, please. Go outside and make sure Elmore isn't out there gathering steam for another run, alright? If he's gone, I'll go upstairs and get the owner under control."

"How was it tonight?" Eva asked. When he came through the door he hadn't said a word while he shed his stuff and poured a glass of bourbon before sitting down on the couch. It was the first weekend without her on the floor, and she didn't know if he was ticked about her leaving.

"A whole new experience," he said, and then told her the story of Elmore and the owner. She knew them both and chuckled a little. As he turned toward her enjoyment of it, she said, "I'd like to have seen his face when little Elmore didn't bow to kiss his ring."

Will couldn't help but laugh. "Yeah, me too. You can be sure he doesn't even imagine Eddie and the others standing around acting it out and laughing their asses off at his expense. He might reconsider his unannounced entrance in the future."

"How was your night?" he asked. Eva had started working breakfast and lunch at Claire's Pantry. That Friday was her first dinner to closing shift and she got home about 45 minutes before he did.

"It was good," she said with a smile. "It's a popular, busy place... non-stop until after 11:00 and the bar is hopping until closing. A lot of regular customers, and lots of people know each other. It's fun compared to the club. Tips are better, too."

"Okay. A net gain all the way around," he said, then leaned over with a warm kiss on the lips they held for a moment. Neither one of them had to be up early for anything in the morning.

There were no deliveries on Saturdays, and he wouldn't be there until 4:00, so they took the Corvette out for a drive through the foothills of the Cascades, stopping to browse the little shops of small towns along the way. Will hadn't taken a day off since starting at the club and regularly thought of a little time away, even a vacation.

The featured band every week played Tuesday through Saturday nights. Will auditioned prospects on Sunday or Monday nights, sometimes local startups who needed a lot of work. But once in awhile there was a promising find. He would occasionally do a one night special on Sundays. This Sunday he had a well-known local Oldies Rock-n-Roll band lined up. Bobby was on the door because somebody had bailed at the last minute.

Will walked over and stood beside him as they cranked up their second song of the night. The club was mostly empty. Sunny, summer Sunday nights were not a big draw.

When the song finished he asked Bobby, "Well... what do you think?"

Bobby turned to him with a sneer, "Nobody's comin' in this place to hear that shit!" he said.

"We'll see," was Will's reply, and he turned toward his office. The huge lighted reader board atop the front of the building proclaimed 10 cent beer and $1 pitchers. He had also put the word out.

Thirty minutes later Will lifted the house phone. "Yeah?"

"Hey!" Bobby grunted. "A bunch of motor cycle suckers are down here. What do you want me to do?"

"Let em' in!" Will said. The reader board also declared NO COVER! "And no cover charge," he told his astonished doorman.

When Will came down stairs, the main floor was half filled with foot stomping, table pounding, beer swilling bikers who were making more noise than a packed house on a hot night of funk. The profit margin was low, but the volume of beer poured was off the charts for a Sunday night, for almost any night, for that matter. Nobody sucks down more beer per person than bikers out to have a good time. No one made mention of the whiskey bottles.

Will walked up to Bobby and slapped him on the back. "Relax, man. They're a little loud and messy, but they're not going to hurt anyone. Besides, none of our people were coming in anyway." A few had, and stood back in awe at the spectacle playing out before them. All of the scooters in the parking lot drew a few curiosity seekers, and the band had their own loyal following. The cheap beer was an added bonus.

Moving On

Other than a monumental brawl on Thanksgiving, things moved through the schedule from month to month with an established regularity. Blues guitarist Albert Collins came to the club for Friday and Saturday night shows one week in October. Collins had a large following and a 200-foot long guitar cord, years before wireless technology, and he fired the place up, strolling among the happy customers while making his guitar cry and pouring passion through the time-honored, soulful lyrics.

By December Will had been running the club for eleven months of his original one year commitment. He had admitted to no one but Eva that he was tired of it all. Though it didn't lack for excitement, there was a predictable monotony to it, and he needed movement. He did, however hope to go the distance with her.

Monday nights were the quietest for the club. Will could trust a bartender or two, and a good doorman to keep things in order while he and Eva had some personal time. They liked to try new restaurants, and pulled the Corvette into the parking lot of a new Steak House in Kenmore, along the north shore of Lake Washington.

When they both worked at the club it was their habit to go out for a late night, early morning breakfast about 3:00 AM, after closing things up. But with her working elsewhere their date experiences had become more infrequent. Will ordered his typical New York steak, in the largest available portion. Eva decided on filet mignon. They both liked their steaks medium-rare with baked potato, salad, and whatever vegetable the house was serving. Drinks before, during, and after dinner made it an expensive proposition, but it had become part of the lifestyle, in addition to stylish clothes. They were both tall already, and platform shoes made them seem unusually so.

The food was good, and Eva lifted her eyes and her fork as she said, "Can I have a bite?"

A slight smirk appeared on Will's face, and he sliced off a piece from the rarest portion of his New York, made eye contact with her and nodded. She reached across the table to spear it, and eased her eyes closed as she placed it in her mouth and began to chew slowly. He continued eating while she experienced the more substantial cut with a smile.

"You want a taste?" she asked expectantly after she swallowed it.

"Sure," he said, and she cut off a nice big bite from the outside of hers with some crispy, charbroiled edge. She poked her fork into it and reached to put the morsel in his mouth. She watched, her eyes wide with delight as he ate the much more tender filet. Smiling she asked, "Good, huh?"

"Yes, it is," he said. "Thank you very much," and mouthed a smooch. She smiled even more and pushed her fork into the steaming baked potato. She loved baked potato and would often finish it, skin and all, while leaving some of the tender meat to take home in a travel container.

"Potatoes are a dime a dozen," he would usually protest. "Why fill up on that and leave that beautiful piece of meat?" he'd ask with genuine perplexity, but not tonight.

"Mmmm. Because I like them," she always responded sincerely.

When he got past her traffic stopping beauty, that was it. Her genuineness. She was transparently honest, and he loved her for it. After more than enough people who weren't, he valued it highly. She may be incapable of deceit. She was also naïve and gullible, but those things contributed to her little girl-like innocence that was not expected of most beautiful women. Too many of them were so convinced of the value of their own looks, they came to care about little else. No doubt about it, she was a keeper.

He finished with crème brulee. She had a hot fudge sundae made with chocolate ice cream. As they sat back contentedly, he pulled the small, felt covered cube from his right-side jacket pocket and placed it on the table between them. She didn't notice it at first, watching the waitress retreat after removing the last of their dishes to get some fresh, black coffee. His hand was back in his lap when she turned and saw it.

At first her eyes registered an almost blank uncertainty, faint puzzlement. They widened slightly as she lifted them to meet his. He was looking straight at her. She looked back at the little box then back at him without a word.

"Open it," he said.

She looked back at it once again, then slowly reached out and picked it up. Placing it down on the table again in front of her, she kept her hand on it and looked at him once more. "Go on. Open it," he repeated.

She lifted it halfway to her face, and peaked inside as she raised the hinged, gold-rimmed lid. Sparkling back at her was the largest cluster of mounded diamonds she had ever seen. Set atop a slender band of white gold, it was elegant with an understated simplicity, if such an attention getting thing could be. When he saw it in the jewelry store it looked exactly like her to him. It belonged on her finger, and he wanted her to have it.

She raised it from the box and turned it around in her hands, fascinated as a new kind of warmth washed over her. She looked back at him.

"Put it on," he said, warming every bit as much as she did.

She slipped the costume jewelry ring off of the ring finger of her left hand and slid the new one on. It fit perfectly.

"How did you do that?" she asked. She had slender fingers.

"When I saw it I knew it was you, so I came back with one of your other rings you weren't wearing when you were at work one day. Do you like it?"

"Like it!?" she blurted out. "I love it!"

"Good," he said. "I hoped you would. I hoped it wouldn't be too much."

"Oh, no," she said. "It's beautiful." She was staring at it instead of him now.

"Yes, it is," he answered. "Just like you."

She looked back at him. "What does it mean?"

"It means I love you," he said, almost choking up. "I've known some women before," he continued. "But no one like you. I don't ever want to be without you. Is that Okay?"

"Oh, yes... it is," she said. She scooted her chair back, walked around their table, bent toward him and kissed him long, holding his head in both of her hands. "It's more than Okay. I never want to be without you, either," and she kissed him again.

He took her hands in his and kissed them, then let go so she could return to her seat on the other side of the table.

Once seated she asked, "What do we do now?"

He smiled warmly and said, "I'm sure we could think of something."

She blinked and almost laughed. "Sounds good."

As the waitress arrived with the coffee, he flipped an excessive amount of money on the table and said, "Thanks. We won't be needing anything else. There's plenty there to cover it."

She smiled, picked up the money and said, "Thank you. I hope you come again," and turned to leave.

Never looking away from Eva, he said, "Let's get out of here."

Sunday night, ten days after Thanksgiving, the club was dead enough to be buried. It could have been the local startup band that stunk, it could have been the time of year, it could have been many things, but at 9:30 Will sent everyone but one waitress and the bartender home. They would probably be bored. At 9:45 he reminded them of some tedious maintenance tasks that should be done, and went home himself. The bartender would put the night's meager receipts in the dead drop behind the bar.

The dead drop had been installed to insure against armed robbery loss during a barnburner night; it was quicker and safer than Will carrying money through the back room and up to the safe in his office. When the money was pouring in like a flood, Will would take everything above an established reserve amount and dead drop it, the whole transaction out of sight. It took two keys to open, neither of which was available behind the bar. If someone went to the time and trouble to make it happen during business, the police could be summoned while the heist was in progress.

Just two months earlier the doorman phoned Will up in his office at 10:45 one Friday night when the place was jammed with a hot band. "There's a dozen cops at the door and you need to get down here now."

As he approached, the officer in charge stepped forward, looked at his watch and said, "We got a phone call that said this place is going to blow up in…" he looked at his watch again… "ten minutes. What do you want to do?"

"Shit!" Will said. "What do you recommend?"

"You ever had anything like this happen before?" the officer asked.

"No," Will replied.

"Then I'd clear the place and let us search, PDQ," the cop said flatly.

"Shit," Will said again, more softly but with resignation.

After telling the head bartender to dead drop, he marched down the nearest aisle and walked up onto the stage to the lead singer's mic, right in the middle of a song. Grabbing the mic, he made a throat slashing hand motion to the band members and they haltingly shut it all down. The whole club went silent in a matter of seconds, and every face in the building was turned in his direction.

"Okay," he said into the mic. "The police are here and have been told a bomb is going to blow this place up in less than ten minutes. We need to clear the building immediately."

The whole crowd sat in stunned silence… motionless. Will blurted out with force, "NOW! People. You have to leave as quickly as possible NOW!"

The boos and insults exploded with vehemence from what looked like most of them. Some people began throwing their drinks at the stage, but as the police officers streamed down the aisles, everyone began picking up their things and heading for the door. Will shouted out, "If you keep your ticket you will not be charged a cover charge tomorrow night." The only responses he could hear were not encouraging.

From the front of the stage Will could see through to the back, above the main floor area, past the mezzanine walkway all the way to the bar. As the word bomb left his lips, he saw one of his three bartenders bolt for the back door like Roadrunner when Wilie E. Coyote reaches for him.

Of course, a thorough search revealed no bombs. He suspected a rival club having a slow night. When the next threat came almost two weeks later, Will greeted the same police officer at the door. "What do you want to do this time?" the cop asked.

"Let her blow," he said. "Thanks for asking," accompanied his nasty grin.

"Okay," the officer replied. "We're required to stick around until the appointed time. We'll be in the parking lot if you need us," he said with a knowing nod.

"I'm sure it will be good for business," Will said. "Thanks."

Will had been home for less than an hour on the dead Sunday night he sent everyone home, when his phone rang. Reaching for it he thought, "What crisis down there demands my presence now?"

He hadn't said a word yet, the receiver not quite to his ear, when a hysterical woman's voice shrieked, "THEY KILLED HIM! Will, THEY KILLED HIM!"

"Who is this?" he almost shouted into the phone.

"Will, this is Angela, Bobby's sister. They killed him, Will!"

"What!?" he blasted. "Who? Who has been killed?"

"Bobby, Will! The killed him. They shot him in the head and he's dead! I'm at his apartment right now!"

"Who all is there?" he asked, only a little less loudly.

"The police are all over the place and they won't let anybody inside. My number was in Bobby's phone book and they called me. They killed him! He loved you, Will. Can you come down here? Can you come right now?"

"I'm on my way," he said. "It will take me 20 or 30 minutes. I'm way out north, but I'll be there as soon as I can. I'll see you soon," and he hung up.

He turned to face Eva, who stood in stunned silence in the doorway from the living room, puzzled and distressed. "Someone is dead?" she asked, fearfully.

Will walked over and wrapped his arms around her, pulling her in as he said, "Bobby. That was his sister. She said Bobby has been shot in his apartment and he's dead."

She burst into tears, convulsing in his arms as he held her tighter and tighter. She loved Bobby and knew how much Bobby had, in his own way, made his love for them known.

After a few minutes that seemed much longer he said, "I have to go. I told his sister I'd be there as soon as I can." He held her at arm's length. "Will you be OK?"

"Do you think I should go, too?" she asked.

"NO!" he said firmly. "I don't want you anywhere near that place. I'll call as soon as I can."

On the drive down to Rainier Valley, Will thought back to when Bobby told him about his drug trafficking involvement. Bobby didn't use drugs. But in prison he became associated with a major west coast drug trafficking kingpin. Anything of value can be traded inside, and Bobby could provide valuable enforcement and protection muscle very few people could match, even in prison.

During the summer Bobby found it necessary to tell Will why he was likely to be absent from the door occasionally. The people he worked for on the side had every number where Bobby could be reached and when he was most likely to be there. His work schedule at the club was known ahead of time every week. The outside line for the general public to call the club, which was usually answered by a recording, had three one-digit variations that would ring directly to the door, the bar, and Will's office.

For security purposes Bobby often had little notice. He would get a phone call telling him of an airline and flight number with a ticket waiting for him at SeaTac, and what time he had to be there. Bobby would get on the plane to wherever it was going on the west coast. When he landed, he would be met by someone who would take him to a major transaction. Bobby was there to make sure everyone involved played according to the rules. If anyone got out of line, they would be dealt with swiftly and forcefully. It wouldn't happen twice.

The call had only come a few times while Bobby was working at the club. He would ring Will in his office, or approach him on the floor and tell him, "I got to go."

Will would ask him, "Do you have the door covered?"

Bobby would answer, "I do."

Will would say, "Okay then. Will you be back tonight?"

The answer was usually, "Probably not", but it had happened.

"Be careful," Will always said.

"I always am," Bobby would promise him.

Before he pulled into the parking lot of Bobby's apartment, or talked to the police or anyone else, he supposed the drug ring he worked for had probably decided Bobby had outlived his usefulness. After he got there, he was almost sure of it.

He learned from the police there were no signs of forced entry, a struggle, or robbery, though some of Bobby's clothing was missing, clothes that wouldn't fit very many people.

He had taken one point-blank round in the head, just behind his right ear, while seated at his dining room table. It was someone he knew, someone he let in and did not think he needed to take precautions to protect himself from.

Will told the police everything he knew. If he could provide any information that would lead to the arrest of Bobby's killer, he would withhold nothing. Though he never lost his composure, there or in private, it rocked him like a gut punch. He had no intention of continuing at the club any longer. Bobby's killing had nothing to do with the club, but Will was just done with the whole environment.

The next morning he delivered the news to the owners over the phone. They were not happy. He did not care. He hadn't called to negotiate.

As it turned out, the radio station had booked a northwest concert tour for a fading four-man soul group, like unto The Temptations and The Four Tops. Will agreed to oversee the business end of things on site the night of each concert in Western Washington and Portland, Oregon. Then he would be done. He would not, however, ever set foot in the club again.

The night of the last concert was New Year's Eve in Portland, and Will took along a young white pool player he had come to know. The kid had never been around black night life, but it sounded interesting. After the concert, the local promoters invited Will to a big party with the singers at an after hours club. Will agreed, but when he pulled up outside of the club, his young friend decided he didn't want to go in.

They were parked in the Corvette at the curb about a half block from the club. Will didn't pull into the parking lot because he didn't intend to stay long. "No problem," he told the young man. "I'm just going to put in a courtesy appearance, and I'll be back within twenty minutes, or so."

At that point he reached under his seat, and pulled out the .357 he had purchased at the club earlier in the year. He extended it to the young man and said, "There is almost twenty thousand dollars in the under-floor compartment behind your seat. If anyone comes to the car and wants in while I'm gone, just shoot them and leave. Don't worry about me. I'll find my way home. I'll meet you back in Seattle."

The kid couldn't have looked any stiffer or whiter if he'd been a dummy in Madame Tussaud's Wax Museum. He looked at the gun, then back at Will as though he couldn't speak. Finally, he said "I don't want the gun."

"Okay," Will said. "If anyone sticks a gun in your face, just get out and run."

When Will came out the kid and the car were both still there. They never spoke of it again, and after turning over the money in Seattle, Will hoped he would never see anyone related to the club again in his life.

Bobby's funeral was large and loud at a well-established black church in Rainier Valley. It was very emotional. Will would remember it and think of him for the rest of his life. He told no one of his thoughts about whether God had redeemed Bobby or not. Bobby had showed no outward signs of relationship with God, and had never spoken of such things to Will. But neither had he, and he couldn't escape the realization that if eternity was real for Bobby, it was for him too.

Most people only knew Bobby as a powerful, dangerous man you did not want for an enemy. Will knew Bobby also had a genuine heart of love for those who loved him. Though Will's God confrontations weren't happening more frequently, his thoughts about God were. He couldn't seem to shake them

(1976)
Old & New

"So, what are you going to do?" Ted asked.

"Hell, I don't know," Will said. "Sell a little dope and collect unemployment, I guess. Hope I don't find a great job too soon." He shrugged and handed the joint back.

"You can come to work for us if you want," Ted said. Ted and his partner owned a collision repair shop in the north end. Will's experience could be put to good use, and paying him under the table would be a financial plus for them both.

"Hmmm..." Will grunted. "A body shop would be a nice, peaceful change from that stinking night club, I'll tell you that. And I don't want to drive all the way out to West Seattle again, or work someplace like Boeing. That was torture. Every night I went to bed hating the next day before it even arrived."

"You know, I'd like to teach you how to do estimates, too. You'd get the hang of it easy. Right now, if I'm in the middle of a spray, someone comes in for an estimate and I either screw the paint job or risk losing the customer. You already know how to prep. Why not come on by and look around?"

He had been working at Ted's shop for less than a week, and being around a bunch of regular working guys in overalls felt like coming home. What the hell was he doing in that night club, anyway?

The distinctive, musical horn of the roach coach pulling into the parking lot signaled everyone who wanted something to eat it was break time. Though every man worked with steady determination at the job in his hands, the general attitude of the shop was pretty laid back. The breakroom upstairs above the spray booth was an original man cave, devoid of any feminine influence.

"I got a call last night," Will said amidst the eating and smoking. Spoken without preamble, everyone's head turned in his direction.

"From who?" Ted asked.

"The owner of Our Place and The Pub," he answered.

After a significant silent pause he continued, "He wants me to tend bar again."

More silence with unspoken questions. "Not either one of those places" he added. "He has a 24-hour place in Ballard with a full-service restaurant kitchen and a bank of pool tables. It stays busy, but fills up when the other bars close. It's a major destination for serious pool players. Lots of nine ball for cash. The guy has a real nose for when, where, who, and how to I.D. a niche and fill it."

"When?" Ted asked.

"Evenings. No problem. I can do both jobs easy. My shift won't start until 8:00 and runs until 1:00 or 2:00, depending on whose following on graveyard. Maybe two of us for the transition on weekends. The place is absolutely hammered on Friday and Saturday nights until at least 3:00 in the morning."

"Cool," Ted said. "Let's get back to work." Everyone started moving.

Floyd, a multi-talented gear-head and one of The Boys, joined the team at the shop in the spring. One day while cleaning up to go home at night he asked Will, "You ever think of getting rid of that Corvette?"

"Depends," Will said. "Right time, right deal… who knows? I'll cross that bridge when I come to it."

Floyd smiled.

The next day when Will pulled into the lot, parked out nearest the street was the cleanest, nicest pale yellow 1966 Chevy Caprice two-door he had ever seen. He got out of his car and circled it a few times, stooping to look inside. He wanted to lift the hood, but didn't know the car's status or why it was there. It sure didn't need any body or paint work.

A very subtle double-line black pinstripe ran from the tip of the front fender to the taillight extension on each side, just below the body crease between the door handles and windows. Black vinyl top, Cragars and T/As filling out the fender wells, it had a nice low aggressive stance. Black satin seats looked like they had never been sat on. The odometer showed 43,000 miles. 396 fender flags announced some serious power. He stood back and admired the car. It looked perfect.

When he walked through the door, he asked loud enough for everyone to hear, "Who owns the Caprice?"

"That would be me," Floyd said confidently as he stepped out from the john, wiping his hands with a paper towel. "Pretty nice, huh?"

"Nice," Will said dismissively. "You sly dog. Where on earth did you get that thing?"

Floyd was only too happy to tell him. "Old Japanese guy in Bellevue bought it brand new. Didn't drive it much. Always garaged. He died last year and it sat while his estate was closed out. His kids didn't want it. They drive expensive European stuff. They just wanted to unload it, and I was happy to help," he said with a smirk… meaning he got it for almost nothing. "I put the Cragars and T/As on it."

"Un-huh," Will grunted.

"If you like it, we can take it for a drive after work," Floyd offered with a wink as he turned toward the car he was working on.

It was a perfect trade, each man happy with what he got for what he gave. Floyd gave the Caprice with some money. Will never drove the perfect Chevy in the rain even once.

Will's parents bought his little house in Lake City as an investment two months earlier. All he wanted was what he had in it, and they knew real estate prices were starting to rise. He just wanted to feel unencumbered again. He and Eva moved into the house his parents owned near Green Lake and Woodland Park, the same house where he had lived in their basement. His parents moved to Ocean Shores, built a new home, and opened their own plumbing company. Not all of the neighbors were thrilled to see Will again, but Eva was having a civilizing effect. They ended up buying the house from his parents the following year because they wanted to buy some commercial property at the ocean.

One lazy Sunday morning he wandered out onto the front porch to get the newspaper and froze before he even touched it. Straightening up he looked down the street, one way and then the other. His Caprice was nowhere in sight. Leaving the paper, he drifted back into the house to the kitchen where Eva was fixing coffee.

"They stole my car," he said matter-of-factly… dazed.

"What?" she asked incredulously.

"My Caprice," he said. "It's not there."

"Are you sure?" she asked in a higher pitch, then marched past him to see for herself.

Joining her on the porch he said, "If we ever see it again, it will be torched. It's already stripped to the bone and burned to a crisp. Shit,", he said. "I really liked that car." He had dropped the insurance when he sold the Corvette.

She turned and hugged him. "I'm so sorry," she said.

Monday evening the phone rang as they ate dinner on trays in front of the TV.

"Yes?" Will said as he lifted it to his ear with one hand and put his fork down with the other.

"This is Detective Mason with Seattle Police, Auto Theft. Are you Mark Wilson?"

"That's me, Detective. What's the bad news?"

"Well, actually, Mr. Wilson, I think it might be better than you expected. We found your car."

"Okay," Will said. "Where and in what condition?"

"It was out by Haller Lake, in the bushes not far from the parking lot. The wheels and tires are gone, along with the engine wiring and the stereo, but other than that it doesn't look like the car is damaged at all."

"No shit," Will said, astonished. "Amateurs. Probably teenagers."

"You're probably right about that, and you're also very lucky."

"You're telling me," Will sighed. "When can I get it?" he asked.

"Any time you want," the detective said. "North end SPD impound lot. Bring a set of wheels and tires, spark plug wires, and $58 and she's all yours. 24/7"

"Wow," Will said. "Is it another $58 if I wait until morning?"

"Nope. You've got 24 hours from the time they hooked it. That'll be about 3:00 o'clock tomorrow afternoon."

"Thanks, man. This is good news. I was sure it was gone forever."

"My pleasure," the cop said. "Glad it worked out," and he hung up.

Later, when Will told his mom she said, "Well, thank God."

"Thank God that my car was stolen?" he responded.

"No, Will. Thank Him that you got it back with so little damage, especially when you had no insurance," she said matter-of-factly.

He never would have thought that.

Life in the night club had left some lasting impact. In addition to stylish clothes and upscale restaurants, Will and Eva had become regular cocaine users. Coke was gaining in popularity over more everyday recreational drugs, except for the old standby, marijuana. As with clothes, food, and booze, they came to prefer high quality cocaine.

Will had no desire to get involved in dealing coke. It not only required a much larger investment, but its surge in supply and use made it a more popular law enforcement target. He would stick to personal use.

Without Malice

He tapped on the apartment door three times. His childhood friend, Micky, opened the door with a big smile. If Will hadn't called first the door wouldn't have been answered at all.

"You're just in time," his friend boasted. "I'm breaking up a brick." He grinned and closed the door behind them.

Some people are gifted in art, music, athletics or academics. Micky was gifted in making money. It just seemed to come to him, and cocaine was serving the purpose well. He didn't look like a drug dealer. He wore neat, clean conservative clothes and a modest, conservative haircut.

They walked into the apartment kitchen where the table had four spotless, rectangular glass baking dishes set out. Will didn't know how much was there, but each dish had a large clump of white powder, far more than he had ever seen at one time. Even more than Matthew Lee had thrown down in front of him.

For everyday personal use, coke was dispensed one gram at a time. This was a lot, and much of it would be sold in ounces to people who would break it up, and often dilute it, known as stomping on it, before selling it in grams. A quarter ounce might cover a weekend of heavy partying by several people.

"Have a seat," Micky said as he took a chair for himself.

Sitting down across from him, Will said, "Shit, man... how much is this?"

Micky looked up smiling and winked. "More than you've ever seen before, huh?"

"No kidding," Will replied. "How much is this all worth?"

"I paid $20,000.00 for it, but it'll be worth a hell of a lot more than that by the time it all goes up somebody's nose."

"Damn," Will said.

"Want a little toot?" his friend asked him.

"Hell, yeah," Will replied.

The mound in the dish in front of him was the most broken up already, and Micky pulled a little away from the larger pile to form up a couple of lines. He sniffed up the one closest to him, and then handed the sliver tube to Will. Will got up from his seat as he reached out to take it, stepped around the table by his friend, and snorted the uncut drug into his right nostril. Blinking a couple of times, he returned to his seat.

Micky gave out a little snorting laugh. "That shit hasn't been trampled by a herd of elephants yet, huh?"

"No shit," Will said.

"You want to help me bust this stuff up?" Micky asked.

"Why not," Will said, and Micky left the room, returning with a second expensive triple beam balance scale.

Will was detail oriented for this type of thing, and Micky was confident he was doing things the way he wanted. Not much conversation interrupted their work as they both concentrated on the task at hand.

As Will finished packaging a quarter ounce and stacked it with the others he had already prepared, he suddenly sensed that all too familiar presence he knew was God. As his mind acknowledged it, he felt what seemed as real as someone's finger poke him in the side.

He glanced up at Micky. His friend was completely unaware of what he was experiencing. Then he recognized that voice in his head… "Will… look at yourself. When are you going to serve Me?"

If he were alone he may have replied out loud, but didn't want to draw his friend's attention. In his mind he responded strongly, "Not Now!" His heart was pounding. There was a brief pause, and then it was gone. Will felt his body temperature rise and he began to perspire heavily in his armpits. He glanced at Micky again. Nothing.

Driving away an hour and a few toots later, he found himself looking over his shoulder, wondering when his stalker would confront him next.

Parking his car a half block away from the tavern, under a street light, he was thankful for the open spot. He didn't mind walking farther, even though this wasn't a great neighborhood to leave a nice car. He double checked to be sure nothing was left in plain sight, locked both doors, and headed for work. As he came through the front door it was as he expected. There were a few casual, novice pool players with a beer perched on the rail while they shot, and a modest after work crowd, including some middle-age, unmarried guys who usually ate out. The food was good.

When he came on shift behind the bar after Jen, he always showed up 30 minutes early. Her body and her mouth never stopped - constant motion and chatter. Many of the men who came in regularly enjoyed the interaction. Will's problem was she would grab a bottle from the well to pour a drink for someone seated at the bar, walk to where they sat, put the bottle down to pick up their dishes or something else, and leave the bottle there. That's just the way she was, and it wasn't going to change. Trying to encourage her otherwise was an exercise in futility.

The bar was "L" shaped, longer on one side than the other, with seating along the inside of the angle. Serving the customers meant traveling around the outside of the angle. He always thought you could serve more customers more efficiently if the customers were on the outside of the angle, but acknowledged it was probably done that way to get the best use of the shape of the room. Oh, well. When it was busy, and being Friday it was going to be very busy, he would spend most of the night in a half sprint from one spot to another. Given his organizational quirkiness, he wanted every bottle in the exact same place in the well all the time. A place for everything and everything in its place. He didn't even need to look. When he reached for something it was there.

So he made himself a casual presence behind the bar, chatting with Jen as she breezed by one way and another, picking up stray bottles and returning them to the well. One at a time he repositioned them in the 4X3, 12 slot well, saying nothing as she continued to spray them around the area. When she exhaled long, smiled, and poured herself a drink before heading out to unwind with the clientele, he would retrieve the last of the strays, settle into his routine, and serve his first customer of the night.

When Ted and Ray walked in together about 9:00, two seats had just opened up at the end of the short side of the bar. Will nodded and waved, Ted held up two fingers, and without breaking his rhythm Will poured two draft beers, glided their way, and set the cold drinks down in front of them, a perfect head on each one. He took great pride in his ability to pour a proper glass of draft beer.

"Good to see ya," Will said as he pivoted away. "I'll be back in a couple of minutes."

He was off to grab a dinner order from the kitchen window while placing another meal ticket on the wheel of spring clips they spun to keep the food moving in a quick and orderly manner. He liked the process, and cooks were often like mechanics. Don't let the customers get too close to them.

It was several minutes before he was back with their second round. "You guys want something to eat?"

"Nah… just dropped in to see how you're doing here," Ted said. Ray worked at the shop, too. "I'll tell you what, though," he continued. "If you moved like that around the shop we'd be making more money." Ray almost spit out his beer laughing.

"Ha!" Will laughed. "Far different environment, man. And the customers at the shop don't tip. I'll check back in a bit," he said and moved off quickly to clear the bar in front of a seat that opened up on the other side. It was occupied before he got there. When he came around the corner of the bar the next time Ted and Ray were gone. Unlike Jen, he had no time for casual conversation.

Unlike Will, Oz was an unapologetic phlegmatic. He ambled along at a leisurely pace, speaking slowly, pausing between phrases, never in a hurry for anything or anyone. His shift was scheduled to begin at 2:00 AM, and he strolled behind the bar at 1:55. The place was hopping, and Will was as busy as he'd been all night, but he still spent the last 15 minutes making sure things were as orderly as possible before he left.

Even more people would begin flooding in about 2:15, after all of the other bars shut down for the night. Duffy's stayed open with no booze between 2:00 and 6:00 AM. The kitchen would explode, and the pool tables would gather crowds watching the money players do their thing, and making side bets. Beer would be replaced by coffee and booze slipped discreetly out of pockets to liven it up. The crowd would thin between 3:00 and 4:00.

"Hey, man... you want me to stick around to handle the rush with you?" Will asked excitedly.

"Nah," Oz drawled slowly. "I'll get to 'em when I get to 'em".

"Okay, then," Will said, poured a cup of coffee and went to sit down and unwind before heading to his car. Before it was stolen that Sunday morning, he mostly thought about it being broken into, but since then he always breathed a sigh of relief to come out and see it at the curb where he'd left it.

(1977)
The Grass Is Greener

As winter looked forward to spring in 1977, Will left Duffy's and was growing tired of the grind at the body shop. Grant took the night shift at Duffy's. He fancied himself a bit of a pool player and liked hanging around the action. Will sat sipping a beer as Grant leaned on the bar and asked, "So… what're you going to do this summer?"

"I'm thinking about mowing lawns," Will said.

"What!?" Grant almost spit the word out. "Mowing lawns?"

"Yeah," Will said back. "I tried to hire someone to mow mine when I was running the club. Man, it's insane what even a kid expects to be paid for it. I figure I'll line up enough to keep me busy and make a few bucks, then go back to school in the fall." His brows arched, eyes shining with anticipation. "What're you going to do?"

"I think I can get on a fishing boat working up in Alaska. Big bucks when you're hauling 'em in. It's worth a shot," he said dryly.

Grant turned to walk away and muttered dismissively, "Mowing lawns."

Six weeks later Will sat down at the bar one night, nodded to Grant, and waited for his beer. When he came back with a fresh one, Will said, "Hey… can you do me a favor?"

"What?" Grant asked.

"Can you cash these checks?" he said, and spread several personal checks made out to him on the bar. "I'll guarantee them. If any come back, I'll give you cash for it immediately."

Grant picked up the checks and shuffled through them, all from people he didn't recognize, all but one from women. He looked back and met Will's steady gaze. "Sure," he said.

The next week Grant brought Will's first beer of the night as he settled onto the barstool. Putting it down, Will pushed a fistful of checks his way. Grant picked them up and looked them over. He hadn't seen any of the names before, and Will seemed to have more and more of them each time.

"Where are you getting all of this money, man?"

"I told you... mowing lawns," Will said, as if Grant was a little slow on the uptake.

"What!? You're telling me you're making all of this money mowing lawns?" he asked.

"Yeah. In fact, there's way more out there than I can do. I'm close to maxing out. There's only so much time in the day. I'm going to have to start turning people down." He shrugged as if it were just a fact of life he couldn't avoid.

"Could I make this kind of money?" his friend asked.

"Sure," Will said. "There is so much out there, I'm amazed. I'm getting better at it, but nobody could get it all."

"What do I need?" Grant asked.

Will replied, "Well... a rotary lawn mower with a bag and something to haul it away with. That and the willingness to work your ass off all day every day."

"How do you find these people?"

Will chuckled, "They find me. I put a little ad in the Ballard/Greenwood weekly newspaper and one in the Green Lake/Wallingford paper, and they ring my phone off the hook. I phone them back at night, and then take the first hour or two in the morning to make bids and get to work. But like I said, I'm about at my limit."

Their shop was in Grant's back yard and Will pulled down the driveway at 6:45 one clear June morning. Not far behind him Bert and Taylor parked out front and headed for the shop. The first pot of coffee was steaming on the bench, the shop door was rolled up, and Grant was wheeling four lawn mowers and two edgers out, the ever-present Marlboro dangling from his lips.

Since forming their partnership in April, they had continued to multiply until they were now in need of a third truck and two more workers to keep up. Some days they didn't turn off their machines until after 9:00 PM, and only because they were running out of daylight.

The office in Will's house had four individual phone lines, each offered in a slightly different ad in four different neighborhood newspapers around Seattle; sixteen ads in all. Some customers called three of the four lines, not knowing they all led to the same company. If someone wanted their lawn cut on a continuing basis, the work was theirs for the taking. Grant and Bert were both available to make bids, too.

Each two-man truck could do twenty or more jobs per day at peak efficiency. One day when they were down two men and one truck, Will and Grant knocked off 34 jobs together before calling it quits. Will did the administrative work, and Grant ran the shop. Bert helped keep the equipment well serviced and in good repair. Each truck had a spare mower engine on board and a supply of parts needed for typical repairs, so they didn't need to come in off of a route when something broke.

At every regularly scheduled job each man used the same machine in the same sequence on each job, every time. Talking was reserved for travel time in the trucks between job sites. Economy of time and movement. They actually charged less than other landscape maintenance services, but knocked out the work so quickly they made more money per hour. They were on and off of some jobs so fast they were strapping down their equipment to leave before the homeowner came out the door to greet them. Every employee was paid a percentage of what the truck produced. Will exhorted them all, "You want to make more, produce more. Time is money."

Their first commercial job was an apartment complex with two three-story buildings bordering two sides of a huge lawn. They scheduled three trucks with six men and did the job like a drill team in less than 20 minutes. Apartment residents would

Without Malice

line the railings to watch them. They challenged themselves to better their best time every time.

Their second commercial job was an old two-story, expensive brick condominium complex. The buildings, built in the 1920's, occupied three sides of an entire city block on the south end of Phinney Ridge near the Woodland Park Zoo. The circular drive had its entrance and exit on the open end facing Freemont Avenue. The grounds were beautifully detailed English style gardens, inside the drive through center, in front of each unit, and around the entire outside of the property. A fulltime, resident gardener took care of the trees, shrubs, and flower beds. Will and Grant's crew did the lawns, very precisely.

Two months into their one-year contract Will came around one corner of the property with a mower, and the lawn he was there to cut was not edged yet. Rotary mowers were like vacuums and sucked up the edging while eliminating another procedure. He shut off his machine and went to find the man who should have done the edging already. Finding him somewhere else on the property, he asked him, "What are you doing?"

"Well, I thought," the man began to say.

Will instantly cut him off and barked, "Do you know how much money you just cost us?" He then proceeded to rattle off, rapid fire, how many collective man-hours would be waisted because things were not done according to plan.

"I'm not paying you to think!" he roared. "If you've got some bright idea about how we can operate more efficiently, tell us about it in the shop. Don't ever do something like this again!" He stormed off to get another edger and help get it done so they could move on.

As with waitresses and waiters, not everyone was cut out for this type of work, and some just didn't get it. It was fast paced and physically demanding. They were encouraged to find work elsewhere.

In August they landed their largest account, a 500 unit apartment complex. They actually increased the owner's landscape cost by almost 50%. But they convinced him the grounds looked shabby, and he could increase rent because of their work, increasing his income. The relationship lasted for years. From fall into spring they worked hard to learn all they could about properly tending to trees and shrubs, and expanded their services accordingly.

As spring approached, Will put up a wall-sized map of Seattle in his office. He bought dozens of six different colored pushpins. He grouped the account locations daily by color, which eliminated unnecessary driving, decreased their fuel consumption, and increased their profits. The company name changed from Seattle Lawn Care to North Seattle Lawn and Tree. The problem was going to be how to accommodate the increasing number of customers lining up.

Adding trucks, equipment, and employees wasn't their first, best option. Where to keep it all? And maintaining more of it took time that wasn't spent generating income, to say nothing of the cost. The other big issue was that they were both workaholics who pursued their task with feverish frenzy all day every day, sometimes for 15 hours per day. Both Will and Grant came to work every day determined to not be outworked by the other. Not everyone was up to keeping up.

Loading the trucks and handing out route schedules one Monday morning, Taylor said, "Hey... look, I like the work and the money, but you guys are nuts. I like a little night life, and getting out of bed to be here at 7:30 six days a week is wearing thin. I can't keep doing this."

Will was fond of saying that a man had to work at least a certain amount of hours in his life, and he was going to get his out of the way as quickly as possible. Grant may not have held that same philosophy, but he was committed to working as hard, or harder, than anyone else around him.

Over the next three weeks they worked out the details that made Taylor the owner/operator of his own truck and equipment, with enough work to give him a full five-day schedule, even if at a more modest pace. They were also now free to hire another man, buy fresh equipment, and continue to expand their customer base. Before summer ended, they put two independent operators in business. The newly minted owner/operators made monthly payments for the buy outs, and that boosted their scheduled income. Everything was sailing along smoothly. Will and Eva also decided to get married in November.

As they worked toward the seasonal downturn, Will talked about more than marriage. He wanted to make the graduation to a much larger scale with their business. As he envisioned it, they would buy some commercial property on the outskirts of town where they could house and maintain as much equipment as they needed. They would set up both a shop and an office, moving the operations away from their homes. He would run the administrative side of things, and Grant would run the hands-on stuff. Grant wasn't happy unless his hands were bloody at the end of the day anyway. Bert would get a raise and keep the equipment operational. They would also be able to compost the cuttings they generated by the ton every day, escaping the high cost of dumping it at the county transfer station. It all looked obvious to him.

Sitting around a gazebo fire by the creek at the back of Grant's property one night after what felt like a light, lazy October day, Will, Grant, and Bert were sharing a pot of coffee and a joint. Will was just pulling out a little coke for a rare workday treat, when a customer from the Mall Pub they had known from their bartending days walked down past the shop to join them.

After they had both left the Mall Pub a few years earlier, Grant told Will that this guy had seen him take the empty wine bottle home to Eva two nights before he was fired. The man assumed Will was stealing it and told the owner as much. By the time Will heard the story, it was water under the bridge and everyone had moved on. Confrontation wouldn't produce anything. Grant played pool with the guy from time to time.

As Will dipped his little cap spoon into the toot bottle he carried and passed a snort to Grant and Bert, Kendal said, "I'll take a little of that," with a smile on his face.

Will hadn't seen him since being fired from The Mall Pub. He fixed his gaze on him and said, "Like hell you will, you lousy bag of shit! After you tell a lie about me that gets me fired from my job, the only thing you're ever getting from me is the hope that I never see your worthless ass again." With that he resumed his conversation with the other guys as if his betrayer were not even there. After a few minutes the unwelcomed guest slipped away.

"Well," Bert offered with a snort, "he's probably not confused about how you feel about that!"

When the wedding day rolled around in November, both partners agreed to take a month off and pick it up again slowly with winter pruning work before the inevitable spring avalanche of vegetation growth. They had taken minimal compensation for their work so far, pouring most of their money back into equipment and savings for future expansion, after an initial small business loan from a local bank. They would now each withdraw an equal amount for vacation. Will and Eva would be taking a leisurely driving honeymoon down through California, while Grant and a buddy were headed for Vegas to hit it big at the poker tables.

Returning home was a blessing. Will and Eva were tired of being away after three weeks, and it turned out Grant still needed to work. (It's not about how much you win. It's about how much you leave with.) The slow winter pace didn't hurt them financially, since they had placed most of their steady customers on annual contracts. Predictable budgeting was a convenience for their retired residential customers, and a requirement for their commercial accounts. For Will and Grant it meant the money kept coming in every month even though they weren't spending many hours in the field. Their talks about the company's future were not progressing as smoothly.

Grant was content. They could see a predictable, profitable year ahead and he liked the steady nature of it all. They had a limited capacity, but how much did they really need? They were in their twenties and both of them had come dangerously close to serious trouble in life already. This felt like a stability they didn't need to fear.

Will liked to work hard physically, but had no intention of doing it for the rest of his life. He wanted affluence that worked his mind more than his muscles. Neither of them had learned how to translate their differences into a complimentary compatibility, and negotiation was seen as the process of getting other people to agree to your way. They were at a stalemate, with no idea of how to get beyond it together.

Will was also thinking about his and Eva's future. Though God had not become a topic between them, Will knew they would have to raise their children to know who God is, and they wouldn't be able to do that from the sidelines. Will's mother's pastor officiated their wedding ceremony in the spacious living room of his friend Howard's parents' house. They also bought a sizeable quantity of uncut cocaine for the evening and their honeymoon. Eva was very well thought of at Claire's Pantry, and the owners sprang for the reception in the banquet hall of the restaurant. Will's mother's friends and his biker buddies were an interesting mix, the church ladies much more aware of the scooter tramps than they were of them.

Sitting at his desk, looking at the city wall map and pondering things one February night before the horticultural tsunami that would consume them in March, Will's home phone rang. He picked it up, "Yeah?"

"Will," Carl said. "What's going on, buddy?"

"Hey, Carl. Nothing, really man. Just sitting here thinking about the coming year and how to proceed."

"You guys going to be busy?" his old roommate asked.

"Huh!" Will laughed. "Are you kidding me? We're about to start working like farm animals for the next eight months."

"You interested in maybe doing something else?" Carl said.

After a noticeable pause he asked, "Like what?"

"Well," his friend continued, "We're going to be hiring a new salesman at Olympia Beer, and I told them I know a guy who would do really well at it."

The Seattle distributorship was owned by former Washington State Governor, Albert D. Rosellini, and Carl had been a top producing salesman for the last two years.

"No shit," Will said. "Interesting. Very interesting."

Carl remained a good friend to both of his former roommates, and didn't know the details, but he knew they weren't on the same page. After a slight pause of his own, he said, "If you want to, I can set up an interview. These jobs don't get advertised."

It was outside sales, where the salesmen called on clients, on-sale and off-sale, and truck drivers delivered the product two days after the salesman turned in the orders. On-sale was product consumed on site: taverns, restaurants, bars, etc. Off-sale was product purchased, primarily from grocery stores, and carried off site to be consumed elsewhere. The largest volume moved through large chain stores like Safeway and Albertson's.

"Listen," he said. "I need to talk to Eva, but yeah… I would like to interview for it. Grant and I are stuck, and it just might be what all of us need. I'll call you back to confirm it, Okay?"

"Sounds like a deal," Carl said. "Talk to you soon."

"Thanks," Will said, and they both hung up. Will stayed in his office, but for the first time his thoughts turned to separation from the bustling business he and Grant had built together.

A New Direction

The great American philosopher Yogi Berra said, "When you come to the fork in the road, take it."

After wearing a beard for several years, Will walked into the offices of Olympia Beer, Premium Distributors, in a new three-piece suit and clean shaven except for his well-trimmed mustache. (Eva had never seen him without it.) He didn't want anything to prevent him from getting this job. He and Grant had agreed to split all of the company's assets 50/50, money, equipment, and most of the accounts. Since Will wasn't sure what he would be doing with his share, it only made sense for Grant to keep the commercial accounts.

After introducing himself to the receptionist, Will took a seat in the outer office waiting area. A few minutes later one of the sales managers came out to greet him and usher him back to an interview room. This branch had 22 salesmen, and as Will walked past their desks five of those present were wearing full beards. It would be a year before he earned vacation time to grow his beard back.

Will's sales territory was a patchwork of disjointed areas, cobbled together from the redistribution of several other territories, spread out around the greater Seattle region. Beacon Hill contained some of Seattle's highest crime rates, and Mercer Island some of the lowest. The Beacon Hill and South Park areas prompted him to carry his trusty .357 under the seat of his company car. Will had decided years before that if someone turned up dead, it wasn't going to be him.

The salesman's first job was to make beer leave the warehouse of the distributorship. His second job was to make the store more money by making more beer leave that store. No sale was complete until a six pack, half case, or case of beer went through a check stand. That meant getting more shoppers to buy his product instead of another brand. Coolers were the most consistent and likely place to do that. Once Will had earned a store manager's respect and trust, he could then justify putting together a scaled drawing of how the cooler could be reset to generate more sales.

The company had ways of expressing their appreciation for those store managers they were able to work more closely with. They had a block of 20 Seattle Seahawks tickets on the 40 yard line of the 200 level in the King Dome. They also had a block of a dozen Seattle Super Sonics tickets, ten rows up from the floor, just off of the center court aisle. It didn't hurt that the Sonics were the NBA World Champions. Salesmen were authorized to host clients at games from time to time, promoting good will as they helped each other succeed in businesses.

His next most effective sales tool was prominent floor displays. Huge quantities of half-case bottle or can packages were creatively stacked in pyramids, columns, or towers. They were offered at reduced prices as incentive to buy his brands instead of someone else's.

He had also adopted a third, and very personal tool, one for which he set a daily goal of four successes. He would watch a cooler from a discreet distance, waiting for customers to linger in front of the selection, uncertain of what to buy. He would then approach, engage a customer in conversation and encourage them to buy his brand. It was most rewarding when he persuaded a customer to put back another brand and buy his instead.

Six months after being hired, Will was recognized as the salesman of the month. What he wanted most was to be known by his management as someone who made more boxes leave their warehouses than other salesmen.

Months later he swapped some of his accounts for the biggest ones in Bellevue, Redmond, and Kirkland after Carl left them

Without Malice

behind to take the job as General Sales Manager of the distributorship in Bremerton. It was an unofficial vote of confidence in Will's performance.

Finishing his workday on the eastside one evening, Will crossed Lake Washington on the 520 floating bridge and turned off of I-5 onto N.E. 45th Street toward their home near Green Lake and Woodland Park. He came to a stop at the traffic light between Meridian and Wallingford. To his right was a family drugstore that had been there since he was a kid. Next door to that was the Food Giant, also a long-established neighborhood fixture. Two blocks ahead on the left was the Wallingford precinct of the Seattle Police Department, a place he had been officially received on three occasions as a teenager. The last time was when he had blasted an undercover Seattle police narcotics detective with a fire extinguisher the night before their opening senior year high school football game. It was an honest mistake. He had no idea the man was a police officer.

Chuckling to himself at these warm reflections, his attention was jolted to the right when a teenage girl burst out of the front doors of the drug store, followed closely by the druggist in hot pursuit. As she ran right in front of him, she held a bag aloft and tossed it down in the middle of the street. Just before the druggist stopped to retrieve the bag, three teenage boys jumped up from the bus stop across the street and were sprinting toward the fleeing girl and the druggist. Something popped.

Will slammed the gear shifter into park and exploded from his car, charging toward the boys. They all arrived at the same time where the druggist was straightening up with the bag in his hand. Will was fuming, on the verge of eruption. The boy closest to him stepped toward him and barked, "What are you doing here?"

Will forcefully took the next step that put them nose to nose and exploded, "WHAT AM I DOING HERE!? I LIVE HERE!!! WHAT ARE YOU DOING HERE!?"

He was at hair trigger and his right foot would have come up like a catapult with the slightest provocation. They were in the middle of rush hour traffic, on a busy arterial, and no matter how it may have turned out, the boys paused. Every muscle in Will's body was as tight as a bow string, ready to fire.

The druggist lifted the bag and said, "Everything is fine," and turned to leave.

One by one, the boys turned away and started back toward the bus stop. The girl had continued running. As he watched them moving away, he realized he was standing alone in the middle of traffic, his car was blocking one lane and he was blocking the other. He walked back to his car and drove the short distance to his home, his temperature slowly lowering, slightly.

Will sat in his car at the curb in front of the house, his mind churning. He had lived in north Seattle since he was 10 years old. Eva had grown up there, too. They were thankful for their house and its convenient location, but the incident was stewing in him, below boil now, but still cooking.

His job was in a highly competitive and stressful environment. During his physical examination for a life insurance policy three years earlier, the doctor said he had the blood pressure of a 10 year old child; 110/70. He had asked, "Is that good?"

The doctor replied, "Have you ever heard of a 10 year old having a heart attack?"

The same doctor had recently expressed concern about his high blood pressure. Two McDonald's quarter pound cheese burgers, wolfed down between accounts every day may not have helped. He sat behind the wheel with his eyes closed, breathing slowly and thinking more slowly, wanting to arrive at some sort of conclusion.

Opening the front door, he walked into his office, plopped his briefcase on his desk and draped his sport coat over the chair. From there he walked down the hall to the kitchen. Eva was at the counter beside the sink preparing whatever delicious meal they would enjoy for dinner.

"Hey," he said, walking toward her.

She turned and smiled. "Hi," she replied, and wiped her hands on a kitchen hand towel before embracing him in the comforting hug they enjoyed nightly.

After a moment he moved his hands to her shoulders and stepped back, gently extending the space between them.

She looked at him in quiet curiosity. He held her gentle gaze for a moment, then said, "I don't want to live here anymore."

"Why?" she asked, emotion creeping into her voice.

He told her about the incident on N. 45th on the way home, just a short while ago and too close to home, less than two blocks from the police station.

"Where would we go? What would you do?" she asked.

"I don't know," he said.

Four nights later they were eating dinner in the living room while watching the news when the telephone rang. Will lifted the phone from its base on the end table beside his chair. "Hello."

"This is detective William Atkins from the Seattle Police Department. Is this Mark Wilson?"

"Yes," Will replied.

"Mr. Wilson, do you own a 1967 Ford Country Squire station wagon?"

"Yes", Will replied again.

"Mr. Wilson, your car has been reported as having left the scene of an accident 10 days ago, out in Lake City."

Will lowered the phone and turned to Eva. "Eva, were you in an accident in your car?"

"No," she said.

"No, it wasn't our car detective."

"We have a witness who wrote down the license plate number," the detective said.

Turning back to her, Will said, "They have a witness."

Eva burst into tears, hung her head and began sobbing.

"Apparently, that was our car," he said to the detective.

After exchanging some required information and promising to appear, Will listened to Eva's story. She was backing out of a parking stall after work late one night. She didn't realize she had hit another car until she was jolted to a stop at very low speed. She hoped no damage was done, but she panicked, dropped it in drive, and left, not thinking about anything but getting away from the sudden and alarming surprise.

She had an unblemished driving record, and after appearing before a judge in a downtown Seattle court room and paying a fine, she was given a 12 month deferred sentence. If her driving was incident free for one year, the charges would be dropped.

They had also began talking about having children, and Will's conviction that they would need to raise their kids to know who God is became regular and persistent. He began asking her veiled questions about her own faith and beliefs. Her parents never attended church, but she had gone to some church services with friends as a child. Though she had some general understanding of the basic premise of Christian faith, he didn't believe she had ever come to the genuine knowledge of who God is, or what Jesus had really done for everyone.

Will made good money working for Olympia, and they continued to enjoy nice clothes, good booze, and top quality cocaine.

Nothing Left Behind

Will and Butter Dog were standing on the roof of a house Butt had purchased out in Lake Forest Park, north of Seattle. The landscaping hadn't been tended to in years, and Will was there to help get things in shape. He left work the night before in a sharp, new three-piece suit, starched shirt, and silk tie. Midday Saturday he looked like a different man in the work clothes he'd worn not so long ago. He had kept all of the equipment he would need to do single landscape jobs on his own: ladders, saws, hand tools, an edger and a couple of mowers, etc. And Big Brown, a 1966 one ton Ford truck that was so ugly nothing was at risk, no matter what he did to it. It was a mule, and could be worked like the toughest beast on the farm.

"Let gravity work for you," was one of Will's axioms, whether landscaping or washing cars. Things head toward the ground all on their own. Use it to your advantage.

Without Malice

There was a huge maple tree growing in the front yard, and many of the long branches were reaching out over the house, some of them touching the roof. Left unattended they would do damage as wind scraped them back and forth against the shingles. Though the tree was 35 feet tall, the branches threatening the roof were the oldest and largest, some of them 10 or 12 inches in diameter at the trunk. If he cut them off in manageable sections, less than eight feet long, they would fit more easily in the back of his truck and require less effort to load.

Will tended to work fast. In reality, he attacked his work. At home or on the job, any job, he labored under the constant internal pressure to get more done. However much did get done, it was not enough. It could have been more. It should have been more. Butter Dog was a career ship yard man and would periodically say to Will, "I've never worked so hard in my life."

Will would laugh and reply, "Being self-employed motivates you to pick up the pace."

Will had begun with the longest, lowest branches, those touching the roof. Each seven to eight foot section was thrown down until he worked his way out to the rain gutters. The large base of those branches would be cut off flush at the trunk from a ladder. He then walked back up toward the center of the roof, and began the same process with the branches that weren't touching the roof, but could be reached and grabbed. Up on the roof he had a small chain saw with a 14-inch bar he could wield with one hand.

He jumped up 10 or 12 inches and grabbed the end of a large branch with his left hand, hanging on as he pulled it down. Then he walked toward the edge, bending it down further until he could reach up and cut it to the proper length with the saw in his right hand. The roof was a gentle slope.

They had been working hard for several hours and he was more tired than he realized. The branch also had more spring in it than he anticipated. As the chain saw cut through it, the branch shot upward and the saw dropped faster than it would have if he'd been paying closer attention. Will jerked the saw back with his right hand, and his left hand fell to his side, his jacket sleeve sliding down to his wrist. His mind snapped back into full clarity. WOW! That was close, he thought. But as he reached to switch the saw off before he set it down, he saw the blood coming from under his sleeve.

He put the saw down and reached up to pull his sleeve back with his right hand. The fountain of dark, red blood was bubbling up strong from his left forearm just above his wrist. This was not good.

"John," he yelled to Butter Dog as he sat down on the roof.

"Yeah?" his buddy called back up from the yard where he was hauling branches to the truck.

"We have a problem up here. Can you come up and help me?"

When Butt came up the ladder Will was sitting down and squeezing his jacket onto the wound with his right hand. "What's going on?" Butt asked.

Will loosened his grip and slid his left sleeve up his forearm, and the blood gushed forth with renewed vigor.

"Holy shit!" his friend said. "You need some help."

Will slid his sleeve back down and clamped it with his right hand again then said, "Go down and call for help, man. Then come on back up and help me down the ladder."

"You should just stay put," was his reply.

"Just call for help first," he said. "Then we'll deal with that."

When Butt disappeared down the ladder, Will stood up and began moving cautiously toward the edge of the roof. When his friend came back outside, Will was standing at the edge of the ladder, but unwilling to let go of his arm to take ahold of it.

"Don't be stupid!" John blurted out.

"Just get up here and help me," Will replied. "It'll be a lot easier for everyone if I'm on the ground when they get here. Come on!"

John came up and steadied him by his hips while Will worked his way around and got his feet on the ladder rungs. Then he leaned on the rail with his left elbow as his friend guided him down from below. When he got to the ground, he walked out by

Without Malice

the sidewalk and sat down. They could hear the siren approaching and Will realized he was feeling a little light headed.

John had called Eva too, and she pulled to the curb across the street just as the paramedics were packing up their equipment. One of them remained kneeling beside Will on the front lawn, his left arm propped on his knee, higher than his heart. They had bandaged him tightly and stopped the heavy flow of blood, but told him in no uncertain terms he needed medical attention immediately. He had refused a ride in their cool red truck. He wasn't big on getting into an ambulance. (He had been hit by a car and knocked to the ground once while walking home from football practice one night in high school. When the ambulance arrived on the scene he had already left. They found him in the locker room at the school.) Eva promised them they would go straight to the hospital.

Will was checked in through emergency at the Northgate Group Health Clinic and was waiting in an examination room when Medix Philips walked in. "You again," he said. "What is it this time?"

Will gave a brief narrative as Philips peeled off the bandages and examined the wound.

"What is it with you?" he asked. "Every time I see you you're all torn up."

The chain saw had ripped away a wide swath of flesh down to the bones of his left arm. Later the kindly medical man told Will he was lucky the saw didn't grab the bones.

"I don't want to see you in here again," he said with a slight smirk as he turned to walk from the room.

Will enjoyed being a salesman in the beer business, and the money was good. But there was something about landscape reclamation that he found very rewarding. Ornamental pruning was his favorite thing to do, both trees and shrubs, but mostly trees. He loved taking on a yard that had been severely neglected, and standing back to look at it after it had been squared away. Periodically he would take on a job, usually by referral, he could do on a weekend and make some decent extra money. He was no longer dealing drugs.

One night while eating dinner after Will had finished a weekend side job, Eva asked him, "Do you think I could do that?"

He looked at her, "What… work on a landscape job?"

"Yes," she said. "Could I earn some extra money, too?"

He smiled back at her. "I don't know why not. But make no mistake, it's very hard work."

"I can work hard," she said resolutely, the glint of determination in her eye.

"I know you can," he said. "Just know that you will be filthy and sore and probably do a little bleeding. If you don't mind that, sure… we can do a job together."

"All right then," she beamed, "when can we do it?"

Smiling he said, "As soon as I line one up."

Two weeks later he took her with him to look at a job he was asked to give an estimate on. A couple in their 40's had purchased a house just off of Sandpoint Way between Children's Hospital and Laurelhurst, one of north Seattle's nicer neighborhoods. The landscaping had not been touched for 15 years and was an overgrown mess. Walking around the unoccupied property as he worked up the bid, he pointed out to her all they would need to do. He figured it would take them two weekends working together, every daylight hour from Friday night until Sunday night, 50 or 60 man-hours.

Will got the bid, and after all costs they would split about $1,000.00 when the job was completed. They would begin the following Friday night.

As they worked through the next weekend he could not have been more impressed. She outworked most men he had employed in the business. She was as relentless as he was. When they were packing things up Sunday night her hands were blistered, but she had not complained even once, and never wavered from the tasks she was given.

Sitting in the truck preparing to leave, he said, "You know… we're scheduled to come back next weekend to finish, but I don't think we need to."

She turned to look at him. "We've done much more than I thought we could," he said, "and quite frankly, I think we could finish it off tomorrow night after I get off if you're up for it."

She met one of Will's criteria and had "Worked like a farm animal." She was scheduled to work breakfast and lunch at Claire's on Monday and could be ready to go when he got home.

Without flinching she said, "Let's do it," and smiled like she was enjoying the challenge.

Line in the sand

"Hi, Honey," Eva called out when she heard the front door close a few weeks later. Her share of the money had turned into some nice clothes and jewelry.

"Hey," Will shouted back as he turned into his office to drop his stuff.

Her hands were free and dried, and she took a step toward him as he walked into the kitchen. Neither of them ever left the house without a little good-bye kiss, and as soon as they were both home at the end of any given day, a warm hug was their first order of business. (Will's mother was a hugger and no one could last long in her family without embracing hugs as a normal expression of love and affection.)

Leaning back without letting go she asked, "How was your day?"

"The usual insanity" he said.

Monday's were monstrous, with 30 to 35 stops, ten of them among the largest major grocery stores on the east side. After a weekend, and this one had been beautiful weather, the beer on hand could be down to bare bones. It was a fine line between goat and hero with some large stores. Too much back stock and the management was not happy. Run out and leave them nothing to sell and you were a failure who cost them money.

The perfect Monday stock level was a full cooler and a one or two day supply of product in the back room. Worst case scenario could sometimes produce an emergency short delivery to tide them over until the scheduled order arrived on Wednesday. Big stores got a second delivery before the weekend.

A good salesman needed to know the tendencies of each store. Substitutes filling in during vacation time were often a disaster. The salesman didn't know the store and didn't want them to run out, so often wrote large orders. Of course, if the order was light and the store ran out, the competition would swoop in and fill your space with their product, after pointing out to the management how you weren't taking care of them. It was a cutthroat business.

"We got something from your mom today," she said.

"Yeah? What is it?" he asked.

"Remember that book she sent us awhile back – The Late Great Planet Earth?"

"Sorta," he said, hesitantly. "You know I don't like Sci-Fi."

"You loved The Hobbit and the whole Lord of the Rings trilogy."

"Come on... that's not Sci-Fi."

"Neither is this. It is about the end of the world, but not alien invasions or nuclear winter."

"So, you looked at it?" he asked.

"I did, but not until her invitation came today."

"Alright... I'll bite. What's it about? And what invitation?"

Her face took on a deeper more contemplative look. She slowly closed and opened her eyes and said, "It's about the return of Jesus," and he could see a subtle warmth spread over her.

His mother had faithfully sent them books about Christian faith two or three times a year, so this didn't surprise him. When he didn't respond, Eva said, "The author of the book is going to be speaking at her church in Tacoma, and she sent us an invitation with a note asking us to join her for dinner first." (She was currently separated from his stepdad.) "It's a Wednesday evening in two weeks."

Without Malice

Though he wasn't speaking, she knew the gears in his head were spinning. He had a certain look. It even showed in some toddler pictures his mother had of him. She didn't know what he was thinking, but knew she wouldn't have to wait long for whatever it produced.

Will loved his mother. Before Eva came into his life, she was probably the only person he was confident actually loved him… real love that was committed no matter what. There were more than enough betrayals in life to convince him to not believe too many people too easily. Butch was entirely dependable, and wouldn't run off when things got nasty, but Will didn't think of it as love.

Will looked her in the eyes. "What do you think?" he asked. "Do you want to go?"

He knew her hesitation wasn't trying to figure out what her reply would be. Her sweet little mouth turned up slightly at the corners, and her big brown eyes looked at him with that soft intensity he knew was absolutely real.

"Yes," she said. "I think we should go."

"Okay, then," he said. "Let's do it. You want to call her?" She knew it wasn't really a question.

"Sure," she said. She leaned into hug him again and said, "It will be good."

He wasn't so sure about that, but neither did he have any sense he should resist.

His mom had talked about this church enough, but he could not have anticipated it before they arrived. The churches he grew up in were mostly classical brick, dark wood, and stained glass with steep gabled roofs. The new First Baptist Church of Everett, Washington in 1960 was light colored stone, concrete, and rectangular. This place was not only enormous, but more the style of a contemporary downtown Seattle concert hall than what he thought of as a church, though it did have a large cross standing prominently from the center of the pentagonal roof. Attendants with vests and flashlights were guiding cars systematically to sections of the multi-lot paved parking spaces spread out over what must have been two acres. The flow of people was merging toward the two giant entry doors like country streams combining to form rivers on the way to the ocean. The entire front of the building was a wall of glass 40 feet tall.

Will had not been in a church for 16 years, except for his sister's wedding, and this was already dislodging many of the predispositions he had held since childhood.

The sanctuary must hold at least 2,000 people Will thought. But when they walked in about 6:40 for the 7:00 meeting, the main floor was already full. Teams of ushers were directing them to the balcony, up either of two sets of stairs wrapped around the outside walls of the cavernous entryway. They found seats on the aisle about half way up the center of the lofty, upstairs seating. It was all so different than what he had imagined for years, he was caught up in looking around at everything and taking in the details of the architecture, materials and great variety of people. It was like going to a Super Sonics game but many people were dressed a little better. Some wore classic church clothes, nice dresses, suits, and ties. Will was business casual. Eva was her usual elegant, stylish self.

After a well-dressed young man, way down at the podium, welcomed everyone, a huge formal choir in robes filed out into the largest multilevel choir stands he had ever seen. A director walked out like the conductor at the symphony, drew the singers to their feet, and commenced an old church hymn Will immediately recognized. He was surprised by the familiarity that swept over him, an odd mixture with the unexpected newness he was experiencing.

After two verses of the hymn they paused, as the director turned toward the audience and lifted his hands, signaling them to rise to their feet as well. The backs of the pews held hymnals for those who didn't know the words by heart. They all remained standing for two more songs, then sat as one. Will was not sure what was going to happen next.

Then, an equally well-dressed older man came out and welcomed them again. This guy was no doubt the senior pastor.

Authority carries its own introduction. After a few warm thoughts, he launched into an enthusiastic recounting of the book that had drawn them all here, followed by an introduction of the author. As he walked onto the stage the whole room broke into thunderous applause, something Will had never heard in the churches of his youth.

The speaker started off lightly, thanking everyone for their attendance and praising the natural beauty of the Puget Sound region. Then he turned to the topic he had written about, and warmed to his subject quickly. Will was pleased and surprised that the man's talk held his interest so well, knowing he had come more than a little critical.

Then it began to happen. Something vast and deep began to seep into the room, like fog on a marine morning, relentless and irresistible. Will lost all track of what the man was saying. His past was drawing him back into something long forgotten, and he knew this guy was working things up for an altar call. It didn't matter that he was raised Baptist and this was an Assemblies of God church. This was not unique to either of them. Slowly, Will realized he had been cornered. If he had somehow showed up by himself, he would have slipped out, but he was sitting next to Eva and his mom in the midst of a crowd whose single attention was focused on the man at the microphone and what he was saying… everyone except Will, that is. There was no clean way out of this and he'd just have to sit and do his best to endure it, keeping his resolve.

Lost in thought, he found himself suddenly face to face with what he was sure had to be God again, though this time there were no distinct words. What he did know was that he was being called to account, and he was sure there would be serious, if not severe consequences for blowing it off again. Two options, and both of them filled with dread.

Then he knew. He had to get up from his seat, high in the balcony, and walk down to the front of the sanctuary, and in so doing, relent and surrender his life to God. In reality, it was very inviting. He understood he was being offered a clean slate. That was both surprising and huge, beyond any of his preconceptions.

He'd known he had dived into inexcusable sin and had been enjoying it with enthusiasm for years. He was quite good at it. And he had feared for years, that turning to God would require him to answer for it, like taking his swats in junior high school for his repeated defiance and rebellion.

But bright lights had just gone on in big rooms of his mind, and he was certain he was being called to a freedom he didn't have to answer for. He knew as never before that the Son of God, Jesus of Nazareth, had voluntarily suffered and died in his behalf so he would not have to answer for his sins. He was being invited into clear, secure standing with God because of what Jesus had done, and he could freely receive this clean, new life if he was willing. If he was willing. His head and heart were converging in his chest and throat like never before.

Will had never considered himself a fool, and he thought, what sort of fool would turn down this deal? Then he heard another voice, just as clearly as God had spoken to him at the inaugural party of his first house.

"If you go down there, you're going to lose your wife. She likes the booze, and she likes the coke, and she likes to party. If you go down there your life is going to change radically, and you're going to lose her."

All of a sudden he was trapped in two corners at once. He loved Eva more than anyone he had ever known, and he was unwilling to lose her.

And then the voice of God spoke as clearly as ever. He said, "I'm not talking to you about her. I'm talking to you about you," and he knew. It wasn't about 'what if' and it wasn't about the fear of losing anything. It was entirely about him responding to God, who had been faithful and patient with him, and the time was now.

"You've been telling Me for 15 years," God continued, "that when your time came you'd be there. I'm telling you your time is now."

Will feared what would happen to him if he turned Him down this time. He had to respond to God, and God alone.

Without looking to his left, he stepped out into the stairway aisle of the balcony, and as he did he felt Eva take his left hand. He turned his head to look her in the eyes, and they knew this was for both of them. Their lives would never be the same.

Three Steps Forward, Two Steps Back

The next several months were not easy. Will kept working at Olympia Beer and they started attending the church in Tacoma off and on. It was a 45 minute drive. They also continued much of their life as it had been with old friends.

"Will!" Carl's voice boomed over the phone. "Hey, how's it going over on the east side Buddy? Are you still tearing 'em up?"

"Carl. Good to hear from you, man. How's life over there in Bremerton? You teach those hicks about the beer business yet?"

"I'm working on it. That's why I called."

"What?" Will asked. "You want me to come over and give a few lessons?"

"As a matter of fact, I do. I want to know if you'll consider coming over here and going to work for me."

"You're kidding," Will said, half amazed. He had actually thought of moving several times since the clash with the teenagers on North 45th street.

"No, I'm not," his old roommate continued. "When can you start? We've got a spot opening up as soon as you can get here."

"Wow," Will said. "You have no idea."

As they continued talking, Will believed it was an opportunity he could not turn down. He told his friend he would talk with Eva that night and get back to him. There was a lot to consider, not the least of which was their house in Seattle.

"Oh, man," he told Eva when they decided it was the thing to do, "I hope they just tell me to hit the road." He was going to tell his boss in the morning and give his notice. Perfect timing.

"Eva," he said when she answered the phone later that morning. "Can't leave yet. They've actually been recruiting an

Albertson's store manager already. I don't know where they were planning to put him, but my notice just created an opening. I have to spend the next two weeks training him for my area. Oh, well… it will all work out fine. It always does."

Sitting on the couch Friday night after the first week of training the new guy she asked him, "So, how's it going?"

Will let out a sigh… "They are going to eat this guy alive. He's not cut out for it. As a store manager, he came up under authority and he's been in authority. He tells people how he wants his store run, and they have to do it. He's a nice guy, and people liked working for him. In this job, the salesmen from other brands are sharks. He won't even know what they're doing until it's too late."

True to his word, Will stayed late every night doing everything he could to prepare the new guy, but he didn't have the killer instinct.

"Hey, Johnny," Will said over the phone Monday night. "I left my coffee cup in the company car when I gave it to Joe last Friday. Get it from him, will you? I'll pick it up this weekend."

"That ain't all you left in that car," his buddy said with his gruff Italian, Chicago accent.

"What?" Will asked.

"He took it home and was cleaning it out in the driveway Saturday, with his kids hanging around. He reached under the front seat and pulled out a loaded .357. He about shit his pants. I've got it, and I'm pretty sure I convinced him to not say anything about it at work."

"Shit," Will said. "I forgot all about it."

"No shit, Sherlock. I don't think this guy had ever even seen a loaded gun before. He had it in a bag and acted like it was a rattle snake."

"Thanks, man. I owe you one."

"No problem. See you this weekend."

After one month of commuting from Seattle to Bremerton, by ferry or driving around, more than an hour each way, Will and

Eva decided it would be best to move to the other side of Puget Sound. They found a nice house in Olalla, near the water, way off the beaten path, half way between Tacoma and Bremerton. They left Seattle behind for a life that would be different in almost every way.

They started attending the church in Tacoma more regularly, and the contrast between their established way of life and what was drawing them became clearer and sharper.

Though they agreed to cut back on their drinking, they still tipped a few when socializing with their old friends, though Will suspected Eva had begun to drink a little during the day. So, one morning before leaving for work he took all of the liquor bottles out of the cabinet and put a tiny mark with a razor blade right at the content level of the label of each bottle.

When Eva was in a back room after dinner that night, he checked the bottles. One of them had more in it than it did in the morning. Walking out to the kitchen she saw him sitting at the breakfast counter with that single bottled in front of him. She stopped several feet away.

After a few moments of silence, he reached out to take the bottle by its neck, slid it close and turned it so the label was facing them both. Pointing to the tiny nick he had made earlier he said softly, "Eva… I marked the level of each bottle before I left this morning. This one now has more in it than it did before."

At first, she looked confused, and then a few tears began to form and slide from her eyes. "I'm so sorry, Will."

He stood and walked over to her, wrapped his arms around her and gently pulled her into his embrace. She put her head on his shoulder and he said, "We can't keep doing this."

It all came to a head after a New Year's Eve party a few weeks later. Neither of them had become drunk, but they both felt awkward even drinking socially since they had made it known they were devoted to following Christ. Waking up the next morning they looked at each other across the kitchen counter and agreed, "We're not fooling anyone, least of all God. Let's either be Christians or don't, but let's get it settled," and they did.

(Epilogue)
Into the Great Unknown

Will toweled off from his shower Monday morning, knowing what he had to do. After shaving and dressing he walked into the kitchen to greet Eva and their new Newfoundland puppy, Bubba, who ambled toward him, tail wagging. Gabe almost moved his head looking up from the floor.

"I have to tell Carl," he said.

"Really?" she asked softly.

"Yeah," he said. "I have to tell him, and tell him that I'm leaving the business. Honey, I walked into a bar last Friday morning about 10:30, and one of their regulars was sitting on the same stool he always occupies, half in the bag already. I'm supposed to slap that guy on the back and be happy he's getting drunk on our product? I can't do it anymore."

Eva smiled knowingly. To do what she could to counter Will selling alcohol, she kept her purse well supplied with Gospel tracts. Whenever she went into a grocery store she would inconspicuously slip one inside the handle opening of every half case box in the cooler. She hadn't been caught.

Will thought his buddy and boss would laugh out loud when he told him. To his surprise he relayed that he had spent some time with a group of Campus Crusade for Christ students when he was in college. He also persuaded Will to hold off giving his notice until he could break it to the owner of the distributorship. When he finally sat down with Carl and the owner, they persuaded him to wait until they found a suitable replacement to take over his accounts. He reluctantly agreed.

Six weeks later Will called Carl on Sunday night. "This has gone on too long, man. I'm telling them in the morning they have two weeks."

The owner asked him to wait until the next morning so they could tell everyone at once, including the drivers before they went out for the day.

Tuesday morning at 6:45 the entire company was gathered in the warehouse before the trucks left. Will kept things short and to the point, and most folks went to their various jobs without a word. A few stepped up and shook his hand.

About 9:15 he walked into the back room of the Safeway store in Silverdale, the biggest, newest Safeway store west of Puget Sound. The manager was waiting for him. The man was old school, hard-nosed. Some salesmen tried to sneak in and out without being seen. Will got along great with him. He gave as good as he got, and the gruff manager respected him. They even enjoyed some playful banter.

On this morning the manager was waiting alone for him in the back room, grim faced. As Will came close he asked, "Are you leaving?"

"Yes," Will said.

"Because you've become a Christian?" he asked.

"Yes," Will replied.

"Where are you going to go? What are you going to do?" he continued.

"I don't know," Will said.

The manager exploded, "ARE YOU CRAZY, Boy? These jobs don't grow on trees! Take some time to get your feet under you before you go walking off."

Will paused, out of respect because he hadn't anticipated the vehement response. "God hasn't called me to starve, Dave. It'll be fine. Just because I don't see the next step doesn't mean I'm not supposed to take this one. But, thank you. You have always been good to me, and I appreciate you."

The older man stood silent for a few moments, then turned and walked away slowly shaking his head.

With his old job behind him, Will and Eva became more and more drawn into life with others who were following Jesus. He and Carl remained close friends, interested in what was happing in Will and Eva's life. One night on the phone Will told him they were going to a party on Friday night. Carl asked him, "Will there be any drinking?"

Will replied, "No."

His friend asked him, "So, what are you going to do?"

Will explained that they would enjoy each other's company as they ate, maybe play some games, and talk about the life and faith they shared.

Will and Eva were settled into the Sunday night worship service at their church, a much more relaxed and casual gathering than Sunday morning. A special speaker was telling her story of how God had intervened in her life, and was inviting those present to consider their own response to Him.

When he left the beer and wine business, Will expected to go back into business for himself in some way and use his profits to finance missions and other ministry efforts. He had always envisioned being financially successful. But as he contemplated his response to the speaker's invitation, he recognized what he had come to know as the voice of God revealing His purposes.

"I don't want your money, I want you," was as clear as if he had heard a voice in his ear. Will instantly knew he would not be going into business, but full-time vocational ministry of some sort. Everything he believed about his own future was changed in a moment. What would Eva think when he told her? Whatever they did they would to it together.

>>>> <<<<

Made in the USA
Columbia, SC
26 June 2019